HIS TOUCH WAS HER UNDOING

"Let's get you back in the saddle."

Chaco tried to give Frances a leg up, but she had trouble, even when she grasped the mare's mane.

"This horse is too big!" she groused.

He laughed and took hold of her waist. Once again, she felt the warmth of each and every finger. Distracted, she let her foot slip out of the stirrup as the mare stepped forward. She fell back against Chaco, making him stumble.

"Sorry!" Turning in his arms, she found herself face to face with him.

His smile faded. He let her slip down farther, her body whispering against his and reacting in kind. She caught her breath. For a moment all differences were forgotten and the world stood still.

Harper Monogram

The Wind Casts No Shadow

ROSLYNN GRIFFITH

HarperPaperbacks
A Division of HarperCollinsPublishers

If you purchased this book without a cover, you should be aware that this book is stolen property. It was reported as "unsold and destroyed" to the publisher and neither the author nor the publisher has received any payment for this "stripped book."

This is a work of fiction. The characters, incidents, and dialogues are products of the author's imagination and are not to be construed as real. Any resemblance to actual events or persons, living or dead, is entirely coincidental.

HarperPaperbacks   *A Division of* HarperCollins*Publishers*
10 East 53rd Street, New York, N.Y. 10022

Copyright © 1994 by Patricia Pinianski and Linda Sweeney
All rights reserved. No part of this book may be used or reproduced in any manner whatsoever without written permission of the publisher, except in the case of brief quotations embodied in critical articles and reviews. For information address HarperCollins*Publishers,*
10 East 53rd Street, New York, N.Y. 10022.

Cover illustration by Diane Sivavec

First printing: June 1994

Printed in the United States of America

HarperPaperbacks, HarperMonogram, and colophon are trademarks of HarperCollins*Publishers*

❖ 10 9 8 7 6 5 4 3 2 1

Thanks to Edward Majeski for his assistance in researching the historical details.

Prologue

Lincoln County, New Mexico Territory, 1880

Chaco Jones tossed and turned in his bed, a top berth in the best bunkhouse on the Ralston Double-Bar Ranch. Though built of adobe, the structure had a real store-bought window, two corner fireplaces and a columned, open portal across the front. Thankfully, the well-patched roof didn't leak when sudden thunderstorms came pounding down from the mountains.

But tonight he hadn't been able to sleep for hours, had lain awake long after the rain had stopped and a restless wind began moaning through the copse of pinon pines out front. His sixth sense, the instinct that set him apart from others and sometimes spooked them, told him something was wrong.

Something was going to happen.

Something as elusive as the wind . . .

Still fully dressed, he lay on his side, face toward

the window, hand on the Colt .45 beneath his pillow.

Even so, he finally dozed off and dreamed of wandering across a gray mesa in the white moonlight, of tracking shadows that flitted and danced just beyond his reach. Wind wailing around him, he followed, refusing to give up until the specters led him back to the ghostly bunkhouse. Once there he entered and climbed into his bed, where he stared at the glowing curtainless window on the opposite wall.

The wind dropped, though he thought he heard a skittering sound, soft clicks that seemed to be coming closer, as if a creature with claws were running lightly along the planks of the portal.

Then a dark form glided into view.

Four-footed.

Predatory.

The beast paused before rising on its back legs to place its paws on the deep window sill and stare directly at him with open jaws and glittering eyes.

A wolf . . . yet not.

Surely no natural creature had such a searching gaze.

With a start, Chaco suddenly realized he wasn't dreaming. His eyes were wide open and he was fully awake. All senses alert, he rose to his elbows, cold chills creeping up his spine.

The wolf watched him expectantly, its muscles tensing as if getting ready to leap . . .

From somewhere deep within, Chaco drew forth an Apache curse, "Go, leave this place, run into the night, evil one!"

Barely a hiss and a whisper.

The beast dropped to all fours and was gone.

Grabbing his gun, Chaco rolled out of the bunk, hitting the floor with a soft thud that didn't awaken the other wranglers. In two strides, he was at the door and flung it open, his finger on the trigger of the Colt.

The portal was empty, but in the distance a large sleek shadow slipped into the junipers.

His breath came fast and shallow as he strode to the end of the porch. He sniffed the pinon-scented air, then searched for a match in the pocket of his denim pants. Striking it, he squatted to examine the nearby ground for footprints. Another chill crept up his spine and made his hair stand on end.

No animal had left its mark in the damp red clay. Instead, he saw indentations made by narrow, high-heeled boots.

The footprints of a woman.

He relaxed his finger from the Colt's trigger, let his arm drop to his side. The weapon was of little use.

Bullets couldn't stop a skin-walker.

1

Boston

Miss Llewellyn's School for Girls offered board and private education for young females, ages twelve through seventeen. Frances MacDonnell had been a scant two years older than some of her students when she'd begun teaching English Composition and Hygiene there a decade before.

Frances sometimes felt so old, perhaps because she was expected to dress and act soberly, to set a sterling example for her young charges. Getting ready to start the day, she secured her thick, brown hair in a tight knot and straightened the white lace collar of her dark, green dress.

The small room she called home offered few amenities—a narrow bed, an old dresser and some wall pegs for hanging clothing. A single window looked down on the courtyard that lay between the teachers' quarters and the other buildings—the massive brick mansion that served as the girls' dormitory, the school itself and Miss Grace Llewellyn's private home.

Since the spring morning had dawned sunny after days of rain, small clusters of students had gathered outside to giggle and gossip before classes officially began. Frances gazed down at them, only wishing a simple event like sunrise could call forth such joy and gaiety from her own heart.

With a sigh, she turned from the window, picked up the text book she'd laid on top of the dresser, and made for the door. Outside, the corridor was quiet, the other teachers still at breakfast, the usual sparse meal of porridge and tea served in Miss Llewellyn's personal dining room. Frances hadn't been hungry this morning. As she swept down the corridor, she turned her eyes away when she passed Emily Bradley's room. Her good friend and fellow teacher had been dismissed several months before, but Frances continued to miss her, probably the reason her appetite was dampened, her spirits down.

At least with Emily's companionship, she'd forgotten for a while her feeling of not belonging.

Descending a narrow staircase and opening the outer door, she entered the courtyard. Dressed in blue skirts with matching blouses, ribbed black cotton stockings and ankle-high black shoes, several students turned to look at her.

"Good morning, Miss MacDonnell," called a twelve-year-old.

"Good morning, Tilly," Frances said before being distracted by raised voices coming from a huddle of girls.

"So you admit you are a savage?" demanded someone so shrill and loud, she could only be sixteen-year-old Amy Dandridge.

"I am half Comanche."

Louisa Janks. Frances had suspected the girl's ancestry and knew that trouble had been brewing since Louisa had arrived after Easter. She squeezed through the tightly packed group so she could see the opponents. Amy was a porcelain blonde with a pouty mouth and the arrogant attitude of a child born to wealthy parents; Louisa was a black-haired beauty with lightly-bronzed features and a proud bearing, though she never spoke of her own family in New Mexico Territory.

"You're a Comanche!" cried Amy accusingly. The blonde glanced about at her audience as if to gather support. A self-appointed leader, she'd been jealous of the other girl from the first. "Comanches are heathens who kill white people!"

Louisa's dark eyes flashed. "White people knew the Indians were there before they invaded their territory. And white people kill plenty of Indians, even women and little children!"

With a pang, memories of the missionary reserve camp—a temporary holding area for Indians being sent to reservations—came to Frances. A desperate mother's face still haunted her two decades after the tragedy.

"Girls, this is no way to speak to one another." Frances met Louisa's gaze, hoping to calm her, then addressed Amy in particular, "We are all creatures of God."

Amy scowled and addressed her disrespectfully. "Savages aren't creatures of God. They scalp people—cut off their hair."

"And part of their heads along with it," Louisa added angrily. "Would you like me to show you?"

The crowd gasped and retreated as one, including Amy.

"Go ahead, run away!" Louisa looked as fierce as any warrior Frances remembered.

"Godless heathen!" shouted Amy, her voice quivering.

The situation was far out of control. Frances grabbed each of the girls by an arm. "Enough! Make peace and go inside!"

Amy shook her off, once more shocking Frances. "I don't have to make peace with a savage!" she hissed. "And I don't have to listen to an Injun-lover!"

"How dare you speak to her like that!" Louisa pushed at Amy. "Maybe I should show you another Comanche trick. Drag you behind a horse until you're a bloody carcass!"

"Louisa!" Frances stared, appalled.

"You don't belong here or any civilized place," cried Amy. "You should be on a reservation with the other filthy savages." She slapped Louisa across the face. "Stay away from me!"

Dark eyes blazing, Louisa struck the other girl with her closed fist. The blonde fell to the ground, and chaos erupted as several friends came to Amy's aid in a scratching, screaming, hair-pulling free-for-all.

"I order you to stop!" Frances waded into the fray and pulled a girl from Louisa's back. "Remember you are ladies!" Then she wrestled with Louisa herself, though the angry sixteen-year-old was as strong as she was. "Stop it, right now!" Even as she spoke, reason overtook the fury burning in Louisa's eyes. Intent on fending off another attack, Frances thrust the girl behind her. "You should be ashamed of yourselves!"

But the other girls were already backing away. Frances suddenly realized several other teachers had appeared. One of them grasped a little girl by the pigtails and scolded her. Miss Llewellyn stood on the rear steps of the mansion.

"Take the girls to their rooms," ordered the elderly headmistress. "Miss MacDonnell . . . to my office!"

Frances watched Louisa being escorted into the mansion and hoped the other teachers wouldn't blame the girl. At least she herself could give a true report of the incident. But she had to wait nearly a half hour before the headmistress was ready to see her. Then she took the suppliant's seat in the straight-backed chair before the great mahogany desk that had belonged to the Llewellyn family for generations. Miss Llewellyn, unmarried and the last of her line, had chosen to use her remaining fortune and estate for the education of young members of the fairer sex.

Frances had sat in the very same chair ten years before when Miss Llewellyn had congratulated her on passing the teacher's exam and welcomed her to the school. That day, the stern lady had smiled and said she was especially pleased to take on a teacher with such good moral upbringing, Frances being the daughter of a minister.

The headmistress wasn't smiling now, however. Her faded blue eyes were cold behind her silver spectacles and her thin lips pursed disapprovingly. The funereal black she always wore gave her pale, wrinkled skin an icy cast. Frances felt a twinge, though she refused to give in to fear.

"What exactly do you have to say for yourself?" Miss Llewellyn began.

"Myself?" The accusatory tone didn't bode well. "Amy Dandridge said appalling things to Louisa Janks." And to her as well. "I tried to stop the ensuing battle to no avail."

"The report I received said that the Indian girl was the attacker and that you defended her."

Surprised that she wasn't being asked for her version of the incident, Frances nevertheless told the truth, "Louisa made some offensive remarks, but Amy started the whole affair and—"

The headmistress cut her off, "Miss MacDonnell! Are you refuting me?"

The twinge she'd felt before turned to anger as she realized Miss Llewellyn was calling her to task. "Someone else heard the argument?" she asked. "And why is this other person's opinion more believable than mine?"

"Exactly *who* heard what and saw whom is not the subject of this interview! I am far more concerned with your proclaiming savages to be creatures of God!"

Frances was stunned, both with Miss Llewellyn's obvious fury and with the older woman's stance, the same as her strident father's. "But you are an educator and a Christian."

"I most certainly am!" the headmistress stated hotly. "And if I'd known that Louisa was a heathen, rather than a Spaniard or a Mexican—which would have been bad enough—I would never have taken her! The girl's mother was intentionally devious."

Frances hadn't considered the possible ramifications when she'd guessed the truth about Louisa's heritage. Stupidly enough, she'd thought she might be able to put a word in for the girl during this interview.

"Louisa is only half Indian," she finally stated lamely.

"Half is the same as whole when it comes to heathens!" Miss Llewellyn's voice and lace cap trembled. "More animal than human being. Why, those savages massacred General Custer and his troops only four years ago."

There'd always been war. Brother had fought brother when the southern states had seceded from the union. But Indians weren't considered men. Instead, they were animals, heathens, savages. Oblivious to her surroundings, Frances again focused on the past, her throat tightening. She saw the Indian woman's face when her children were torn away from her, never to return. The woman hadn't wept, but Frances knew she had wanted to die.

"You have harbored outlandish opinions before, Miss MacDonnell," the headmistress went on, "though I have tried to overlook them—spiritualism, women's suffrage."

Subjects of flyers Frances had picked up in bookstores and discussed with some of the other teachers.

Miss Llewellyn added, "You kept Miss Bradley's marriage a secret."

True. Frances had indeed known about the forbidden marriage—teachers had to be single—but she had remained silent as her friend had asked. Emily's new husband was a lowly clerk in a department store, and they had needed even a teacher's small wages to get along.

"You flaunted the rules."

Frances swallowed, wondering how best to defend herself. "I am sorry if you believe I would intentionally break rules." She had learned to be careful with words after all these years, but she had never actually lied.

"Be that as it may." Miss Llewellyn adjusted her spectacles. "There were problems concerning Louisa before this day. I had heard that you were befriending her after lessons."

Had there been gossip all along? "I helped Louisa, but no more so than some of the others." And Frances had enjoyed introducing the bright girl to her favorite stories and poems. In return, she'd been rewarded with tales of wild New Mexico.

"Nevertheless, I have heard you were decidedly partial to Louisa. I don't know why you have taken this course, after serving here for so many years. Perhaps it is the result of the vile books you keep hidden in your room."

Startled, Frances cried, "Someone invaded my privacy?" The cheap novels were harmless entertainment. "Surely it isn't a sin to read about romance and adventure." The books had brightened her spirits when she'd grown tired of her stagnant life.

Miss Llewellyn wagged her finger at Frances. "It is not your place to say what is sin and what is not. Such books are the works of the devil. And you a minister's daughter! Those horrid texts have obviously poisoned your mind." She took a deep breath. "We can't have your sort of person teaching young ones at my school."

Frances flushed, her reaction a combination of fear and anger. "What are you saying?"

"The Dandridges are an upstanding, God-fearing family. We can't have them withdrawing their daughter because a teacher allowed a savage to attack her. You are dismissed!"

"Dismissed!" Frances rose from her chair. "That is unfair! Outrageous!"

Miss Llewellyn rose as well. "Must we call a policeman to escort you from the premises?"

"Of course not, but—"

"Then see to your bags." The headmistress pointed at the door. "You shall leave the school this very night."

Shocked to her core, Frances could not think what she would do now. Having existed on so small a salary, she had been able to buy a few books and articles of clothing, but had very little savings.

The thought of being on the street, penniless, was enough to make her normal mettle crumble.

New Mexico

Don Armando de Arguello had never been a man to spend much time praying. A hard-riding caballero in his youth, the scion of an old Hidalgo family who had lived in northern New Mexico for more than two centuries, he had passed his time in more amusing, earthy pleasures.

But after the death of his only remaining legitimate child a month before, a grown daughter who had succumbed to difficult childbirth, Don Armando had started visiting the modest *oratorio* of his *estancia* every morning.

Today he lit a votive on the altar of the Virgin and crossed himself before allowing his accompanying servant to help him sink to his knees. There he prayed for the soul of the son who had been killed a year before and for the souls of both his daughter and stillborn grandson. Would the de Arguello bloodline survive? Armando worried. His second wife, the beautiful and much younger Ynez, seemed to be barren after three years of marriage.

Would he himself live much longer?

At seventy, Don Armando expected aching bones, but not the constant digestive problems he had been experiencing of late. Perhaps his days on earth were numbered. Perhaps his house and vast land holdings would go to some stranger . . . unless he took an action he considered questionable.

Above all, Don Armando feared mortality.

That was why he prayed, God forgive him.

And that was why he wanted his land to go to someone of his own blood.

Not to mention that Ynez would need a strong person to take care of her after he was gone. Don Armando's final prayer was for his modest wife, a woman who had long ago asked him to represent her to the Virgin and the Saints. She did not feel capable of doing so herself and never entered the oratory or any church except for Sunday mass.

Crossing himself one last time, Don Armando motioned for the servant to help him rise again. Once on his feet, however, he pushed the man away and took up the staff he used for walking. He hated being weak.

Outside, he stood for a moment, enjoying the spring sunshine in the *placita,* a welcome open-air space inside the sprawling wings of the *estancia's* great house. Two cheerful kitchen maids gossiped and ground corn near the great well in the center.

Ynez approached. Always aware of the sunlight's effect on her delicate skin, she had draped a black silk shawl over her upswept hair.

"Good morning, Doña Ynez," he greeted her politely, his wife having always preferred formality to forms of endearment.

"Good morning, Don Armando." She was tall for a Spanish woman and had arresting dark eyes that could make her appear severe at times. But, as usual, unassuming, she lowered her gaze, her lashes rich and black against her cheeks. "Are you feeling better? I have been worried about the illness you suffered last night."

"I am recovering."

"Have you eaten yet today?" Her eyes flicked over him. "If not, I shall bring you some eggs and tortillas hot from the oven."

"I would like both very much." She was kind and liked to serve him food when she could, whenever his housekeeper Mercedes did not do so first. He suggested, "Let us eat outside."

She made no objection and walked toward the kitchen. Armando followed, intending to sit at the little table some yards from the well and near the newly blooming wisteria.

The cook had left the door of the kitchen open to the air. Ynez stopped with a gasp at the threshold.

Don Armando frowned and moved nearer. "Is something wrong?"

"Nothing to worry you, Husband."

But now he could see the crude cross drawn on the kitchen wall. Yellowish-brown, the peon's sign against witchcraft had been sketched with ground mustard plant.

"Superstition!" Ynez sounded annoyed. She pointed at the cook and commanded, "Wipe that off at once."

The woman obeyed, but Don Armando wondered why Mercedes, who'd been with him for forty years, had not taken charge of the situation herself. No one was to touch his house's dutifully whitewashed walls. While Ynez entered the room, Don Armando sat himself at the table and glanced at the kitchen maids. No longer gossiping, they looked frightened. Perhaps one of them was to blame for the witchcraft sign.

But he was more concerned with his own health than domestic squabbles. Closing his eyes, he rubbed his middle and basked in the warm rays of the sun until Ynez returned with a plate of food and set it before him.

About to thank her, his words were cut off by a scream.

"Ai-i-ii!" One of the kitchen maids stood near the well, wide-eyed and frightened.

Heart beating hard in his chest, Don Armando struggled to his feet. "What is wrong?"

"Mercedes!" The maid pointed to the well. "She is dead!"

"Mercedes?" he murmured, not wanting to believe it.

He went to look for himself. Far below, the elderly woman floated face up in the dark water, head at an odd angle, eyes and mouth open as if to scream, her wrinkled skin swollen and distorted.

"God help us!" Don Armando crossed himself as other servants gathered, cries rending the air. Weeping softly beside him, Ynez stroked his arm.

But he could not be comforted. Perhaps he himself should make signs against witchcraft. Surely there was a curse on this house, on his family. How else could so many bad things happen in so short a time?

"The boss wants you to head up to Santa Fe tomorrow," John Gates told Chaco Jones as they sat on their horses and oversaw some branding on one of the farther ranges of the Ralston Double-Bar.

"What's going on?"

The center of territorial government was a hundred miles away, several days ride, an excursion Chaco wasn't looking forward to.

Gates' narrow eyes turned on Chaco. "Somebody important's coming in from Dodge City, one of Ralston's old friends." Lighting the cigarillo he'd hand-rolled, the foreman took a long drag. "Ralston thinks The Boys might have heard about him, too."

So one of the boss's cronies needed protection. Well, protection is what he'd been hired for. He only happened to be on this range below the Capitan Mountains to guard against cattle rustlers in the area. Not a regular hand, he did little branding or any of the other backbreaking, day-to-day work.

Instead, he dodged bullets from time to time and fired a few of his own. Knowing that under the circumstances he'd been lucky to see thirty-five, Chaco was growing weary of the job.

"So you think the Lincoln County problems are heating up again?" he asked. The feud had begun with two warring merchants, had gone on to involve the county sheriff and various ranchers, and finally had escalated into a sporadic war between rival gangs of gunfighters dubbed The Boys and The Regulators. Ralston had taken sides with the latter. "If things don't calm down, there's gonna be another blood bath like in '78."

"Just so long as the blood that's spilled is *theirs.*"

Chaco said nothing. He had no personal investment in either of the factions, but he was being paid well.

"I'm gonna send Martinez to Santa Fe with you."

Again, Chaco remained silent, though he was disapproving of the Mexican hired gun, a man who often liked to load up on tequila then go after the women when he hit town.

"The train stops in Galisteo Junction," Gates went on, referring to the town that had been built to accommodate the railroad a year ago. "Place is eighteen miles south of the capital and is real small, only a few saloons and some shacks."

Meaning Martinez wouldn't be so tempted? Rumor had it he was as good an aim whether drunk or sober, but Chaco didn't want to test that out.

"Don't know if The Boys would really go as far as Santa Fe," Gates went on. "But you'll need to get the man on a horse and take the high road down to Lincoln."

"And watch his back all the way."

"Goes without saying." Gates stubbed out his cigarillo. "You'll leave in the morning."

Chaco nodded, watching as the foreman rode away.

Then he gazed toward the north, the direction of Santa Fe. Not that the ancient town's surrounding mountains were visible along the endless expanse of bright blue sky.

When a gust of wind came up, he had to grab his wide-brimmed hat to keep it from blowing off . . . and he felt the familiar chill again. For a moment, the breeze seemed cold as ice.

Damn. No matter what logic told him, he was still certain something was awry in this familiar world of red-brown dust, high desert and wind. He'd felt something was wrong since the night he'd locked gazes with the wolf creature, seen its human prints, though he could find no prints at all the following day.

But whether or not the skin-walker had been real, Chaco honored his premonitions. They had kept him alive years longer than the average gunfighter. He'd taken some lead, of course, once on a cattle drive to Mexico, and again when he worked a short-term job as a deputy in Texas. But he'd been half-expecting the bullets and they hadn't kept him down for long.

What bothered him now was that this premonition seemed so different, more subtle, as if a shadow could sneak up on him and crawl right under his skin. This feeling of danger had more to do with dreams or visions than with gunfire.

Once again, he thought of the wolf creature, its open jaws, the bold way it had looked at him. He thought about the words of the curse he'd uttered and the way the creature had fled.

At least it *had* fled.

Chaco's mother had been a half-breed Apache and her people had told him he had the makings of a medicine man or *di-yin*. They'd said he had the heart and strength to defeat evil.

He only hoped that included evil beyond the ordinary world.

2

Boston

Frances stared out the grimy boarding house window at the incessant rain. There hadn't been one sunny day since she'd been dismissed from Miss Llewellyn's.

Brooding, she jumped when a knock came at the door.

The tight-faced woman who ran the dismal place stood in the hallway. "That man's here to see you again."

Frances cracked open the door of her room a little wider. "Mr. Nathan Gannon?" That would be a welcome surprise.

The woman nodded, appearing cold, if not disapproving. "He's in the parlor." Then she shuffled off down the dim hallway.

Quickly, Frances glanced in the cracked mirror over the washstand and rearranged her shawl. Not that doing so would make her any less plain and not that Nathan Gannon had any more interest in her than a shared concern for Louisa Janks.

"Uncle Nate" had taken a lengthy train trip from New Mexico to Boston to take Louisa home. Upon his arrival, Louisa had insisted he find the teacher who'd befriended her. Renting a carriage, the two had spent an entire day searching every boarding house and hotel within walking distance of the school.

Their sudden appearance had been a ray of sunshine among the heavy clouds for Frances. Louisa had hugged her and begged for forgiveness, thinking the dismissal her fault. The girl might have a temper, but she also had a kind heart. Then they'd all gone out to supper together.

Expecting to find Louisa with her uncle now, Frances hurried down the stairs and into the parlor. But Nathan Gannon stood waiting, seemingly alone. A man who looked to be in his early fifties, he had attractive features, silver hair and a small, neat mustache.

He flashed his infectious smile as he took her hand. "I hope you don't mind that I've come calling on my own today."

"Is Louisa all right?"

"Right as rain. She's packing to get on the train tomorrow."

Frances felt a twinge of sadness. She'd really be alone once they were gone. Worse, considering how fast her meager savings were being used up, she'd probably be in the street.

"You're having a bad time, aren't you?" asked Gannon, sobering. His eyes were sympathetic and as blue as the satin brocade vest he wore beneath his dapper gray coat. "No prospects?"

Frances knew he meant her search for employment and she didn't want pity. "I shall find a position yet. I simply am not the sort of woman shop owners usually hire as a seamstress." More than one had appeared taken aback and said she was too educated.

"And you can't get a governess job, can you? That old biddy at Llewellyn's would never give you a reference."

"I'm sure she'd rather have her tongue cut out."

Gannon smiled. "Seriously, what will you do?"

Questioned point-blank, Frances could hardly avoid telling the truth. "Return to Pennsylvania, if I must. My family is there." Her mother would force her father to take her in.

"Doesn't sound like you want to do that, though."

She nodded. "My father and I had a falling out when I left years ago."

Frances still didn't appreciate her father's approach to religion. Because it had been expected of her, she'd gone to chapel at the school but had no desire to join a church, making her wonder about the depth of her own faith.

"I can understand bull-headed fathers." Nate frowned, as if dredging up memories. "Have you thought about any other alternatives?"

She wished he wouldn't press the matter of her future. "Please, do not be concerned."

"Sorry." His tone was warm. "But I can't help but worry about you, Miss MacDonnell. It can be a cruel world and I am ever sympathetic with those who break its rules." In the next breath, he asked, "Have you considered marriage?"

She almost laughed, in spite of the situation.

"Is the idea so ridiculous?"

"Speaking of rules, Mr. Gannon, I am twenty-nine years old, a spinster in the eyes of society. And even when younger, I wasn't to many men's liking. I was considered too strong-minded and outspoken." Not to mention plain.

He raised his brows. "What kind of men called on you?"

"Oh, missionaries, churchmen—"

He snorted. "Well, they must have been a bunch of milk-toothed cowards." Once again, he took her hand to press it between his own. The gesture made odd little goose bumps rise on her forearm. "You have real gumption and intelligence. At least you can think and speak for yourself. No one else at that school accepted Louisa's background, and no one else stood up for her."

"I only did what my heart told me."

"You're a special sort of woman."

Embarrassed, she lowered her eyes at the compliment. "Why, thank you."

He stepped nearer to tip up her chin. "And you're much better looking than you think."

The goose bumps spread. She hadn't been this close to a man . . . well, ever. "I—I hardly know what to say."

"Then don't say anything." His gaze was steady. "Just listen. How about marrying me and coming out to New Mexico?"

Her jaw dropped and she moved away in shock. "M—Marry you?"

"Would that be so bad?"

"Not bad at all, Mr. Gannon," she said hurriedly, in case he thought she didn't find him attractive. "But . . . well, we hardly know each other." And they hadn't been courting, at least to her knowledge. Furthermore, she feared he was making the offer purely out of kindness. "You are certainly generous, but marriage is too much to ask."

spree, and had finally spent their wedding night in an impressive hotel. Frances now wore a gold ring on her left hand and possessed an expensive new wardrobe, as well as an entirely different outlook on life.

If nothing else, she was no longer a blushing maiden spinster.

Thinking about that as she held hands with Nate in one of the plush dining cars of the Atchison, Topeka & Santa Fe Railroad, she smiled, then lowered her eyes. Well, then again, perhaps she was now a blushing wife.

After some initial discomfort, she'd found lovemaking pleasurable. She looked forward to trying it again when they had privacy and a real bed to share, rather than a curtained Pullman berth.

"Would you like some dessert, sweetheart?" Nate asked, bringing her out of her reverie.

The waiter stood at the table.

Frances smiled at him, then at her husband. "No, thank you. I found the antelope steak very filling." Not to mention the blue-winged teal, new potatoes and corn on the cob that had been served with the gourmet meal. "Some more coffee, please. That's all."

"Brandy with that?" Nate inquired.

"Perhaps a small glass." Her new husband had nothing against ladies imbibing alcohol from time to time. Never having tasted it before she met him, Frances had more than once gotten a little tipsy during their journey.

At which Nate had only been amused. He was a very liberal-minded man.

"You can have some, too, if you want," he told Louisa, seated on the opposite side of the table.

The girl made a face, but she was only teasing. "I don't like anything stronger than sarsaparilla, Uncle Nate."

"Oh, I forgot about that." Indulgent as always toward the girl, he ordered the waiter, "Bring her a nice big glass."

The man moved off but soon returned with a tray of drinks. An expert at traversing the rattling cars, he didn't spill a drop.

Frances had watched the dining car servers in amazement during the first meal she'd taken on the train. But then, nearly everything about this modern mode of transportation amazed her, from the reclining chairs in the first-class cars to the speed with which the outside world passed by the windows. The only discomforts were the ever-present coal dust that settled on her clothing and the intermittent delays. They'd been held up for three hours in Kansas when a herd of long-horned cattle had to be driven off the tracks.

What a visual spectacle that had been. After days of traversing increasingly flat prairie grassland, Frances had enjoyed watching dusty "cowboys" herding the cattle. She had also liked looking out on infamous Dodge City as they passed through, noting its many livestock pens and the ugly false-fronted buildings Nate had told her were saloons. With a laugh, he explained that men who went to those places regularly got drunk and were cleaned out of their money by professional card players. He sobered when Frances admitted she thought that more appalling than funny.

She would have to learn to live and let live in this brand new world. The scenery itself had changed as they steamed across Colorado and into New Mexico. What Frances had assumed were clouds on the horizon became tall mountains as they approached. The soil had gotten redder and rocky, while the usual broadleaf trees changed to aspen and fir.

"This is high desert," Nate told her, noticing her staring out the window at rugged red buttes. "Like in Santa Fe. It doesn't rain much and the snow usually melts in the winter, but the weather's pretty comfortable all around."

Louisa also gazed out the window, a big smile on her face. "Only a few more hours and I'll be home. And Ma better not send me away again or I'm going to take my horses and head for the mountains!"

Nate rolled his eyes. "How many schools is this—three?"

"Four."

"Oh, dear," murmured Frances. Nate had told her that Louisa had been dismissed before, but she had no idea there'd been that many institutions.

Louisa tossed her head, her cloud of black hair now loosened from its braids and tied back with a simple ribbon. "Half-breeds aren't very welcome in cities like Boston."

"Or St. Louis or Chicago or San Francisco," added Nate. He told Frances, "I got the job of rescuing her from all those places."

Which was kind of him, Frances thought, considering Louisa was only the daughter of Nate's business partner Belle Janks, rather than his own flesh and blood. She'd learned much on the train ride, though there was far more she wanted to know. She hadn't yet found the right moment to ask about Louisa's Comanche father, how Belle had managed to take up with an Indian warrior. And neither Nate nor Louisa seemed inclined to tell all. Though they kept up a lively patter, Nate obviously doting on the girl he said was like a daughter to him, they spoke more of the present than the past. Frances supposed she could ask questions outright, but she was enjoying herself so much she hesitated to cast a serious pall over the partylike atmosphere.

"Now you know your mother only wants what's best for you," Nate was telling Louisa. "She wants you to be an educated lady, someone who doesn't have to lead a hard life like she did."

The girl shrugged. "I can already read in both English and Spanish."

The latter being the second language of New Mexico Territory, a tongue Frances was also going to have to learn.

"And I don't want to be a lady," Louisa went on. "I want to be a rancher and a horse-breaker."

Nate shook his head. "It's that damnable Comanche blood." When he noticed Frances gazing at him curiously, he explained. "Comanches are just about born on horseback. It's a toss-up whether their warriors or the Sioux are the best light cavalry in the world."

"But I don't even remember any Comanches," Louisa put in. "I was only four when we left Texas."

"Still, it's in your blood." Nate took a sip of brandy.

Frances saw an opening to appease her curiosity. "You didn't know your father, Louisa?"

"He was killed before I was born." Which was all the girl would offer. She turned around in her seat, gesturing to a beckoning mesa outside. "I'd love to be galloping across there with the wind in my hair. There's nothing else like it in the world."

"Really? I've never ridden a horse myself," said Frances, though she intended to try it.

"Don't worry, I'll teach you." Louisa grinned. "And it won't be on any old sidesaddle either." She looked at Nate. "Susie is gentle enough for her, don't you think?"

"Your old paint? I would think so." Again, he

obviously felt it necessary to make an explanation to Frances, "A paint is a pinto, a horse with two colors."

"Oh."

The day before, Nate and Louisa had gotten into a long discussion about horses—claybanks, buckskins, blue roans, Appaloosas, as well as the blooded horses from Nate's childhood home, Kentucky. Thus Frances had learned another tidbit of information about his background. Many of the other details brought up in the horse discussion, such as how to tell if an animal were sound or a good runner, simply made her head spin.

Not that Nate and Louisa left her out of conversations. One day, they'd told her the history of Santa Fe, a city that had been founded ten years before the Pilgrims landed at Plymouth Rock. They'd also given her an overview of food and customs in New Mexico. She'd learned many new words such as mestizo, pueblo, hidalgo, fandango, chili. That's when she realized she'd eventually have to study Spanish, especially if she were to be of any use around the Blue Sky Palace, Nate's establishment.

Nate spoke little about himself, even when they were alone together. It was always Frances who ended up talking about her past and sometimes she worried about that. She didn't want her husband to be a stranger and, for a moment, had allowed herself to wonder if she'd been a rash fool to marry him.

Not that she'd had many options from which to choose, and she truly did care for Nathan Gannon. Frances even fancied she might be in love.

The winds of change had simply blown her out of her usual path, she decided, and she would have to cope with the place where they finally put her down.

Louisa was still staring longingly out the window.

"How I've missed you, Sangre de Cristos!"

The Blood of Christ Mountains—Frances had looked that up on a map and realized with a start they weren't that far from their destination. "How soon will we reach Galisteo Junction?"

Nate took out the heavy gold watch he kept in his vest pocket. "A couple more hours. Then it'll take another hour before the shuttle train gets into Santa Fe."

So their arrival was imminent.

"I have to repack my bag." The one Frances kept beneath her seat with her night things and some new books she'd purchased in Chicago. "And I have to freshen up." She wanted to look nice.

Nate rose and pulled out her chair. "I'll walk you back there, sweetheart."

On the way, he crossed between cars first and offered a gentlemanly hand to help Frances over, the wheels clacking beneath her while the wind tore at her skirts and hair. She didn't know how he'd gotten to be a hotel and restaurant owner in New Mexico, but from his manners and bearing, as well as his tastes for first-class hotels and train tickets, she suspected he'd been raised by a family of some means in Kentucky.

Their passenger car was sparsely populated now, had been since they'd left Kansas. There was only one other couple sitting near the back and, on the opposite side, a grandmotherly-looking woman with a small child.

Before Frances could start going through her bag, Nate slid an arm about her shoulders. "I want to have a little heart-to-heart talk with you before we get to Santa Fe, Frances."

"To tell me about your background, your family?" Which had been foremost on her mind. "I'd love to hear about it."

"Well, that, too."

She gazed at him curiously.

"I guess I'm kind of used to being mysterious," Nate admitted, his free hand fiddling with his heavy watch fob. "Out West, most everyone has a few secrets to hide. You don't ask too many questions. You take a man or a woman on what they do and say right now."

For a moment, Frances grew concerned. "You have secrets you want to hide?"

"Don't worry, I'm not married already." Nate laughed.

She hadn't even thought of that. "Thank heavens!"

He laughed again, sounding a bit uncomfortable. "You and I have had very different experiences in life, sweetheart. We need to talk about that."

She couldn't help but feel relieved. "I'm curious about your experiences."

"Well, I'm going to tell you all . . ."

Then the woman seated in the back cried out, "Indians! Look at the Indians!"

The woman's male companion leaned over to gaze out the train window and the grandmother and child rose to stare as well. Curious herself, Frances rushed to look, Nate beside her.

Outside, a band of warriors galloped alongside the train on their ponies. "Look," said Frances, awed. "How can they ride without saddles and bridles?" The Indians had only simple ropes looped through their animals' mouths. "And how colorful they are, even if they aren't wearing war paint!"

"I would hope not." Nate chuckled. "They're probably some of the bucks off the northern reservation. They're not going to attack us, like the redskins in Ned Buntline's dime novels." Frances had admitted she'd riffled through one of those in a bookstore.

"They're minding their own business. Seem to be Navajos."

"Navajos? How can you tell?"

"Their looks—arrogant and lean. And see how their hair is clubbed up in back? You can tell the different tribes apart, once you get used to seeing them."

"Will there be a great many Indians in Santa Fe?"

"From time to time, but they'll mainly be Pueblo." Then he told her, "On first sight, Santa Fe isn't exactly pretty, you know. It's an old city but it's also a frontier town. There's an army post right off the central plaza and new people always coming and going, some of them the rough sort."

"I'm not expecting Boston." She admitted, "And I'm very excited!"

Nate drew her against him. "I hoped you'd think it so." He kissed her softly, lowering his voice. "And I can't wait to get you all to myself again."

They were pressed so tightly together, Frances could feel his watch chain against her ribs, even through her corset and silk bodice. Little butterflies of excitement danced inside her.

Hearing someone clear her throat, Frances glanced to the side to see that Louisa had joined them. Nate released Frances with a last peck on the cheek and the girl giggled. Louisa hadn't said much about the sudden marriage, yet she seemed approving, having acted as Frances's bridesmaid in Boston.

Everyone got busy then, readying themselves to disembark. Frances herself forgot about the heart-to-heart Nate had promised until they were pulling into Galisteo Junction.

Then she stared out the window at the western town and buttoned the jacket of the elegant suit her husband had bought her in Chicago. The plum purple velvet skirt was the newest fashion, the sort that hugged a woman's front and ended in a bustle in back. Frances thought the outfit the height of luxury, especially when Nate had insisted she purchase accessories to go with it—purple kid boots, green gloves, green silk hat with veil and small purple feathers. She felt quite the lady.

Louisa, on the other hand, had assumed a completely different style. Glancing at her now, Frances had to admire the girl's bright red shirt worn with a long brown skirt, high leather boots . . . and no corset. Some people in Boston might think such clothing outlandish, but it fit Louisa's personality. The closer the train had approached New Mexico, the more alive and free Louisa seemed to be.

Frances also inspected Nate, who appeared as dapper and well-groomed as usual. His plaid vest might be a bit bright for Boston but he wasn't a conservative banker. He was a man of the West.

The West—Frances could hardly believe she was here.

Her heart raced as the conductor helped Frances down onto the rough-planked railway platform. The sight of Galisteo Junction wasn't terribly inspiring. A few dusty brown streets led into the surrounding hilly terrain and a couple of buildings sat near the railroad. They sported false fronts like the saloons of Dodge City. Other structures seemed to be mere shacks.

"Is the shuttle leaving right away?" she asked Nate.

"Not for a few minutes."

"Can we go look at the town?" Frances was curious about everything.

"There's not much to see, but if you want, sure." He asked Louisa, "Care to come with us?"

"Thanks, but I've seen it. I'll wait for you here."

The other passengers were also disembarking, Galisteo Junction being the end of the line. Nate and Frances followed a man carrying a red carpet bag as he stepped off the platform and into the street. A few yards away, a brown boy herded goats and in the doorway of a nearby building lurked a tall, hard-looking man with long black hair and a huge pistol strapped to his thigh. He actually might be considered attractive if he weren't so dirty and scruffy, Frances thought, staring.

A subtle aura surrounded him, an aura of danger.

"It's not a good idea to be looking at that hombre so hard, sweetheart," advised Nate, sounding uneasy. "He's likely a gunslinger."

Unfortunately, that only made Frances stare harder. She watched as the man with the red carpet bag headed directly toward the gunman.

Then, from behind them, came the sound of galloping hooves. Frances glanced over her shoulder to see several mounted men riding down the middle of the street. As she and Nate tried to get out of the way and the boy with the goats started running, the scruffy gunslinger straightened and took out his pistol. "Watch out!" cried Nate. "Gunfight!" He pushed Frances sideways so hard, she landed on the ground with a thump.

Crack, crack, crack . . .

Cheek against the dirt, heart beating wildly, Frances heard several more shots exchanged between the mounted men and the gunslinger. She was so afraid, she lay quite still, though from her position, she could see the churning hooves of the horses as the mounted men rode on, one of them slumped over the saddle.

The man with the carpet bag also seemed to be a casualty. He lay on the ground near the scruffy gunman, who still had his weapon drawn. When he groaned, the gunman glanced down at him.

The gunman motioned to an approaching man who was wearing a leather coat. "Take care of him, Martinez."

Was the violence all over?

Concerned for her husband, Frances raised her head as soon as she dared. He lay a few feet away on his back.

"Nate?"

He was lying very still and didn't answer.

"Nate!"

Frightened, she struggled to her feet, not an easy task with her heavy skirt. She saw the bloody hole in her husband's chest before she'd even reached him. His eyes were open, staring up at the sky.

"Nate!" she cried yet again, falling to her knees, pulling a lacy handkerchief out of her reticule to staunch the flow of seeping red.

3

"Everything will be all right," Frances told her fallen husband, worried at the blood that soaked the handkerchief and his vest. "I'll get a doctor."

A crowd of men had slowly gathered about her, though all she was aware of were boots and dusty trousers and murmuring voices.

A big, gentle hand touched her shoulder. "He don't need a doctor, Ma'am. He's dead."

"Dead? He can't be!" But with sinking horror, Frances realized that Nate wasn't breathing, that his eyes were already clouding over. Her heart froze and she shrieked, "No!" Then tears streamed down her face. "Oh, Nate!"

The same gentle hand again touched her shoulder, though she barely noticed, she was shaking so hard. He brushed Nate's eyes shut. "I know it's hard, Ma'am."

Louisa suddenly pushed her way through the crowd. The girl caught her breath sharply but she didn't scream. "Oh, no! Uncle Nate!" Eyes full of tears, she ran to Frances.

Frances clung to the girl but was unable to feel comforted. "How could this happen?"

"Someone shot him!" Louisa gazed around at the crowd. "Who?"

"It was an accident." The emotionless voice came from the scruffy gunman. "He was in the line of fire."

Frances gazed up at the tall man through a film of dust and veil and tears. Eyes oddly pale in a bronzed face stared back at her. "You? You killed him?"

The gunman offered, "I'll pay for his funeral and burial."

He was blithely suggesting he give poor Nate a funeral? As if that would make everything better? He had taken a life in an act of terrible violence! Frances was beside herself.

"Murderer!" she screamed, rising to throw herself at the man. "Cold-blooded killer!"

The surrounding crowd parted like water. Thoughtless of her own safety, she pounded her fists against the gunman's chest.

"You murdered my husband!"

And snatched away her new life!

The gunslinger took hold of her shoulders, easily keeping her at arm's length. Her fists flailed the air.

"Look, I'm sorry, I really am." Though his voice remained cold and distant-sounding. "But it was an accident. I was defending myself against those men on horseback."

"Murderer!"

"No, it was an accident, not a murder, all right," said an onlooker as the crowd began to mutter louder. "I saw it. And so did Will here. There's no need to have anybody arrested."

"Killer!" Frances shrieked as Louisa pulled her away from the gunman. Sobbing, she gazed about, finally seeing the individuals who'd gathered round, a mixture of Anglo and Spanish men. "No need for anyone to be arrested?" she asked disbelievingly. "What kind of place is this?"

"New Mexico Territory, Ma'am," said the man who'd touched her shoulder and closed Nate's eyes. He had a kind weathered face with a big brown mustache under a dusty wide-brimmed hat. "We don't hang men unless they steal horses or kill somebody a'purpose."

"That's the truth," Louisa told Frances, her eyes red and sad. "It's the law of the West."

The law of the West.

Emotionally drained, Frances was barely aware of the next half hour as a lawman arrived, papers were signed and Nate's body covered with a blanket before being placed on the shuttle train. The poor man might have been stripped if Louisa hadn't had the wherewithal to remove his valuables. Frances glanced at the items quickly before placing them in her bag—a money belt, which wasn't heavy, a wallet, the big gold watch with its fob and a small pistol Louisa called a derringer.

Louisa also spoke to Nate's killer when the tall gunman drew the girl off to one side. Frances had no idea what they talked about, but she couldn't help hating the man who'd destroyed her life. She hadn't felt so helpless since she'd seen soldiers put Indians in chains and take away their children at the missionary reserve camp.

She stared at the gunman anyway, noting the proud way he held himself in spite of his shabby appearance and beard-stubbled face. He shouldn't be proud; he should be ashamed! And his expression was so hard and emotionless.

Didn't he have a heart?

Belle laughed. "Satan? I'd need horns and a forked tail."

She surely would like to know what secrets Minna Tucker had hidden away. In her experience, a person that loudly devout was usually covering up terrible guilt of some kind. Minna was wasting her time trying to make Belle feel guilty, though. Having done what she thought she must to exist, if on the boundaries of proper society, she had little or no shame.

Belle's attitude toward Louisa was completely different, of course. Her dream had always been to see the girl accepted. She knew her daughter's Comanche blood didn't help matters any, but surely education and manners counted for something. Hopefully, a respectable man would marry her.

Damn Louisa for causing trouble again! She'd saved good money to send her daughter to four schools now, only to have the girl be sent home every time. Didn't Louisa realize how hard she'd worked, how much she wanted to see her rise above the sordid life she herself had had to lead?

Insane asylums and jail.

Belle would do anything to keep Louisa from seeing the inside of either one of those institutions.

The shuttle train climbed upward as it cut through the mountains rimming Santa Fe. Clear golden sunlight spilled over bluish-green shrubs and layered red rock. More mountains hovered on the horizon, lavender with distance.

Frances would have thought the scenery beautiful if she hadn't gone through the hellish scenario in Galisteo Junction. Despite her desire to forget him, she kept envisioning the gunfighter, the cool gray eyes that had chilled her to her bones, the aura of danger that he exuded, which should have warned her. She only half-listened as Louisa babbled about Nate continuously and intently, as if she were trying to exorcise his murder from her soul.

"Uncle Nate ran away from his family in Kentucky, you know, when he was only eighteen. Then he traveled west and ended up on one of those riverboats from New Orleans. That's where he learned card playing. He was good at all the games, even blackjack and keno. You never saw such a fast hand with cards. Sometimes he even did tricks with them."

Frances cleared her throat. Her dark state of mind made her suspect the worst. "You mean cheating?"

"No, actual tricks—making cards appear and disappear." Louisa paused. "I guess he did do a fair amount of cheating, too, though he never actually admitted it. All card players do. You know how they trim the edges a tiny bit or mark them?"

No, Frances had no idea.

"But Uncle Nate had a heart," Louisa went on. "He never took advantage of men with families."

"How nice," Frances said sarcastically and then immediately felt badly about it. After all, Nate was dead.

"He was kind," Louisa insisted. "He loaned money to people that he knew would never repay it, and he always gave to churches who were taking up collections for the poor."

And he'd married a spinster who had nowhere to turn, Frances thought with mixed feelings. Now she remembered the remark she'd made about card players when Nate had pointed out the saloons in Dodge City. She must have made him uncomfortable, too much to even try explaining anything to her.

"Uncle Nate was good-natured. He meant well,

though he didn't always tell the truth, especially if he thought it would hurt someone." Louisa's remark made Frances wonder if they were thinking along the same lines. "He was understanding. If I wanted someone to talk to, he always listened—"

Then the girl was silent, which made France look at her. She had her fist pressed against her mouth, silently weeping.

"Oh, dear, I've been thinking entirely about myself. This has been terrible for you!"

She put her arms about Louisa, who sobbed against her shoulder. How selfish she'd been. But the sixteen-year-old had handled the situation so capably, and Frances herself had been so upset, she simply hadn't worried about Louisa. She'd assumed the girl must be used to sudden violence like gunfights in the street.

When Louisa got herself together, she raised her head. "Thank you. I appreciate your kindness, too. I know you're a special sort of person. So did Uncle Nate, or he wouldn't have married you."

The remark caused Frances's eyes to burn, though she'd thought she was cried out for the moment.

Then both women sniffed and wiped their eyes.

Louisa patted Frances's hand. "It'll be okay. You'll see. You'll live in Uncle Nate's quarters at Blue Sky Palace. He has two rooms upstairs with a real bathtub that came over the Santa Fe Trail."

"The rooms are above the casino?"

"Uh, huh." Louisa frowned at Frances's expression. "You know, there's a lot of gambling in Santa Fe. It's a popular and accepted form of entertainment."

Well, maybe such a place wasn't too disreputable then. If Frances didn't like the looks of it, however, she intended to find the nearest boarding house.

At least Nate would be spared breaking the truth to her, a truth he was probably attempting to reveal before they reached Galisteo Junction. She thought of him lying cold and dead in the baggage car. "What will we do with . . . with the body when the train stops?"

"You don't have to worry about it. Chaco Jones is back there. He's going to take care of everything."

"Chaco Jones?" What an odd name. "Who's that?"

"Well, um, the gunfighter." Louisa met her gaze.

Frances's mouth dropped. "You *are* letting him pay for the funeral and burial!" She hadn't agreed to that.

"Why not?" Louisa frowned and sounded defensive. "He owes us that much. I gave him the name of an undertaker in Santa Fe."

"But it's blood money!"

"I guess it is," said Louisa unwaveringly. "One of the men in Galisteo Junction said his word could be trusted."

"The word of a gunfighter?" Frances thought of those riveting gray eyes again. "The man is a criminal!"

"Probably. But there are those with a code of honor."

"I can't believe you're acting so calmly about this!"

"I know." Louisa's eyes were wise beyond her years. "But this isn't Boston. And I don't think Chaco Jones meant to kill Uncle Nate. We'll let him do what he can."

Frances still didn't understand. Though she tried to forget about the awful gunfighter riding with her husband's body as the shuttle pulled into Santa Fe, his spooky gray gaze remained burned in her memory. She couldn't believe she'd thought him attractive in a dangerous way. She would never forget that he was a cold-blooded killer or that he'd destroyed her dreams.

Gazing out at the small train station, beyond which

were a mix of clapboard and adobe buildings, she thought the place as nondescript and dusty as Galisteo Junction. But then she would have had a completely different view of the old city if she'd been arriving at her new home on Nate's arm. When the train stopped, they went to the door of the car to let the conductor help them disembark with their bags.

"There's Ma!" cried Louisa, waving.

Frances gazed in that direction to see a smiling, middle-aged, red-headed woman approaching. Dressed in a tight, gray-silk dress with ruffles around the low neck and several flounces about the fashionable skirt, lace mitts, a hat with tall white plumes, a sparkling necklace and dangling earrings, Mrs. Belle Janks was a bit overdressed but presentable, Frances thought.

The redhead immediately hugged Louisa, complaining gently, "You bad, bad girl!"

"Oh, Ma!"

Then the woman pulled back to look at her daughter's face. "You been crying. What's the matter?" She also glanced at Frances. "You're Nate's wife?" And as her eyes swept over Frances's appearance, she exclaimed. "Damnation! Where did all that blood come from?"

Frances took a deep breath, ignoring the language. "Nate was shot down in Galisteo Junction."

"Shot down!"

Belle's eyes widened, large brown orbs, which Frances suddenly noticed had been outlined in black. And the woman was also wearing lip and cheek rouge. Perhaps face-painting, like gambling, was accepted in Santa Fe.

"My God," the woman gasped, "is he dead?"

"Yes, Ma," said Louisa, holding onto Belle when her mother gave a little cry. "But it was an accident. A stray bullet from a gunfight."

"Dead!" Now it was Belle's turn to deal with grief. Her face twisted. "No, not Nate!"

Frances herself felt numb and completely cried out. She watched the other two as they sobbed in each other's arms.

But as Belle regained control of herself, she offered sympathy. "You poor, poor thing! And just married, too!"

The redhead embraced Frances so hard, her ribs felt squeezed. For a while, the three women simply stood on the platform and commiserated. Belle cried some more and wiped away the rivulets of black on her cheeks with a silk, lace-edged handkerchief. Louisa sniffled. Frances even found a few more tears to burn her already irritated eyes.

"I still can't believe it," Belle mourned. "Old Nate could'a been shot dead a hundred times at the gaming tables. And look what happens . . . a stray bullet gets him!"

Frances suddenly realized she herself could be at fault. "Oh, dear!" She pressed her hand to her mouth. "I was the one who asked Nate to go for a walk. That's why we were in the middle of the street in Galisteo Junction!" Her knees went weak as guilt nearly overwhelmed her.

But Louisa was quick to intervene. She grabbed Frances's arm and held her up. "That's not true! A stray bullet can get you anywhere."

Belle also had her say-so as she grasped Frances's other arm. "Now you listen here, Frances." She shook her finger. "Don't you be swallowin' guilt, now. That's the way a person makes herself think she has some kinda control of the world. But she usually don't. Never forget that!"

Frances managed to nod. She was feeling odd at

being lectured, but the woman meant well. Belle and Louisa took charge of the situation, finding everyone's baggage and having it loaded onto Belle's regal-looking carriage by a brown-skinned driver. Belle also checked on the whereabouts of Nate's body, learning that Chaco Jones had already arranged for the undertaker to cart it away.

"The funeral'll be tomorrow," Belle informed the other two as they all climbed into the carriage. She glanced at the big fancy new trunk Nate had picked out for Frances in Chicago. "You got quite a load there."

"Uncle Nate bought her a trousseau," explained Louisa.

Belle raised her brows.

"She was my teacher at Miss Llewellyn's School, Ma," Louisa went on. "The one I wrote you about. She was dismissed after I got into the fight with that other girl."

Belle gazed at Frances so closely, she felt uncomfortable. "A schoolmarm, huh? No wonder you're so proper-looking."

"She stood up for me, Ma."

"So you got courage," Belle said.

"I've always hoped so." Though Frances wasn't sure she would have been brave enough to defend Louisa if she'd guessed it might get her dismissed. But she wanted to make a more important admission. "I believe Nate may have married me because he knew I had no way to earn money and nowhere to go."

"Hmm." Belle sighed and shook her head. "More to it than that. I don't believe Nate would up and marry you for the hell of it, no matter how sorry he felt for you."

Louisa added, "He really liked her."

Belle smiled. "Loved her, you mean. The old fool finally fell head over heels."

Which Frances had to admit made her feel a tad better, even in her awful state. And even with the swearing. Belle Janks was definitely a rough-speaking woman.

For a while, the carriage passengers remained silent as the driver took the matched set of trotting grays along winding, narrow streets, mostly lined with high adobe walls. Trees and open spaces finally began to appear as they neared what seemed to be the edge of the town.

"I'm gonna leave Louisa at my house," Belle told Frances. "Then we'll go on to the Blue Sky Palace."

Frances noticed that Louisa suddenly sat up straighter. The girl seemed nervous. "Um, Ma? Uncle Nate didn't tell her about the casino, you know."

Belle frowned. "What?"

"He didn't even tell her he was a gambler. She learned about that from me on the train ride up here."

Mother and daughter exchanged what appeared to be meaningful looks, though Frances wasn't at all sure what that meaning was.

The carriage came down a hill toward a neat little house built partially of weathered logs and partially of adobe. Tall trees—the kind Nate had pointed out as cottonwoods—grew in the yard in back, which was surrounded by adobe walls. A large fenced-in meadow adjoined the place and a couple of horses grazed on the sparse grass.

"Home!" Louisa sighed happily.

"Tell Elena to get you some supper," Belle ordered her daughter. "I'll be comin' back later."

The driver unloaded Louisa's luggage and with a last hug for her mother and Frances, the girl disappeared inside. Then the carriage turned and headed back for the main part of town.

Once underway, Belle turned to Frances. "I guess it's up to me to explain things." She took a deep breath. "Damn that Nate. Always giving me the dirty work."

Frances immediately became uneasy. "What else is there to explain?"

"You seem to be a well-bred lady. How do you feel about living above a casino?"

"Louisa said gambling was an acceptable form of entertainment out here."

"Well, that's true." Belle tapped her fingers on the edge of the carriage. "Even when *La Tules* opened a casino twenty-five years ago, she was accepted by local society."

Frances relaxed a little. But she noticed that Belle kept tapping her fingers.

"The only thing is, the Blue Sky ain't just a casino. We also have ladies there who . . . well, they entertain lonely gentlemen."

"Gentlemen?" Frances felt confused for a moment, turning Belle's statement over in her mind. Ladies who entertained? Surely Belle didn't mean what she feared. "You're not referring to a—" She couldn't quite bring herself to say the word.

Belle put in hurriedly, "I call it the Blue Sky Gentlemen's Club." She insisted, "But I run an honest, clean place. Nothing to be ashamed of."

Frances's heart thudded against her ribs. Belle *did* mean what she had feared. "Ashamed?" Her voice rose and quavered. "You are telling me not to be ashamed of a house of ill repute? That's what a gentlemen's club is, isn't it? A brothel?"

"Afraid so, Frances. And you own half."

A brothel! She fell back against the seat, her heart pounding so hard, she felt the stays of her corset pressing in.

"You all right? You look peaked."

Frances didn't answer, hardly able to catch her breath.

"Damnation, you're turning purple," said Belle, concerned. She whipped out a fan from somewhere, a gray silk one with bright painted flowers. "Your lacing must be too tight. Now don't faint on me. It ain't the end of the world."

The moving air from the fan cooled Frances's heated skin. She took several careful breaths, before blurting, "I'm the daughter of a minister!" Though she'd never dreamed she would be proclaiming her father's occupation so stridently and to a madam, of all people.

Now it was Belle's turn to act shocked. She dropped the fan. "Nate married a minister's daughter? I can't believe it!"

Frances didn't intend to explain her estrangement from her family. Still catching her breath, she simply said, "I can't stay in a brothel!" Not if she ever had any hope of obtaining decent employment again.

"You can't?" Belle raised her brows. "Well, the only thing is, I don't know where else you *can* stay, honey."

Frances glanced about desperately, the continuous flat-faced adobe walls seeming to close in. "Surely there are boarding houses in this city."

"Not where a woman on her own would be safe, especially a tenderfoot like you." Belle glanced back at the trunk and bags. "Besides, you'd have to have enough money to pay for the lodging. Looks like Nate spent all he had on you."

All he had? "But he was the owner of a business."

"Uh, huh. Though I can't afford to buy you out, at least not now. Schooling for Louisa has been very expensive."

"But I have his money belt and a wallet. There must be something left in them."

"I hope there's some of that three-hundred dollars he borrowed from me before he went on the trip." Belle explained, "Nate got cleaned out at the tables a few weeks ago and hadn't recouped." She shrugged. "Sometimes he was loaded and sometimes he was broke. You know how gamblers can be."

"No, I don't."

The other woman gazed at her. "I guess you wouldn't." She shook her head sadly, then turned away, face toward the street. "What on earth was Nate thinking?"

Frances wondered that as well, though there would be no asking him now. Drawing herself together, attempting to be practical, she reached over the seat for her smaller bag. Opening it, she took out the money belt and wallet. Though it probably wouldn't matter, she found the latter empty and only a few low-denomination coins in the money belt.

"Not even enough to buy a return ticket to Boston! What am I to do?" The same question she'd asked herself the day Nate had proposed. She told Belle, "I would gladly sell you my entire half of the Blue Sky Palace for a ticket, plus the three-hundred Nate owed you, of course."

Belle smiled sadly. "I wouldn't let you settle for so little. No matter what you think about my profession, I'm honest. But I simply don't have much capital at the moment, and we have a slew of outstanding bills."

We. Frances had a difficult time thinking of herself as a brothel and casino owner.

"You don't know anyone in Santa Fe, do you?" Belle went on, musing. "Your pa and ma must still be back east. So, who's to care where you live?"

Frances supposed that was right.

"I don't see why you can't stay in Nate's quarters and work for a while. Unless business falls off completely, you should be able to go back home in a couple of months."

Work? Frances's eyes widened.

"You should be comfortable enough. Nate bought some new rugs and curtains a few months ago. Both of the rooms are large and the four-poster has a real feather bed."

On which Frances would be expected to earn her money? Her heart raced. "I simply can't!"

"Stay where Nate used to live? Don't worry, I'll sort through his belongings, if you want. Save you some pain."

"No, I mean I can't . . ." Again, she struggled with the words. "I can't entertain gentlemen!"

Belle stared, her expression rapidly changing from concerned to puzzled, then to amused. "You thought that's the kinda work I was talking about?" The redhead threw back her head and laughed. Then she hurriedly assured Frances, "I meant you'd do Nate's job. The book work and supply ordering, overseeing the casino. Think you can handle that?"

Frances wasn't certain at all. But the idea looked reasonably appealing, especially after fearing she'd have to do the unspeakable to earn money. She took a deep breath and hardened her jaw. "I *will* handle it."

"Course you will." Belle reached over to pat her hand. "We all gotta do what we must, that's the rule of existence. Welcome to Santa Fe."

So this is where the wind had brought her, Frances

thought—plopped her down in a casino, in the midst of a pack of ladies of the evening. Perhaps even that would be safer than the wild desert land outside the town or the sudden gunfights that could erupt on its open streets.

Shivering as she thought of Chaco Jones yet again, of the cold-blooded way he'd shot Nate down, Frances stared out at the alien landscape from the safety of the carriage—red earth, bright blue sky, the seemingly endless vista of blank adobe walls. The brown-skinned driver shook the reins and called out to the horses, *"Vamos, caballos!"*

There was even an alien language to get used to, not to mention a mix of several cultures. Would she be able to adjust? Frances wondered. As Belle had suggested, she supposed she would do what she must.

Indeed, she thought bitterly, welcome to Santa Fe!

4

Chaco had shot many men over the years, but never an innocent bystander. Feeling low as a snake, he had ridden the train to Santa Fe, then had gone through the motions of contacting and paying the undertaker, all the while haunted by the anguished screams of Nathan Gannon's widow ringing through his head. He could still feel her fists flailing at him helplessly, could see her husband's blood staining her clothing.

Remembering cut him to the quick.

Nathan Gannon. The name had held a familiar ring when he'd gotten it from the half-breed girl. Then it had come to him. Blue Sky Palace. He'd visited the place more than once and knew Gannon had a reputation of being a decent man, of running an honest game.

Well, he wouldn't be running games anymore, not unless faro and poker tables were part of white man's heaven.

Having left Martinez in Galisteo Junction to take care of the wounded man, Chaco had no reason to return to the smaller town. And the way he was feeling now, real sick deep down, he wasn't certain he wanted to return to Lincoln County. Might only return to Ralston's to quit. He'd had his stomach full of gunfighting.

Feeling dead to the world, he strolled down the streets of Santa Fe, paying little attention to who or what he passed. Still, a couple of times, he thought he sighted the same raggedy old woman in a black *rebozo*. Trailing him? If she was, he thought sardonically, what could he do—shoot her?

He wasn't certain how he ended up on a corner across from a small church. He stared at the adobe building with a simple cross on its bell tower for a few minutes before deciding to go inside. More Apache than Catholic, his mother hadn't taken him to church often but he could remember the singing and the prayers and the strong smell of incense.

He followed a middle-aged Mexican woman into the outer vestibule and emulated her ceremonial actions. Dipping a hand in the holy water, he quickly crossed himself. Then he started to follow the woman into the sanctuary when he realized he was still wearing his gun. He had misgivings about leaving the Colt on the gun rack near the door, but this was a holy place. He finally undid his belt and hung it beneath his hat.

The inner sanctuary was nearly as simple as the church's exterior. Beneath the vigas of its corbeled roof, a few rows of wooden benches were set on a packed earthen floor. Chaco eased himself onto one of the benches and let his eyes adjust to the dimness. Only a few other people were present, their heads bowed. Behind the altar was a painted wooden screen of sacred figures, a reredos. To one side hung the crucifix, a cross with a blood-speckled Jesus wearing a gold crown of thorns.

Small alcoves offered altars to other heavenly personages. Chaco immediately recognized his mother's favorite, the Virgin of Guadalupe. Oneida Jones had said she felt easier with Guadalupe, who was often portrayed with the brown skin of an Indian and the rays of the Aztec sun shining behind her back.

Which had been as positive as Oneida had gotten about Catholicism.

His half-breed mother had raised him in the Apache beliefs she'd grown up with. Spirit power imbued everything in the universe and could either be used by the wise for good or by the self-serving for evil. The Apaches had addressed that power in their ceremonies, including those performed for the dead.

But Nathan Gannon had not been Apache.

Though he'd probably been as decent as Oneida's bullwhacker husband Reuben Jones. The man had given Chaco his name and treated him like a son during his few brief years of marriage to Chaco's mother. Oneida had lit a candle for Reuben when he'd been killed on the Santa Fe Trail.

Would a candle help Gannon's soul? Chaco wondered, watching the Mexican woman slide a coin into the box near Guadalupe, then take a votive candle, light it and place it on the Virgin's altar.

The tiny flame glowed and flickered like a star in the darkness. Reminded of the starry, moonlit night when he'd seen the wolf, he dredged up the uneasy feelings he'd been having the past week or two. Had they been leading up to the shooting today?

To bad magic? Was a *bruja,* a skin-walker, on his trail?

He didn't want to consider that. At heart he might be mostly Apache, but he didn't like to give in to outright superstition.

As Chaco sat there brooding, he saw the church's padre come out of the confessional set up to one side. Surely a holy man's prayers would have more weight with the white man's God. If the padre prayed, perhaps Gannon could be moved to forgive Chaco in the next world, and perhaps her God would smile on Gannon's widow in this one. He couldn't forget her bravery in attacking someone like him. And her dirt-streaked face and heart-wrenching cries haunted him and invaded his dreams.

Chaco rose to approach the priest, who was short, balding and kind-faced. When caution flickered over the padre's features, Chaco realized his two-days growth of beard and hard expression probably frightened him. "Have no fear," he said in Spanish. "I'm here for prayer, not trouble."

The padre relaxed visibly. "Good, good. And would you like to make a confession as well, my son?"

Did the man know what he'd done? Chaco wondered uncomfortably, then decided the question was probably asked of everyone. "I'm not Catholic." He'd never been baptized. "I wouldn't know how. But I'd like a prayer said for a man who was killed today." His mother had told him that was possible. "How do I go about it?"

"For a small fee, I can say a mass for him," the padre offered. "That would be best."

Chaco didn't even bother asking how much the fee was. Instead, he reached into his pocket and brought out a crinkled piece of paper, then several twenty-dollar gold pieces. He placed some coins in the padre's hand.

"So generous! Thank you, my son."

"Do a real good mass for him. Name was Nathan Gannon." Chaco paused. "And could you say a prayer for Mrs. Gannon, too? Don't know much about her but she's all alone." Chaco could understand the situation, having been raised by Oneida.

The padre smiled. "Of course I will mention the widow. *Pobrecita!*"

Poor little one. Yeah, she was, Chaco thought, already feeling better.

Glancing at the paper he still held in his hand, the missive that had been hand-delivered days ago, he also realized he was now in the position to do something about it.

"And is there anything else, my son?"

He looked at the priest, surely a learned man as well as a holy one. "Can you read a letter for me? My Spanish isn't too good."

"You are speaking it well."

"Yeah, speak, not read." Chaco smoothed out the piece of paper, once again inspecting the flowing handwriting. To him, it was only a fancy design, except for his own name at the top and the signature at the bottom. "I didn't learn Spanish in school." Actually, he hadn't learned English there either. He'd attended school for only a few days at a time and couldn't read or write in any of the three languages he spoke. Not that he intended to admit that to anyone.

The priest motioned. "Come over here and we shall read your letter." He added, "And you need make no further donation. You have given enough."

He led Chaco to a small room that opened off the

sanctuary. Chaco sat on a bench in front of the padre's desk, where a kerosene lamp burned. The priest took a pair of spectacles from a drawer and read:

> *"To Señor Chaco Jones,*
> *You do not know me, but I have been aware of your existence since you were born. Your mother was my servant. I do not know exactly how to state this, Señor Jones, but I have come to believe that I should inform you that I am your father.*
> *If you would like to speak of this with me, you may find me at my estancia north of Santa Fe. Ask anyone of knowledge for directions if you do not already know your way.*
> *Don Armando de Arguello "*

The padre was visibly shocked. "Don de Arguello is your father?"

The priest, like everyone in this part of New Mexico Territory, was certainly aware of the wealthy, centuries-old Hidalgo family. And he probably wouldn't have expected such an announcement to be given to a dust-streaked mestizo gunfighter. Chaco simply sat and stared at the floor, emotions and thoughts awhirl. When he had seen the name de Arguello, he'd figured on some kind of job offer having to do with his reputation with a gun—one he'd already determined to turn down—but he had not expected this.

The padre shook his head in amazement. "Don de Arguello!"

Still in shock, Chaco suddenly became concerned. "You won't speak of this to anyone?"

"If you do not wish it. I am a man of God." The

padre folded the letter carefully and gave it back. "You are going to ride north and see the Don, are you not?"

"I don't know."

"But such an offer—"

"I don't need the money of a *rico*." A rich man who lived off of others. At least Chaco didn't need the money that bad. "I can take care of myself." He had done so since his mother died twenty years before.

"But you are of his blood."

"And that of a half-breed slave." On whom de Arguello may have forced himself, for all Chaco knew. Then, when she was pregnant, the wealthy man had given Oneida her freedom and some money to get her out of his house. "The Don hasn't bothered with me for thirty-five years," he said angrily. "Why should I be in a hurry to bother with him?"

At last, she had seen her enemy in the flesh, she rejoiced.

Having acted on the word of one of the spies she had sent to watch him, she had come to Galisteo Junction, then back to Santa Fe, dogging his footsteps.

Filled with hatred, she wanted to rip the meat from his bones, to smell the acrid odor of his life's blood seeping slowly out of his body.

And she could have that pleasure soon . . . if it were not for that peculiar aura of strength he exuded . . . and if her own mortal weaknesses did not hamper her. Her enemy was a well-made man, handsome beneath the dust and grime. His walk was graceful, gliding. He had the bearing of a fierce Apache warrior.

Apache!

She must remember that ancestry and how very much she longed for his death. She envisioned him dead now, ants eating his eyes, blood leaking into the sand from his torn throat, draining his life away.

His life—what a virile and tempting one, indeed.

Despite her passionate desire for his death, she also longed to feel him beneath her, wanted to ride his body like a bucking horse, wanted him to spill his heat and seed into her womb.

Life or death—she felt torn between them.

And power over either was not easy.

Meanwhile, she had followed him and watched him enter a church. Cursing, she also decided to go inside, though she hadn't had time to take her usual precautions.

Her muttering became low snarls as she felt the burning pain upon entering the vestibule. She tried to ignore the flames that flowed up through the earth and seared the soles of her feet through her shoes. Sighting his gun hanging on the rack, she was elated—she could take a piece of him with her. Drawing the knife from beneath her rebozo, disregarding her pain, she quickly cut off the piece of rawhide that had fastened the gunbelt to his thigh.

Then she fled, growling deep in her throat, pausing only long enough to spit on the threshold of this cursed holy ground.

Outside, she scurried down a narrow street, finally resting against an adobe wall until her feet cooled. Yet her burning hatred was not assuaged. Having always existed on the fringes of society, she prowled the streets for some time afterward, undetected, dreaming of special tortures while filled with itching desire.

Damn him!

Then she spotted a slim Navajo youth fastening his horse to a hitching post. He wore a bright blue shirt and around his head had tied a printed scarf from which flowed hair as black and sleek as a raven's wing.

Hmm. Rippling muscles, a glimpse of firm brown hip between his loincloth and leggings.

Yes, he would do.

Quickly, she straightened, threw aside her rebozo and opened the throat of her blouse. She swayed toward him, her eyes bold, hair loosened, breasts inviting. Knowing exactly how to influence him, she removed the packet of herbs from about her neck.

Thankfully, she would be able to take the edge off both her appetites.

Frances had traveled beyond the boundaries of her dreams. Every day she awakened in a strange, faraway land she could never have envisioned in Boston. Though its unpaved streets were rutted and much of its populace crude, Santa Fe bloomed like an exotic desert flower, face toward the eternally bright sun, petals fluttering to soft Spanish music, roots sunk deep in ancient soil.

She'd arrived little more than a week ago, but had managed to see some of the more picturesque parts of the city. Louisa had come by with a carriage one day and had driven her around. The girl had pointed out the central plaza, a small open square of paths and trees where a military band played on Saturday evenings while handsome caballeros paraded past giggling maidens in pretty shawls. Later on Saturday night, she suspected, other sorts of ladies made the place a rendezvous.

On one side of the plaza lay the Palace of the Governors, a long, seventeenth-century adobe building with a great portal and several heavy wooden doors. Having belonged to both the Indians for a short time after the Pueblo Indian revolt in 1680 and, mainly, the Spanish, the structure now housed the offices of the United States territorial government. The U.S. Army itself had taken up headquarters in the buildings north of the Palace, leaving barricaded Fort Marcy empty on its hill above the city.

Frances had seen plenty of soldiers come and go as clientele at the Blue Sky Palace. Not that she rubbed shoulders with the establishment's customers if she could help it. She had done her book work upstairs and had arranged for purchasing and delivery in the mornings before Blue Sky opened. And Belle had been kind enough to keep her "girls" confined to the saloon or the farthest wing of the hotel.

Frances hadn't had any trouble with the work and had even managed to make herself at home in Nate's rooms after Belle had helped her remove his clothing and personal items. The funeral over but not forgotten, she still felt shocked and sad, but she'd just about gotten settled in when yet another crisis loomed. The floorman who'd managed the casino, a traditional Mexican who'd worked for Nate for years, had quit, saying he simply couldn't be bossed by a woman.

She herself would now have to fill in and she was terribly nervous, even though Belle tried to reassure her.

"You don't have to worry about most of those

men," Belle said while Frances prepared for her first evening on the floor. "They'll treat you like a lady, especially since you act like one." The older woman looked over her high-necked black dress. "What are you wearing anyway? Not that, surely."

Frances stared in the full-length, gilt-edged mirror hanging on one whitewashed wall. Standing in the midst of couches and a four-poster all covered with bright Navajo blankets, she supposed she did resemble a pale-faced crow.

"The black is nice and I know you're still in mourning, but that red dress'd do a whole lot better for tonight."

"My ball gown?" The fancy beaded one Nate had picked out in Chicago? Frances cleared her throat. "It's a little too revealing, don't you think?" With tiny cap sleeves and a low-cut bodice, she'd be lucky if she didn't catch her death of cold. High desert evenings tended to be chilly.

"Well, you want to look dressed up, don't you?" Belle argued. "You want the customers to think you're making enough money to run a high-class game. At the same time, of course, you need to make them feel at ease." She knit her brows. "You know, speaking of feeling at ease, we really should do something about your hair. With it all slicked back like that, you still look like a schoolmarm."

Frances patted the brown strands self-consciously. "So?"

"You'll scare the customers away, honey. Not good for business."

Frances sighed. "I suppose not." And she needed their money to make a new start.

"Then I'll fetch the curling iron," said Belle, before sweeping out the door onto the roofed balcony that curved about the Blue Sky's inner *placita* and connected the building's C-shaped wings.

Hoping she wasn't going to regret what she was about to do, Frances laid the ball gown out on the bed and changed into a fancier corset and a stiffer satin petticoat. She had to remember that no one knew her in Santa Fe and that no one would be shocked at the idea of her sashaying through a gambling parlor in a blood-red dress.

She should also remember that she'd been dismissed by Miss Llewellyn of Miss Llewellyn's School for Girls and that there wasn't a chance in high heaven that she'd ever get another decent teaching position, even if she crawled all the way back to Boston and wore black for the rest of her life.

Teaching itself hadn't been a thrilling experience, especially its cramped dormitory living and the teaching of English Composition and Hygiene according to Miss Llewellyn's outdated, dried-up rules.

"Old prune," she muttered, thinking of the headmistress as she drew a casual wrapper around her. "Old prune face." Simply saying the words seemed to free her somehow. "Nasty, dried-up old vulture!"

When someone laughed, a soft giggle, Frances nearly jumped out of her skin. She whirled around to see a young blonde lounging against the half-open door that she hadn't thought to lock.

"Howdy." The girl smiled brightly. "Having fun?"

"I'm afraid you caught me talking to myself."

"Well, if no one else is around, why not?"

The blonde wasn't exactly pretty but she had long, abundant pale hair that hung down past the loose neck of the embroidered blouse she wore with a bright red skirt, bare legs and open sandals. The traditional outfit of most lower-class Mexican women, it kept them cool but would nevertheless be quite shocking to easterners.

Belle suddenly appeared at the door. "What are you doing up here, Ruby?"

"I got curious, thought I'd wander around a bit."

Belle said firmly, "You're new, I know, but you're supposed to stay downstairs."

The girl appeared downcast. "I guess I'll go then."

Frances noted that Ruby was young, no more than a year or so older than Louisa, and she was one of the "girls." Was there no other work the young girl could get? she wondered sadly. "No, wait, that's all right, Ruby can stay."

Belle was openly surprised. "She can?"

"Maybe you can use some help."

"I bet you can." Ruby immediately made herself useful. "You're gonna heat up that curling iron?" She grabbed it and stuck it in the corner adobe-style fireplace. "I'm real good at doing hair." She glanced at Frances, then at the gown on the bed. "And sewing, too. I could lower that bodice for you."

"Thank you, but it's already quite low enough."

Belle pulled out a straight-backed chair for Frances to sit on and searched the pockets of the apron she wore over her gold satin dress. "Damnation, I forgot my scissors."

"I'll go fetch them," Ruby offered, eager to be of help.

"Top drawer of the cabinet by the storage room."

The girl hurried outside.

"You're going to cut my hair?" Frances asked with trepidation.

"Only the front. When we're done, you'll have some nice curls around your face."

Hoping she wouldn't end up with an elaborate

style like Belle's own fussy ringlets and puffs, Frances asked, "How old is Ruby?"

"Says she's eighteen."

"More likely she's not much older than your daughter."

The lines around Belle's eyes deepened. "Maybe. But what can I do? She has to earn her way somehow and they beat her at that place on the other side of the plaza."

Frances shivered. "Good heavens!"

"No one will touch her here, you can be certain of that."

Belle employed several men as "protection" for Blue Sky, another reason she assured Frances that managing the casino would be safe enough.

"Ruby's popular with the Mexicans," mused Belle. "With that blonde hair, they call her *La Rubia.*"

Which meant blonde in Spanish, Frances knew.

When Ruby returned, she brought a couple of other women with her. Though they'd never officially met, Frances recognized Avandera, a plump and pretty Mexican girl, and Magdalena, an attractive woman despite her slightly flat face and coarse black hair she wore in multiple braids. Belle had told her Magdalena was half Pueblo Indian. Both girls were dressed in loose, free-flowing garments like Ruby's.

Belle arranged several brushes and combs on a side table. Everyone was so enthusiastic and sweet, Frances didn't have the heart to act cool or to ignore the younger women because of their profession. After all, perhaps some females simply didn't have much choice in what they did to survive.

How open-minded she was being, she realized, once again startled at her own rapidly changing logic.

But then, why shouldn't she be liberal in her judgments, considering her only friend at the moment was a madam.

She closed her eyes tightly as Belle started to cut her hair. The blades of the scissors snipped softly.

"Don't worry, this is gonna look real nice," Belle assured her.

When she was done, Ruby and Avandera wound Frances's hair around the hot curling iron.

Imagining flames, Frances wrinkled her nose. "It smells like I'm burning!"

"It's just hot," said Ruby. "It'll only take a minute."

Even so Frances was ready to squirm with the pulling and fussing before they finally finished. Still, Belle wouldn't let her look until she'd plaited and looped up the long hair in back as well, piling it on top of her head.

"There! Now all you have to do is get dressed. You really are pretty, Frankie," Belle said, startling Frances with the shortened version of her name. "You simply don't make as much of yourself as you could."

"Very pretty! *Bonita!*" added Avandera with a dimpled smile.

"You have nice hair but you could make it more shiny if you washed it with yucca leaves, Señora Gannon," added Magdalena, toying with the little pouch she wore on a cord around her neck. "I have some in a jar in my room if you would like to try them."

"Or she could use lemon juice," put in Ruby. "I rinse my hair with that when I can afford it."

"Thank you, I'll think about that," Frances told the beaming group as she rose to look in the mirror. With surprise, she realized the new hairdo *did* look good on her. Smiling, she gingerly touched a curl softly falling over her forehead. "Nice."

"Isn't it?" Belle grinned. "Course, a little dab of paint around the eyes and mouth wouldn't be a bad idea, either."

"Paint?" Now that was too much. "I don't think so."

"Only a little," Belle wheedled. "You'll hardly be able to tell."

It took some doing to convince Frances to try a trace of brown at the edges of her eyelids and the tiniest touch of rouge on her lips. But she had to admit she really couldn't tell that the additions weren't natural when all was done. Ruby and Avandera left, but Belle and Magdalena helped her into the red gown.

"Now you're ready for the evening," Belle announced. "And don't take any guff off of them men. Like I said, they'll treat you like a lady if you act like one. In fact, some of them behave themselves better around a woman. Keep your eyes on the tables and try to smile once in a while. If anyone gets too drunk, have Adolfo show him out. That little hombre loves to flaunt his authority."

"Watch out for drunken men. Wonderful," muttered Frances. "As if I could tell when they're drunk."

"You can tell—they stagger when they walk."

"And they swear," added Magdalena.

"And they can't talk right," said Belle. "Also watch out for problems at the tables. Some men stick cards up their sleeves or under their shoes. Have Adolfo throw them out also."

Still uncomfortable, Frances merely nodded. Her policing activities had always been limited to young girls. She decided it would be best to have a word with Adolfo, a wiry little Mexican with a fierce reputation. He'd been so courteous when she'd met him crossing

Blue Sky's *placita* a couple of times, she could hardly believe he was the same man who reputedly carried several knives.

"Meanwhile, have you tried finding someone else for this job?" she asked Belle pointedly.

The older woman laughed, which didn't make Frances one whit happy.

However Magdalena tried to be helpful. "My Uncle Tomas knows someone who would like to manage a casino."

"He does?" She gazed at the girl hopefully.

"He's a friend of your uncle's, right?" Belle asked Magdalena. "I suppose it wouldn't hurt to ask him to drop by. Frances and I will interview him."

"He is already coming. Tonight." Magdalena checked the mirror and straightened one of her huge silver-and-turquoise earrings. "Tomas told him to wait at the bar."

"I guess you can talk to him then," Belle said. "I'll be busy." She turned to the Pueblo woman. "What does this man look like?"

Magdalena shrugged. "Dark, black hair."

"Which describes three-quarters of the people in Santa Fe." Belle looked irritated.

"He's tall," added Magdalena.

Frances inquired, "What's his name?"

"I think it's Pedro, Pablo, Chico, well, um . . . " Magdalena looked embarrassed. "Truly, I forget. Only ask him if he knows Magdalena, Señora Gannon. That will be good enough."

"All right." Frances only hoped she could find someone to manage the casino floor. Perhaps she'd be lucky and tonight would be her one and only experience.

After Belle and the Pueblo woman left, she gazed

into the mirror one last time. A woman with curls, pink lips and a shockingly cut garnet-hued dress stared back at her. Even if Miss Llewellyn saw her dressed like this, Frances thought, she'd never recognize her.

In the space of a few short weeks, Frances hardly recognized herself.

5

Chaco Jones roamed the streets of Santa Fe, heading down one of the narrow byways that opened off the central plaza.

He no longer worked for the Ralston Double-Bar, having returned a little over a week ago to quit, collect his pay and pick up his belongings. Afterward, he'd headed back north, unsure of what to do next but sick of being a hired gun.

Taking a room at a cheap hotel in the territorial capital, he'd gotten into the habit of wandering at all times of the day and night, strangely alert for any danger. The dreams that haunted him when he slept—moonlight and restless wind and eyes that suddenly glowed out of the dark—made him wonder if something was actually stalking him in waking life.

Not that he'd had any unusual experiences, not unless he counted the afternoon someone had sliced the rawhide strip off his gun belt while he sat inside that church talking to the padre.

Then he'd been too distracted to pay much attention

THE WIND CASTS NO SHADOW

to anything except the letter from de Arguello. Leaving the church, he'd thrown the piece of paper away and cursed a blue streak. He had nothing to say to de Arguello unless the old man wanted to hear what he thought about the Spanish practice of enslaving mixed-breeds and Indians.

Tonight, Chaco suddenly found himself approaching the Blue Sky Palace. Nathan Gannon's place. He hadn't thought much about the man since he'd paid for the prayers at the church. He hoped the widow was getting along.

Pausing before the double doors that led into the building's open air *placita*, he listened to the guitar music strumming from within, to murmuring voices and the soft laughter of a woman. He felt drawn to the sounds, wanted to go inside.

And why not? Chaco decided, though he didn't linger with the small group gathered about the guitarist in the *placita*. Instead, he handed over his gun belt to the man outside the door of the casino and entered. It was early, so only a few gamblers were placing bets at the roulette table and none of the poker or faro games had started. Looking around, he passed through the area and went on into the saloon where he ordered a shot of tequila.

The liquor traced a burning path down his throat and into his gullet. Chaco ordered another.

"Señor Jones!"

Glass of liquor in hand, he turned to the throaty voice.

"I have not seen you in so long a time!" the woman went on, an attractive Pueblo-breed Chaco used to ask for at Pedro's in Burro Alley.

She sidled up beside him and lowered her lashes seductively. "Don't you remember me, Señor? Magdalena?"

"I remember." He smiled, touched her cheek. And now that he recalled the sort of evenings they'd had, he realized he could use one tonight. Magdalena had acted like she had a special fondness for him, and he couldn't remember how long it had been since he'd slept with a woman. "Are you working here now?"

"Yes." Then Magdalena's mouth turned down. "I am busy tonight, though."

"Too bad."

"You can come back tomorrow?"

"Suppose I could."

Magdalena's expression closed when he didn't act anxious. "Or you could ask for one of the other girls." She tossed her head as if she'd been forced to say that. "*La Rubia* is pretty."

"An Anglo?"

Her dangly earrings were still jingling. "She is wearing a red skirt and is very friendly."

"Well, if she comes by me, I'll buy her a drink." And see what else developed, now that he was in the mood. After all, it wasn't a personal thing with Magdalena. Not for him, anyway. But he assured the woman, "I'll bet she's not as fiery as you."

The compliment drew her slow, measured smile. Chaco slugged the second tequila as Magdalena moved reluctantly away. This time the warmth spreading from his belly made him think about soft bodies, smooth thighs, round breasts. He turned to lean back against the bar. That's when he saw *her*.

The Anglo woman dressed in red was moving directly toward him. Her abundant golden-brown hair was piled on top of her head, ringlets escaping to curl about her heart-shaped face. Her mouth was soft, her greenish eyes clear and direct.

Chaco's first thought was that she was the fanciest-looking whore he'd ever seen, a woman pretty enough to have stepped out of one of those photographs from a newspaper back east. His second thought was that she looked slightly familiar . . .

"Do you know Magdalena?" she asked, her low articulated voice as cultured as her appearance.

Mesmerized by the creamy breasts whose tops swelled from the low-cut bodice, Chaco silently stared down into the soft shadow of her cleavage. He was already aroused. And he became irritated when she stepped back, not a friendly thing to do. But maybe she was new at this and still shy. The way she was gazing at him made him think she was not only interested but attracted. "Well, do you?" she repeated.

"Do I what?" He frowned, then forced himself to focus on the words. "Know Magdalena? Sure." He remembered to add, "Can I buy you a drink?

"No thank you." But she glanced at the bartender, an older man with gray hair and a big handlebar mustache. "I guess I could have a sarsaparilla."

Perhaps that was promising. Chaco thought her manner a little cool but then he hadn't been with many Anglo women and maybe that was their way. Besides, he really liked this one's looks. Tall, she could nearly gaze square into his eyes, and she surely must have real long legs. He imagined those legs wrapped around him and immediately grew hard.

"So you're interested in the job?" she asked.

He had to focus on words again. "Job?" And on her face, again thinking she seemed familiar.

"You have done this kind of work before?"

He had to laugh. "I wouldn't call it work." At least not for the man. And not for the woman either, hopefully. "But I've had plenty of experience, sure. You won't have to show me anything . . . unless you want something that's newfangled." The very thought of which was highly exciting. He leaned closer to inhale her scent and get another look at that cleavage. "I'm ready for some relaxation now."

"Relaxation?" She stepped backward, her finely drawn eyebrows shooting upward.

"When a woman's with me, she doesn't know she's working at all."

"A woman? Working?" Her voice rose, quivering, now also sounding familiar. "What on earth are you talking about?"

"Going upstairs." But even as he added, "Or wherever you have a room," Chaco had an odd feeling.

She took a shuddering breath, blinked, backed up some more and flushed. She made as if to turn and leave, then seemed to think better of it.

"Sir, I don't know who you are, but I am certainly not talking about . . . going upstairs!" She gulped another big breath of air. "I am the manager of this casino and if you aren't looking for an honest day's work, I have made a terrible mistake!"

The manager? Suddenly, Chaco felt as embarrassed as she looked. Not to mention disappointed.

"I thought you were Pablo or Chico," she went on. "Whoever Magdalena's uncle sent."

"You aren't *La Rubia?*"

"Certainly not! I'm Mrs. Frances Gannon!"

A thrill shot through Chaco. "Mrs. Gannon?" The veil and the emotions and the dirt had obscured the widow's face in Galisteo Junction. She cleaned up right nice.

"And who are you?" she demanded.

He straightened, figuring he'd better leave. "Nobody you'd want to know."

"Your voice . . ."

Well, he was truthful, if nothing else. "Name's Chaco Jones."

Her expression immediately changed and a load of guilt burdened him once more as Chaco wondered how many other widows held such hatred for him in their eyes.

Unable to believe the gall of the man, Frances stared into the pale gray eyes she should have recognized immediately. The gunfighter might have bathed and shaved, might have tied his long black hair back, but his voice and eyes were a dead giveaway.

"You dare to proposition me?" she finally sputtered, not caring if the bartender or the other saloon patrons heard. "You killed my husband and then you come here to sully his wife? You are lower than base vermin!"

"Vermin?"

"Rats!" cried Frances. "You are a murderer! That lawman in Galisteo Junction should have arrested and hanged you!"

His eyes remained cool, his face expressionless. How could anyone show so little emotion? she wondered. But then, perhaps the scoundrel didn't have any emotions.

"I told you it was an accident, Mrs. Gannon," he said, his voice also cool now.

He started to leave but she stepped right in front of him. "As if that exonerates you. Your very profession should be considered a crime—walking around with a gun and killing people!"

"I never killed anyone unless I had to."

"Except my husband!"

His expression actually seemed to change, to harden and intensify, making him look dangerous and attractive at the same time, a fact that angered her the more.

"I paid for his funeral and burial," he said evenly. "Do you want more money?"

"Money won't pay for a life!"

"Then do you want to kill *me,* seeing as the lawman wouldn't do the job?"

That startled her. "Of course not!"

"I can't offer you anything else."

She couldn't decide if his manner was more disquieting or calming, but she felt her pulse slow down. "You *can* give me something else. You can at least act sorry."

"I paid for prayers for your husband."

He had? Not wanting to soften toward him, she demanded, "And you can stay out of the Blue Sky."

"I was just about to leave."

She moved out of the way and he started to go, then paused. "Do you yourself mourn your husband, Mrs. Gannon?"

As his eyes swept over her garnet-red gown, she felt ashamed and defensive. "Certainly." It had been little more than a week since Nate's death, but this costume hadn't been her first choice. "I have to work in the casino."

"But you could wear a dress that didn't show so much of your breasts."

Her face flamed. Was this the way men spoke to a woman in a place like the Blue Sky? Her shame intensified as she felt warmth also creep up from her lower parts. Forced to live in a house of wantons, was she becoming one herself?

Furious again, she cried, "How dare you!"

And he kept staring at her, making her want to shiver. "That kind of dress gives a man ideas."

She'd give *him* ideas! "Get out of here!" She gazed around desperately. "Adolfo? Where is he? I want him here right now!" The bartender was already gesturing and the little Mexican came running. "Escort this man outside!"

Adolfo stared at Chaco Jones. "*Compadre?* You are causing trouble?"

They knew each other? Holding onto the last shred of her dignified authority, Frances straightened her spine. "Throw Mr. Jones out, Adolfo. He is not welcome here."

Thank goodness, Adolfo saw fit to obey. With one last questioning glance that flicked from her to the gunfighter, then back again, he took hold of the man's arm and moved him away. "*Si*, Señora."

Frances stood in place until the two went out the door. Then, keeping her eyes straight ahead, she strode to the nearest stairway and ascended, heading for her rooms. She didn't have time to change her clothing, but she could at least drape a shawl over her bare shoulders.

"Damn Chaco Jones!"

Damn him for even making her want to use such language!

The man had given her nothing but trouble and sorrow since the day she had first sighted him in Galisteo Junction. First, he had robbed her of her husband, had taken away the shield who surely would have helped her better deal with her new and confusing situation.

Now the gunfighter had barged into the awful place where she was forced to work and had tried to rob her of her dignity. For Frances MacDonnell Gannon was no longer sure of exactly who she was. How could she be wearing a gown that exposed half her breasts? And have actually been titillated because her husband's killer had admired them?

* * *

Louisa was bored. Arising early as usual, she went out to take care of Susie, the old paint, and Mancha, her other Indian pony. But there would be nothing else to do today unless she took yet another ride across familiar countryside.

Maria Rodriquez, the young friend who'd lived next door for years, who used to gossip and wander about town with Louisa, had gotten married at the age of fifteen and moved to the southern part of the Territory. Fifteen . . . Louisa had been appalled.

And the neighbor boys on the other side of the road, the ones who'd traded boasts and raced their horses against hers, had left to work on their cousin's *rancho* through the spring and summer.

Louisa was spending far too many hours alone, with only the choice of sitting in the house with a fussy old housekeeper or waiting for her mother to come home. She wasn't allowed to visit the Blue Sky, though she knew full well what went on there. She'd managed to take Frances out for a carriage ride earlier in the week anyway, but the poor woman had been distracted. With a new home, a new profession and no Nate, Louisa could understand.

Louisa missed Uncle Nate, too. She immediately thought of him when she read the hand-printed sign tacked onto a young cottonwood growing outside the pasture:

SALE OF HORSES BY U.S. CAVALRY
SOME GAITED AND BLOODED STOCK
THURSDAY AT FORT MARCY

Blooded. Wasn't that the sort of horse Uncle Nate had talked about? The kind of animals that had fire in their eyes and hearts, the long-legged

THE WIND CASTS NO SHADOW

steeds he'd grown up with in Kentucky?

Drat, and the sale was today, she thought, wanting more than anything to go. Uncle Nate would have gone with her. Louisa felt another wave of sadness for his loss.

Still, neither tears nor sorrow would bring him back. Deciding he'd want her to go to the sale anyway, the only possibility for excitement in the near future, Louisa entered the back door of the house and smiled at Elena as she walked through the kitchen.

"I'm going out for a ride."

"When will you be back?" asked Elena, glancing up from the task of making tortillas.

A small, sharp-eyed woman with several children of her own, she was kind to Louisa but careful that the girl obeyed the rules set down by Belle.

Thank goodness, horseback rides had always been allowed. "I'll only be gone a couple of hours."

"Where are you going?"

Louisa waved casually. "Oh, that way." Though she wasn't about to mention her exact destination.

Before the housekeeper could ask more questions, she sped down the hallway and vaulted up the narrow staircase leading to the attic. The entire second-story area was her domain. She'd placed her bed beneath a window so she could stare out at the surrounding mountains and straight up at the sky. She piled clothing, saddles, books and other personal items wherever and whenever she wanted to, thus driving Elena and her mother to distraction.

Searching for her best boots, Louisa threw aside a Navajo saddle blanket and looked behind the trunk she'd brought from Boston. The boots weren't there but she noticed the silver-clasped leather purse lying in the open trunk. In the confusion over the shooting and the funeral, she realized, her mother had forgotten to collect the refunded tuition money Louisa had carried all the way home.

Louisa opened the purse now and counted the money. How much would one of those blooded horses cost? Though she knew she ought to return the full amount to Belle, she was tempted to borrow a little. After all, she had no intention of going to another expensive girl's school, but she could certainly use a spirited horse. She'd be willing to work for the loan—she could replaster and whitewash the house's interior walls, if nothing else.

Reassuring herself that she was not a thief, Louisa stuck the purse beneath her jacket, found the good boots and was out of the house in mere minutes. Avoiding Elena entirely, she ran out to the pasture and saddled Mancha.

They took the quickest route across town, then headed up the hill to the fort. The roads were busy, as were the grounds inside the great barricade. Men and horses milled about there, the crowd full of blue uniforms. For a moment, when a grizzled trooper stared hard at her as she tied Mancha to a hitching post outside the fort's gates, Louisa felt uncomfortable. But she forgot about being one of the few females present as she strolled about and concentrated on her purpose—finding a spirited horse.

Unfortunately, that goal seemed more and more unlikely as Louisa inspected the animals being sold, a mixture of aging beasts and big shaggy mounts that seemed to be at least half plough-horse. None of the horses struck her fancy until she had circled the grounds and headed back for the gates.

Then she saw him—a beautiful bay gelding with a fine head, great dark eyes and long, long legs.

Unfortunately, the horse was also being inspected by a young caballero, no doubt the spoiled son of some Hidalgo family. Such wealthy young men always demanded good horseflesh beneath them.

The caballero, dressed in the traditional short jacket and tight leather pants trimmed with silver buttons, tried to open the gelding's mouth. The horse tossed his head and made as if to rear.

"Hey, watch out there!" The red-headed trooper holding him yanked on the rope fastened to the gelding's halter. "You don't have to check his teeth. He's got papers that say he's six years old."

"Still, I would like to see that for myself," said the caballero. "If he is so young, why do you sell him?"

"I ain't sure, this being Lieutenant Strong's animal." The trooper scratched his jaw. "But I believe it's 'cause he's a bit high-strung for cavalry work. This hoss threw Strong a coupla times."

The caballero wasn't put off by that. He waved the leaded end of the whip he was carrying in the gelding's face. The horse reared as the soldier yanked and cursed.

"Too high-strung for soldiers, yes," said the young man with a laugh. The gelding continued to prance around. "But a fine horse for racing, for *gallo.*"

Louisa tightened her jaw. Though she admired many qualities about Spanish men—their pride, passion and courage—she disliked the streak of cruelty that seemed to run through the more arrogant of them. *Gallo* was a sport in which a rooster was buried up to his neck in sand, then pulled out dead or alive by men racing by on horseback. The huge roweled spurs this *rico* wore with his high-heeled boots didn't bode well for the bay. She'd hate to see them cut into the gelding's rippling coat. She simply had to put in her own bid.

"I'm interested in this horse, too," she told the trooper. "How much is he?"

The caballero turned, surprised. His glance raked over Louisa, taking in her split riding skirt and boots. "And what is this? A cowgirl?"

She raised her chin. "I want this horse."

"You are very determined," said the young man with a flash of white teeth.

His smile made him even better looking, but Louisa wasn't distracted. She could flirt quite well when she wanted, but she knew too much about the ways of men with women to take it very seriously.

"Shall we roll some dice to see who gets to buy this horse?" she asked, knowing *ricos* loved to gamble. The dice she was carrying, a treasure from Uncle Nate, always came up four. "Pick a number from one to twelve. Whoever's closest gets first dibs."

"Eight," said the young man.

"Five." Smiling, already tasting victory, she took the dice out of her pocket and started to shake them.

"What's going on here?"

Drat, it was a young officer! Golden blond hair curled from beneath his dark hat, and his fair skin glowed with a light tan.

The red-headed trooper saluted. "Lieutenant Strong."

Strong cleared his throat and saluted back, obviously trying to look stern and gruff. Which wasn't easy, considering he wasn't that much older than the caballero, twenty-one or two at the most. "We're selling stock here, not running a gambling parlor." He gazed from Louisa to her competitor. "Is she with you?"

Louisa felt insulted. As if she needed someone to hold her hand.

The young Spaniard laughed and smiled flirtatiously

at her. "She is not with me, at least not yet." He took off his sombrero and bowed slightly from the waist. "Eusebio Velarde y Pino, Señorita."

At least he was being polite. "Nice meeting you, Señor Velarde. Louisa Janks."

"So it's Louisa, is it?" Strong said. "And where might your parents be, young lady?"

Louisa frowned. "Where are *yours?*"

Strong frowned. "Are you trying to be insolent?"

Louisa merely crossed her arms. "My parents have nothing to do with this. I'm the one interested in your spirited horse." She added, "I heard he threw you a couple of times."

That remark made both Velarde and the red-headed trooper laugh as Strong turned ruddy. Tall and slim, his posture very erect, the lieutenant wore a clean, crisp-looking blue uniform with fancy gold epaulets and spotless tan gauntlet gloves. He obviously hadn't been on the dusty frontier for long. Furthermore, with his shiny boots, handsome square jaw and aquiline nose, Louisa thought he looked like a pretty tin soldier she'd once seen in a Boston toy store.

"The horse's behavior is not the most important issue here now." Strong tightened his nicely shaped mouth. "*You* are, young lady. If you are alone, you are asking for trouble. The fort is full of rough men."

What a priss! Louisa hated being lectured! "Thanks for the warning, but I don't need your protection. I can take care of myself."

"I believe she might be stronger than she looks, Señor Lieutenant," teased Velarde. "And I am sure she has a gun."

Strong ignored Velarde. "I shall be most happy to escort you through the gates, Louisa."

Now she was really getting upset! "You can't kick

me out of here! I haven't done anything wrong." She glanced at the gelding. "And I want to buy this horse."

Strong didn't look impressed. "As you say, he's very spirited. Not the sort of mount for a young girl."

Louisa immediately challenged, "I bet I can ride him better than you! And I won't even need a saddle and bridle."

"Come, let her try, Señor Lieutenant," put in Velarde. "If she can ride, the horse is hers. I was interested in the animal myself, but I will gladly step aside."

Louisa could see that Strong wasn't happy, but he was wavering. She added one last boast, "He won't throw *me*."

"Shall we place a wager on that, Señor Lieutenant?" asked Velarde.

"I told you this isn't a gambling parlor," Strong growled. However, he took the rope from the trooper and offered to give Louisa a leg up. "All right, you've got your chance. But if you break your pretty neck, it won't be my fault."

She took a handful of black mane and mounted. Usually, she let a strange animal get used to her smell and her presence before she tried to control him. She was perched so high! Glancing up at the sky, she wondered if there really was a Comanche horse spirit—if so, she hoped it was on her side.

Then she ordered Strong, "Make a loop with the rope and slide it around his lower jaw."

"You said you would ride him without a bridle."

"That's not a bridle."

He did as she asked and led the gelding outside the gates to an open piece of ground, a place where she wouldn't trample anybody. "His name is Defiant."

Defiant. A good name for a graceful, headstrong beast. The gelding took off at a fast canter when

THE WIND CASTS NO SHADOW

Strong let go of his halter, Louisa barely managing to guide him in a wide circle with the loop of rope. Luckily, the method taught her by an Indian friend was sufficient for that, if not strong enough to stop the horse when he was most rambunctious. Louisa clung to the animal, allowing herself to feel his rhythm through her legs, to become one with him. The wind flew by and she whispered soothing words. The horse listened, his ears pricking back. Then he slowed some, having a kinder nature than his name implied. Or perhaps he just liked her. Louisa smiled, knowing the gelding would probably be willing to stop when she pulled on the rope. Meantime, she waved to Velarde and Strong, who were standing at the gate watching. The lieutenant looked annoyed. Good!

For she had won—the horse wasn't going to toss her off.

She didn't care what price the lieutenant would ask. As far as she was concerned, Defiant was hers.

"A dead body!" screeched Minna Tucker once again as several men inspected the horrible remains her son had found near the old irrigation ditch right behind her house. "This is the work of the devil!"

"I'd say it was devilish all right," said a bearded man, holding back a branch of the juniper bush under which the body lay. "Seems to be murder."

"Murder! And near my home!" Minna couldn't help feeling as outraged as she was horrified. She pressed a handkerchief to her nose and leaned against Billie, thankful the eighteen-year-old had been home to support his lonely, widowed mother.

The odor and flies had attracted Billie Tucker in

the first place. He'd come running in to tell his ma immediately.

The bearded man clucked. "Somebody went and messed up this fellow's throat real bad."

Minna felt sick but she had to get a better look. Try as she might, though, all she could see were leather-encased legs, discolored flesh and the remains of something blue, perhaps a shirt. Dried blood and black hair stuck to the fabric. A printed scarf lay on the sandy clay nearby.

"Is that a savage?" she asked suddenly.

"Believe it is an Injun, Ma'am," said the bearded man.

"An Indian?" Who'd managed to get himself killed near her house? "The filthy heathen!"

Behind them, more and more people were gathering from all parts of the neighborhood. Several women gave little cries. A man who said he was a doctor forced his way through. But it was far too late for doctors now.

Nevertheless, he knelt by the body. "Hmm, been dead for at least a week," he said finally, looking up at the bearded man. "You're saying this was murder? Not unless someone set a dog on this man. Only an animal could tear out a throat like that."

The crowd murmured and Minna stepped forward when she feared they were going to shut out her view. That's when she saw the hand print on the chest of the corpse. "What in God's heaven is that?"

The doctor was puzzled, too. "Seems to be a burn."

"A hand print burned into the flesh?" said a Mexican man with wide eyes. "*Dios, a bruja!*"

A witch! Even Minna knew the Spanish word. She took a shuddering breath. "Lord, protect us from Satan!"

The doctor stood up and faced the crowd. "Look,

don't get yourselves all riled up. There's got to be a logical explanation. As I said, someone obviously set a dog on this Indian."

"Then why are there no paw prints?" asked the bearded man.

"After a week?" said the doctor.

The Mexican man pointed. "There's a print—a human one! I tell you it is a *bruja!* They can take the shape of an animal! They can even fly on the wind!"

"That's enough of that!" the doctor interrupted. He told the bearded man, "Somebody get the marshal. I'll help him make out a report."

"A witch!" muttered Minna, who believed in evil far more than she did doctor's opinions. She was truly afraid. "A servant of Satan!"

"Now, Ma." Billie patted her, trying to calm her down. The boy was a Godsend. "They'll take the body away and then you won't have to worry about it."

Walking back toward the house, they passed a blowsy, plump neighbor Minna particularly disliked.

"A witch?" repeated the woman, staring directly at Minna. "More likely this is the work of an insane, drunken woman who hates Indians."

The woman's tone was accusatory and Minna paused. "And what do you mean by that?"

"Don't pay any attention to her, Ma," said Billie.

But the blowsy woman went on, "Don't deny you were three sheets to the wind more than one night last week, Minna Tucker. Why, I looked out my door and saw you raving in the street in your nightgown!"

"Liar! Sinner!" Minna screeched.

"Ma!" Billie led Minna forward whether she liked it or not. "Don't listen to them!" He pulled her toward the house. "That patent medicine makes you a little strange sometimes, that's all."

Such a good boy! "I have to take my medicine when I have that terrible dry cough," murmured Minna. And it had seemed to grow worse since she'd been widowed. "Why, I hack so much, I can't sleep."

"I know, Ma."

"You're a God-fearing, righteous boy, Billie."

She would never believe the horrible people who claimed her son smoked and drank and chased loose women.

Just as she would never admit how often she'd awakened mornings with the hem of her nightgown soiled and no memory of the night before.

6

Don Armando de Arguello owned a spread that was something to see. Riding one of the northern roads down out of the mountains, Chaco took in the sprawling, traditional adobe house that lay in a narrow valley between rugged peaks. Cattle and sheep grazed in the meadow off to the west. Expansive adobe walls connected the house itself to stables, barns and numerous other outbuildings. The man was definitely rich.

So what did de Arguello want with a bastard son? Chaco wondered. Having received yet another hand-delivered letter at the hotel in Santa Fe, he'd decided to act on his promise to tell the old man off.

Several servants came running as he rode up. Carrying a rifle, one man asked him to identify himself, then accompanied him to the door. He wasn't packing a gun today, except for the one he'd placed in his saddlebags, but he supposed the rifleman had been told to be careful.

The house had thick, aged walls and only a few high, narrow windows on the outside. About to knock, Chaco stared at the heavy wooden door instead, suddenly bothered by a strange and unpleasant feeling. It wasn't so much that he feared something bad was going to happen. He simply didn't like the atmosphere.

He pushed the feeling aside when a servant girl opened the door a crack, obviously having heard the approach of a visitor. "*Si*, Señor?"

"I'm here to see Don de Arguello." He showed her the last letter the man had sent with its distinctive signature. "He told me to come. I'm Chaco Jones."

She motioned him inside. "Please wait in the *sala*, Señor."

He glanced around the main hall that served as a reception room as she scurried away. De Arguello or his wife must have a taste for eastern goods, as several imported red-velvet chairs were set among the traditional couches covered with Navajo blankets. A long expensive mirror hung on one wall, reflecting the great fireplace across from it. Native-weave black-and-white checked rugs lay on the floor.

The girl returned, followed by an attractive woman whose narrowed gaze never left his face. "I am Doña Ynez, Don Armando's wife."

"I'm here to see your husband."

"And why is that?"

Her smile was cool and he sensed a hardness in her, unusual in a Spanish woman.

"Don Armando sent for me." Again, he showed the letter. "I came up from Santa Fe."

Doña Ynez's long fingers toyed with the fringe of the fancy black shawl she wore over her equally costly-looking silk dress. "I will tell my husband you wish to speak to him, but he is not well."

"Tell him. He'll see me."

Chaco wasn't certain whether she was aware of his true identity. Perhaps she did know and didn't like it. Nevertheless, she left the room.

Good thing, for he wasn't leaving without having a few words with the old man. He'd been too angry after having received a second letter. De Arguello displayed the usual Hidalgo arrogance, thinking Chaco would drop everything and run to answer his call. He probably expected his bastard to sit up and beg for a few crumbs. Chaco had no intention of doing so. He still hated the man for what he'd done to his mother.

Finally Ynez returned. "He will talk to you," she said curtly. "Come with me."

He followed as she swept out into the corridor that led past other rooms. Like most old adobe houses that belonged to the wealthy, this one cradled a central *placita* and was laid out every which way with connecting corridors and steps and doors that joined older sections with new additions.

He stared at Ynez's ramrod straight back. Don de Arguello had obviously married a second time, since she was much younger than the wife his mother had mentioned. He thought she might be around thirty-five, his own age. Ynez was of the same Hidalgo stock as her husband, though, and her proud bearing showed that more clearly than her rich clothing.

Upon turning a corner, climbing two steps and passing an open door that led out into the *placita*, Ynez halted and motioned to a set of double doors ahead. "Don Armando awaits you there."

Chaco nodded curtly, unwilling to voice a thank you. His past made him resentful. He walked away from her without looking back.

De Arguello sat in one of the high-backed chairs before the fireplace of his sitting room. White of hair, strong of profile, the old man still possessed a fierce gaze despite the illness that was wasting him. He looked very thin and a cane leaned against the chair.

"Please sit down," he said, polite but unsmiling.

Chaco took a seat across from him.

"So you are my son."

"Oneida's son," Chaco emphasized.

"Did she tell you about me?"

"She didn't say much about you at all, except that you gave her freedom and some money to leave when she was pregnant. She didn't say that you were my sire." For *father* was too kind a word, and Chaco wondered why his mother had kept silent about that truth. "Did you rape her?"

For a moment, de Arguello stared measuredly at him. "No." The answer was definite, decisive.

Chaco tended to believe him.

"I cared for your mother," said the old man. "But she was, of course, a—"

"Slave."

"A servant," corrected de Arguello.

But the Hidalgos would never admit they kept captured young Indians and mixed breeds against their wills and even to this day to be used as unpaid workers.

De Arguello went on, "My first wife was alive then, as well. But that is in the past. That is not important now."

"It's important to me. My mother died in poverty, in a filthy shack."

To his credit, de Arguello seemed taken aback. "I knew she was gone, though I did not know how. Did she die of disease?"

"A fever. We didn't have money for a doctor or any medicine." Not that medicine would have necessarily saved her, but he would have paid anything to try. "She did all kinds of work to feed and take care of us." Including a little whoring, he suspected, after Reuben died. "She had a hard time, being a woman on her own."

De Arguello said nothing.

"You sent her packing years ago," Chaco went on. "And now you're writing letters to me. I'm not interested in you or anything you have to say. I rode up here to tell you that to your face."

Again, the measured stare. "You are not interested in an inheritance?"

Chaco was unmoved. "I don't want your land or your money." Which was probably some sort of bribe, in return for which de Arguello would want something back. Not to mention that taking such would insult Oneida's memory. "Why would you consider leaving anything to a mestizo?"

The old man gazed at the fire. "You are a child of my blood—not that I have made out my will to that effect. I had to see you, to judge you first."

"Judge?" Who the hell did the old man think he was? "You have no power over me. Not like you had over my mother."

"You are the *only* child left of my blood," stated de Arguello.

So that's how it was. "I may have been sired by you but that's the only thing we have in common."

De Arguello's eyes swept over him. "I am not so certain. I have inquired about you. You are a brave man, you have worked as a gunfighter. I was brave when I was young."

"Not brave enough to marry my mother." But then,

de Arguello would have had to buck society, the church and his own relatives. "Or to see that she was taken care of through the years."

"Unfortunately, what is past is past."

"Is that all you can say?" But what had he expected, an apology? Chaco rose, seeing no reason to stay longer. He gazed down at the old man. "Don't write me any more letters."

"Is that an order?"

"If I get another, I'll come back up here and stuff it down your throat."

De Arguello remained silent as Chaco strode out of the room, almost running into Ynez in the outer corridor.

Once outside, he mounted his horse and rode away, only glancing back once. The strange feeling he'd had at the front door came back full force. Instinctively, he wanted to dig his heels into the sides of the buckskin and take off at a gallop. The horse was nervous, too, prancing and tossing his head about.

Nevertheless he reined the animal in, refusing to react to whatever was bothering him. By the time he was a half-mile down the road, the horse relaxed and the strange feeling receded.

There were plenty of reasons for feeling strange. He now realized he *had* wanted to see the Don, to hear his side of things. He'd wanted more than the chance to tell the man off.

Still de Arguello had surprised him in some ways, hadn't been as arrogant as he'd expected. But then, the old man was getting on in years and had no legitimate children to whom he could leave his land. That was why he'd sent letters to a bastard son.

He wasn't tempted by the idea of an inheritance

from de Arguello. For one, he refused to be judged and measured by a man who thought himself so high and mighty, who'd sent a pregnant young woman off into the world alone. For another, he knew that no one ever got anything without trading something back, and that the price of any part of de Arguello's holdings would be very high. He preferred independence. He liked to do what he wanted and to go where he wanted. He'd rather let the wind decide his fate than some selfish old buzzard who was feeling close to death.

Mood soured, he figured on dropping by the Blue Sky Palace as soon as he got back to town. Mrs. Gannon might have thrown him out and demanded he never return, but the place was open to the public and he had done nothing wrong.

More importantly, he also sensed a feeling of connection with the Anglo woman—though *that* feeling was neither strange nor unpleasant—something that went beyond the desire he'd felt when he'd seen her in that red dress.

"I would like some more rice," Don Armando told the girl who was serving supper that evening.

"Your appetite is improving," Ynez noted from the other side of the table. Perhaps the talk with Chaco Jones had somehow made her husband feel better.

"I will have to live, at least for a short time longer."

"You are not dying, Husband. Please do not speak like that."

"We both know I am old. Life only lasts so long." Don Armando wiped his mouth and thick white mustache. "And even if age does not overtake us, accident can. Who would have thought Mercedes could have fallen in the well and broken her neck?"

"That will not happen to you."

For a moment, there was silence as Don Armando ate more beans and rice. Then he went on, "You are still young, Doña Ynez. I was hoping to find a way to take care of you. But we are both cursed with small families."

Was he going to bring up the unpleasant subject of her barrenness again? Ynez wondered.

"I had only one hope and now that, too, is gone." He sounded more fatalistic than sad. "I believe Señor Jones could be a worthy successor for me, but he is not interested." The old man gazed at her questioningly. "You know he is my son?"

As if she hadn't been listening outside the door of his rooms this afternoon! Ynez said, "I have heard gossip—some of the servants."

"Ah, servants. Señor Jones is the son of a former maidservant, you know." When she nodded, he asked, "More gossip?"

Ynez toyed with her food, not at all happy. She thought of telling Don Armando that she would be able to take care of herself, but knew he would neither believe that, nor like it. Husbands preferred to think of their wives as mindless property.

"Señor Chaco Jones is very rude, a peon. He nearly pushed me into the wall coming out of your sitting room."

"The boy is not polished, that is certain."

"Then why would you think him a worthy successor?" She didn't usually question her husband about such things, but she felt she must in this case.

"He has courage. And intelligence, despite his lack of education. He also has a sense of loyalty and responsibility—he took care of his mother until the end. I believe he would take care of you," said Don Armando. "If he would accept his inheritance, that is."

"But you are saying he won't." Chaco Jones *was* strong or else very stupid. "And he is mestizo." Part Apache, part Spanish and, she'd heard, also part Anglo on his mother's side.

Don Armando shrugged. "He is of my blood." Sighing, he finished the food on his plate and changed the subject. "Did you make the *natillas* you promised, Doña Ynez?"

"Yes, I shall bring it from the *soterrano*."

She rose and went out to the half-buried storehouse that kept things cool, once again brooding about the way Chaco Jones had treated her today. He could not say thank you; he could barely acknowledge her presence. And her husband actually considered the ignorant heathen a worthy man.

With a vengeance, she dusted the baked custard with a special powder. The spices would cover any bitterness. Then she returned, hearing voices as she approached the dining room. Don Armando had summoned Pedro, his foreman.

"I must change my will. Tomorrow you will fetch the Padre and some witnesses."

"Yes, Don Armando."

"I am afraid I must leave everything to the church."

To the church? Ynez's hands would tremble if they weren't holding the bowl of *natillas*. Her face felt cold as she entered the room, locking eyes with her husband.

"Of course, the lands you brought from your first marriage will be yours to do with as you will," he said, seeing her. "And, hopefully, we can find a relative of a relative to be responsible for you."

"You are not going to die, Don Armando, not yet." Her dowry wasn't half the size of the de Arguello holdings.

Again, the shrug. "That is up to God." But Armando smiled when he saw the custard. "Ah, I can taste it already."

Upset, she set the bowl on the table, only to have it teeter on the edge. She tried to catch it but her clumsy motions merely sped the crash to the floor. Custard and shards of pottery flew through the air.

"Oh!" Ynez held her hands to flaming cheeks. "I am sorry!"

Don Armando fell back in his chair, surprised. Then his expression changed to disappointment.

"Do not worry." Ynez called for a servant to clean the floor, then told her husband, "You *must* live, Don Armando. I will cook *natillas* every day to make sure that you do."

Every day of every week of every month until she found some way to change her husband's mind. The thought of his leaving such a great amount of money and land to the church, of leaving her to rot with some money-grasping relative of a relative, made her soul sick.

Frances had survived a week of working as a casino floorman, but she didn't think she'd ever get used to it. Especially difficult had been learning to ignore the way some men undressed her with their eyes. She was uncomfortable enough policing a room of gamblers; she didn't want to play hostess.

At least none of the men's glances had titillated her, which gave her more faith in herself and her feelings. She was no wanton. She must have been in

"Um, hmm." Sophie's beautiful slanted eyes looked knowing. "Or worse." Then she laughed.

Frances found the whole conversation fascinating, but it ended when Magdalena drifted out of the room. Sophie and Luz soon followed.

Ruby had finished pinning the hem and was ready to sew. Frances slipped off the dress and put on the wrapper she was carrying.

"Are you interested in witchcraft?" asked Ruby. "Magdalena knows a lot about *brujeria*—that's what they call it in Spanish. She keeps all kinds of feathers and stones and herbs in her room. One time she took a bowl of water and some ink and showed us how to read the future."

"How can you see the future with ink and water?"

"I don't know, but Magdalena swirled the ink around and stared into the bowl and told us things that would happen."

Like a crystal ball she'd read about, Frances decided. She admitted curiosity, but doubted folk beliefs only a little more than religion. "And did her predictions come true?"

"Some of them."

"But I'm sure they were general."

"Probably." Ruby said reassuringly, "Magdalena only does good witchcraft. She'd never try to hurt anybody. She said people who do are really *diableras* not *brujas*."

As if Frances would know the difference. Sometime she'd have to have a longer discussion about witchcraft and voodoo with someone more knowledgeable, perhaps Magdalena herself. Meanwhile, as soon as Ruby finished the hem, Frances headed for the casino, meeting Belle on the way. The older woman had just arrived and looked flustered.

"You won't believe it! Louisa's getting out of hand. She took some of my money and bought a big, fancy, galumphing horse! Do you know how much hay and grain it'll take to feed a thing like that?"

Frances focused on the most disturbing news. "Louisa took some money?"

"Well, she didn't exactly steal it and she says she'll pay it back somehow, but she didn't ask me first. I'm worried."

"I don't blame you."

Belle sighed. "I don't know what I'm gonna do with her. She was never this hard to handle when she was younger."

"Perhaps she's only going through a period of adjustment." Considering her age, her recent problems with school and her mother's profession.

"I only hope that's it."

"If I can be of help, please let me know."

"I will, Frankie." Belle glanced around, noticing Sophie motioning to her. "Some other time, though, seeing's how we both gotta get to work."

Work, indeed.

The gray-haired bartender, Jack Smith, had said the troopers would be invading tonight, after receiving their monthly pay. Frances found herself wading through a sea of blue-and-gold uniforms. She had a difficult time trying to tell who was doing what, and there were so many drunks that Adolfo was constantly escorting men outside.

While Adolfo worked alone, an incident in the Gentlemen's Club kept the Blue Sky's two other "protectors" busy. At least most of the men in the casino moved aside respectfully when Frances asked them to, so she could glance at the poker and faro tables, trying to make sure both customers and professionals were happy. The gamblers who worked for the Blue Sky had been told to notify her if they suspected cheating going on or if one of the customers became unruly.

Still, Frances felt tense in the crowd. The troopers seemed high-strung and ready for trouble, as if they'd been waiting impatiently to let their emotions flow freely with the alcohol and their money. More than once, someone got angry at a card table and raised his voice.

That's when Frances would appear in her official capacity and the unhappy customer would either settle down or leave. Loud voices from the poker table near the saloon alerted her. A trooper and a big rough-looking man with a black mustache were arguing.

"You're cheating," said the trooper. "Admit it."

"Now boys," said the gambler in charge of the table. "Nobody's cheating here or I would've known it."

The mustached man scowled. "Anybody says I'm cheating, I'll kill him."

"With your bare hands?" taunted the trooper, who'd left his weapons outside like everyone else. "I'd like to see you try." Not liking the fierce way the men were speaking, Frances thought she should probably get hold of Adolfo. But before she could do so, the trooper slugged the other man and knocked him into the saloon.

The man with the black mustache scrambled to his feet with a roar. "Now you've done it!"

An answering growl seemed to rise from the surrounding crowd, as if this was what they'd been waiting for. Customers started to gather from both sides to watch.

Frances hurried forward. "Adolfo!"

But the little Mexican was nowhere to be seen. Black Mustache threw himself at his attacker. The trooper tried to strike again, missed and was knocked to the floor.

"Stop it!" Frances yelled, seeing she would have to act herself. Violence sickened her. Pushing her way through, she placed herself between the struggling men. "Get out of here, both of you!"

Seemingly blind with rage, the trooper pushed her aside, slamming her into the bar. Her arm throbbed with pain. Worse, as she stood there breathlessly, Frances saw the other man reach down to draw a hidden pistol from his boot. The trooper backed away.

Frances was too outraged to be frightened. "Get out of here this instant! Guns aren't allowed!"

"Who says so?" His mustache bristled. "You?" He took hold of her and shook her.

Now she was frightened. "Adolfo!" she yelled.

"Shut up, I hate mouthy women!" The man backhanded her hard across the face.

Little pinpoints of light danced before her eyes. Slumping backward, Frances was caught by Jack Smith.

"Hit a lady? What kind of man are you!" shouted the bartender.

"You're gonna be a dead one if you say anything else." The man laughed unpleasantly. "Maybe I'll kill you anyways and the big-mouthed woman to boot."

The entire crowd was held at bay by the pistol and the big man's bullying strength. Frances saw them through swirling vision. Faces came forward, then retreated again.

In the middle of everything, Chaco Jones walked in.

Chaco Jones?

He gazed directly at her, then swung out hard and fast to the side, hitting the mustached man in the chest. The man roared like an injured bull but dropped the pistol. Chaco grabbed it, then slammed the weapon into the man's face. Blood spurted, not a pretty sight, but, at this point, Frances couldn't care less.

The troublemaker fell to the floor and lay there groaning.

"Get out of here," ordered Chaco, nudging the big man none too gently with his boot. "If anybody's going to be killed tonight, Ugly, it's going to be you." He waved the pistol and looked around. "Anybody else want to pick a fight?"

"Hell, man, we were just watching," said someone, who was moving back like everyone else. The threatened trooper had already disappeared.

"Go about your business or get out," Chaco told the crowd, his cold, hard voice carrying over the bilingual muttering and the stamping. Then he approached Frances, who was shaky but had managed to regain her feet.

"Why don't you take her upstairs?" Jack Smith suggested. "She could stand some looking-to."

Frances shook her head. "There's nobody else—" But she moaned as pain shot through her jaw and the room spun.

"Adolfo's back from wherever the hell he went to." The bartender pointed. "He'll take care of things."

Obviously aware there'd been trouble, the Mexican was patrolling the casino like a feisty little rooster, his eyes glittering, his curly hair seeming to stand on end.

Jack Smith added, "And I'll also go over to the Gentlemen's Club and fetch those other two men."

Before Frances could object again, Chaco scooped her up in his arms and headed for the nearest stairway. He carried her effortlessly, the crowd parting before him.

"Where's your room?" he asked when they reached the second floor.

She motioned and managed to extract the key from her pocket. Chaco turned the lock, carried her inside and laid her on the four-poster. Then he went over to the washstand and poured water into the basin. Cradled by the soft feather bed, Frances watched, amazed. She would never have believed the gunfighter would be acting as her savior. She reminded herself that she hated the man and should turn him out immediately.

Yet if Chaco hadn't appeared when he had tonight, both she and Jack Smith might have been killed.

"Got anything to use as a cloth?"

Reluctantly, she motioned, then gingerly touched her mouth. Her hand came away with a smear of blood.

Chaco tried the second drawer of her clothing chest rather than the top one. He came up with a satin corset and silk bloomers, more items from the Chicago shopping spree. Frances didn't have the energy to be embarrassed. Besides, he shoved the underwear aside impatiently and opened the top drawer, finally pulling out a cotton handkerchief. He wadded that, dipped it into the basin, and brought it back to the bed.

Wiping off the blood, he touched her face carefully. "Looks bad, but it's only a split lip and a big bruise."

She winced, though his touch was far more gentle

than she would expect of a man of violence. And he didn't seem as cold and removed as usual. She gazed up at the intense face above hers, admiring the strong nose and high cheekbones, the startling paleness of the gray eyes in contrast with his bronze complexion and black hair.

"This is going to swell up a bit. You're going to be black and blue."

"Umm, hmm." Her entire head ached, as did the arm he was now examining.

"Can you move your fingers?"

She did so.

"Good, it's not broken. Too bad you don't have some *moradilla* for a poultice, though. Or some horse liniment. Might help you feel better faster."

Frances assumed *moradilla* was some sort of herb. "Magdalena has dried leaves . . . downstairs. Ask Belle."

Chaco left and she closed her eyes, allowed herself to sink into semiconsciousness. She already felt slightly better and her head had cleared when the gunfighter returned. Carrying a steaming teapot, a cup, a bowl and several other items, he placed everything on the table by the bed.

Then he sat down beside her. "Lucky for you Magdalena has something for any ailment." He poured hot water in the bowl, then crumbled a handful of leaves into it. "*Yerba buena* and other herbs—you can drink it and use it as a poultice, too."

She'd felt strange before when Chaco had merely been in the bedroom with her. Now he was sitting on the bed itself. And, horribly enough, she was beginning to experience those little thrills of awareness again. Her breasts seemed to swell against her bodice and warmth spread outward from her belly.

Good heavens, this was Nate's bed and she was attracted to his killer. How could she?

She inched away nervously. "I'm feeling better. I don't know as I need that now."

"You need it."

He calmly filled the cup with the steaming mixture and leaned over to let her drink. She kept her eyes lowered, refusing to look him in the face. The herbal mixture was bitter but had a minty aftertaste.

"Now we'll see if we can get that swelling to come down."

He straightened and added more leaves and some sort of clay to the water, mixing it together with a spoon. Then he took the cloth from her jaw and scooped some of the poultice onto it.

"Don't think you should be going back to work soon. Even with this, you're going to look bad."

Which wasn't very complimentary. But then, she shouldn't care what he thought about her looks.

"I only wish I didn't have to go back to work at all, at least not in the casino." And she wished Chaco Jones would get out of her bedroom. "I'm only filling in down there because my husband's floorman quit."

"That's why you were looking for a new man the other night."

At least he now understood she'd been trying to interview someone for a job. Just as she'd quickly realized he'd thought she was *La Rubia*. Her own interest and embarrassment had been the true reasons for her anger.

Finished with the poultice, he gently placed it on her jaw. "Hold it there awhile."

As he arose from the bed, Frances took a breath of relief and stared at Chaco's broad back and trim hips. He was a fine figure of a man.

If only he weren't a killer...

To distract herself, she talked. "I don't mind doing the book work or ordering the supplies but I hate playing hostess to a bunch of gamblers."

"I don't blame you." He turned to gaze down at her. "That's why I've decided I'll take the job."

She blinked, startled. "What?"

"I said I'll take the job. I need another line of work, and you shouldn't be dealing with rough men."

"B—But I didn't hire you!" She didn't want to work with Chaco Jones. The very thought shook her.

"That's all right," he went right on. "Jack Smith and Adolfo can show me everything downstairs." Noticing she'd let the poultice slip, he came over to slide it back in place, his callused hand warm over hers. "If you don't hold this tight against your face, it's not going to do any good."

"But—"

"Don't worry, it'll feel better by tomorrow."

Before she could make another objection, he turned on his heels and left. And Frances was in too much pain to go chasing after him.

Chaco Jones, the gunfighter, as the new floorman of Blue Sky's casino?

Frances thought about the situation long and hard. As Louisa had said, he owed them and they should let him do what he could. Maybe it was destiny that Chaco should pay in part for Nate's death by seeing to his widow's interests.

She only hoped she could keep those interests in hand.

* * *

She had been forced to come to terms with her hatred. Humming a half-remembered chant, she spread assorted treasures on the hearth before the fire—several long hairs, the yellowed fang of a snake, a vial of the sugary powder that was one of her specialties.

Holding up the hairs, she straightened them, then began plaiting them together. Several were her own but most were his.

"You belong to me," she whispered, quickly binding, tying, intertwining. "You desire me more than water or safety or rest!"

When she had finished, she stuffed the tiny braid into a small leather pouch and added the snake's fang.

Then her hatred crept through anyway. "And may your own desire pierce your heart!"

Closing her eyes, she drew herself together.

When she was once more calm, she poured in the sugary powder, something that was both very sweet and very poisonous. The pouch already held a few shreds of the rawhide cord she'd stolen. She'd save the rest for the future.

Meanwhile, she finished her present incantation. "You will only look at me! Your loins will burn with desire! You will do as I bid!"

Then, tying the top of the pouch tightly, she pinned it beneath her skirt to keep it safe until she could place it on his person.

The time was not right for death and his strength was too much for threat.

But surely he was weak enough for sex. If she could not yet have his life, she would at least possess his body.

7

Chaco Jones had not only acted as Frances's savior, he'd given her two days of badly needed rest. After assessing her injuries, Belle had insisted she stay in her rooms. Except for a few visits from Magdalena, who'd brought more healing herbs, and the delivery of meals by servants, Frances had slept and rested. She'd even had the claw-footed bathtub in the adjoining room filled with heated water to ease her soreness.

For the first time since arriving in New Mexico, she'd actually had time to think. And feel. Mourning Nate, she'd cried, though she'd begun to realize she'd hardly known her husband. He'd tried to be kind but he hadn't been honest with her. She'd married him under false pretenses.

Frances also decided Chaco had paid off his debt, at least as best as anyone could who'd taken another life, accidentally or no. Though she would never forget Nate, it was time to try to forgive, to move on.

On the third day after the attack, she spent the morning catching up with her bookkeeping. With satisfaction, she noted that the Blue Sky had paid off most of its creditors, owing only the loan to a local bank. In preparation for the order of more supplies, she wrote out two lists, one each for the saloon and the casino.

Patting some of Belle's powder on her discolored jaw and taking one last look at herself in the mirror, Frances thought how much she had changed in so little time. Feeling almost a stranger to herself, she exited her rooms, went downstairs and out into the sunny *placita*.

Seated next to Ruby and Sophie on one of the benches, Avandera asked, "Señora Gannon, how are you feeling?"

"Much better, thank you."

"We're real happy to see you up and about again," added Ruby.

Luz and Adolfo stood talking under one of the flowering trees. He gazed up at the slim young woman worshipfully, obviously not caring that she was half a head taller. He didn't notice Frances at all until she walked by.

Then the little Mexican sprang to attention. "Señora Gannon!" As she halted, he approached shame-faced. "I am so sorry that I was not there Saturday." He looked at her bruised jaw. "There were two drunks and—"

Frances waved the apology away. "I know you were busy."

"If I had known that dog would touch you," Adolfo went on, scowling, "I would have slit his throat."

An appalling image but Frances knew the man meant well. "Luckily, I am fine."

"Thanks to Señor Jones. He is doing a good job,

you know. He watches the customers with a sharp eye."

And his reputation helped, as well, Frances was certain. He'd been a gunfighter in the area for quite some time, Magdalena had said, also adding Señor Jones had led a sad, hard life. Frances hadn't wanted to hear more about that part. The less she knew about him, the better.

"I am happy everything is working out," Frances told Adolfo. "I'd rather take care of the bookkeeping and the purchasing anyway."

"A far better task for a lady," Adolfo said, smiling. "And do not be worried about Señor Jones's honesty—I have known him for many years."

"So I gathered." Smiling in return, Frances moved away.

In the saloon, Jack Smith also put a word in for Chaco. "A floorman who can speak both Spanish and English can be right helpful. Some nights we have more caballeros than Anglos."

A bit tired of hearing the gunfighter's praises sung, Frances murmured a curt reply and handed Jack the list she'd made out. "Check that off, will you? Let me know what I should order?"

The bartender examined the piece of paper. "Sure."

Then Frances took a deep breath and went toward the casino. She didn't look forward to seeing Chaco again, but she knew she was going to have to get used to dealing with him. If he was going to remain in his job, that is, and if she was going to continue to live in peace. The night after she'd been hurt, the army had descended on the Blue Sky again. She'd heard the ruckus from upstairs and, no matter that Belle claimed the attack on her had been unusual, she was glad she lay safely in her bed.

She almost didn't recognize Chaco when she saw him standing near one of the poker tables talking to a dealer. His clothing, brown trousers and a black coat worn over a white shirt and ribbon tie was far more formal than his usual dusty denim. His long hair was tied back neatly, as black and straight as an Indian's.

"May I speak with you for a moment?" she asked, angry that her heart speeded up when he looked at her.

Chaco nodded.

Why couldn't he simply respond verbally like a normal person? Instead, he stood silent and grave, gazing down at her with those spooky eyes. But she wasn't about to show him he made her nervous.

"I have a list to give you." She handed over the second piece of paper. "I'm ordering supplies."

"What kind of supplies?"

"For the casino. You know, cards and dice and so forth."

He glanced at the list but said nothing.

She noted his high cheekbones and the bronze cast to his skin. "If you can think of anything else, you're welcome to add it."

He nodded again.

Ordeal having been faced and overcome, she nearly turned to leave, then decided she'd try to ease future situations by being forthright. "Are you, perhaps, part Indian?"

Just as she asked it, she realized the question could be offensive, since some establishments in the city didn't allow entrance to Indians or mixed breeds. Because of that, not everyone admitted to their heritage.

But Chaco answered easily, "I'm a quarter Apache, half Spanish and some Anglo."

"About me?"

"Well, it wasn't seriously bad."

His eyes were cold as stone. "You know I can't read."

She admitted, "I'm a teacher. I can tell." She added quickly, "It doesn't mean you're not intelligent."

"I need to read for this job, though."

"Not necessarily." She had struck at a vulnerability and felt very badly. Many people didn't know how to read on the frontier. "It would help, of course. And I could give you lessons, if you wanted. I have some books." Though perhaps he would feel odd about that, being a grown man.

"I don't take anything unless I can give something back."

She suggested the first thing that came into her head. "You could teach me some Spanish."

"I can't write or read that either."

"I meant speaking the language."

"I could help you, I guess." He sounded reluctant. "Is there anything else you don't know how to do?"

She shrugged. "I need to learn how to ride."

"Then I'll teach you that."

She had been about to say that Louisa would be taking her riding, but she supposed she could change her plans.

Chaco seemed more satisfied. "That'll be fair. We'll trade." Everything settled, he got back to business and held out the paper again. "So what does this say?"

She read off the casino supplies.

"And this." He pointed at her first addition.

"Can you read?"

"And now the bad thing."

Oh, well. *"You are a big donkey."*

For a moment, he seemed stunned . . . until his face split into a wide grin. Then he laughed aloud, teeth flashing white against his tanned skin. Even his eyes warmed up. He looked like a completely different man.

"A donkey?" He laughed again. "You think that's bad?"

"Would you like me to come up with something worse?" she joked, smiling.

But she didn't make any other suggestions, simply glad she'd made some sort of peace with the man.

Doña Ynez came to Santa Fe to see Chaco Jones a few days after his encounter with Don Armando. The hotel where he was staying said he spent most of his hours working at the Blue Sky Palace. A casino and brothel? With a sigh, Ynez tightened her shawl and climbed back in her carriage. She was alone, not having wanted her husband to know of her activities. And though it was hardly proper for an upper-class Spanish lady to enter such a place as Blue Sky, she had no servant to protect her so she was going to have to do so.

As if the horse knew she was upset, it reared and whinnied as she took up the reins. Wanting to curse, she instead laid her whip on the beast and demanded he go forward.

What was Don Armando thinking of, sending letters to this mestizo bastard? And why must he demand an heir of his blood or else leave his land to the church?

But then, if there had been no bastard at all, Ynez would not have this chance . . .

Her chin high, she asked for Chaco Jones at the front desk of the Blue Sky. A red-headed, middle-aged woman showed her to a private office where they could talk. As Ynez had expected, he looked surprised when he saw her.

"Señora de Arguello," he said in cool greeting.

"Señor Jones. But please call me Doña Ynez." She smiled, keeping her voice low, fluttering her hands prettily as she adjusted her shawl. She had worn the red flowered one today over an elegant yellow silk dress. "I am sure you must wonder why I have come to see you." If he was in the least curious, he didn't show it, throwing her off track. "M—My husband is very disappointed that you will not recognize your kinship with him."

Jones frowned. "And he sent you to talk to me?"

"No. He does not know I am here." Ynez tossed her head, aware of the ruby earrings that would sparkle in the light from the office window. She had also made sure that several dark strands of her upswept hair were loose enough to fall about her shoulders. "You are making a mistake, Señor Jones. You have more to gain than you can possibly know."

"Some acres of land? I could care less."

"I speak of far more than a few acres. Don Armando owns the valley in which his house sits and all the mountain meadows surrounding it." She stepped closer, allowing her shawl to slip. The bodice of the yellow silk was cut deeply. "And there are also many cattle and horses, Señor Jones. My husband is very, very wealthy."

"I don't care about cattle and horses either." He quirked his lip. "Besides, it's hard to believe a Hidalgo would up and give all that to a bastard son he'd never seen before."

Ynez agreed, but she had come to believe her husband meant what he threatened. "Don Armando will bequeath his kingdom to you if you will honor him as your father."

"*And?*"

He was rightfully suspicious. "He may ask other

tasks of you, but I do not believe they will be so odious."

"I'm an independent sort of man."

She could respect that, bound by rules and conventions as she was. "But what do you have with your independence? Nothing." She added carefully, "Don Armando does not have long to live." Though he seemed to be feeling much better after the interview with Jones. "Soon, the land will be yours without his supervision."

Now she thought he appeared interested.

"Of course, you would be expected to take care of your father's widow," she went on. And if she were very clever, she could thereby retain control of much of the wealth. There was no such hope with the church. "You may be assured I would not make unpleasant requests of you."

Perhaps she would even grant favors. Which wouldn't be unpleasant for her either—despite his base-blood heritage, he was a very handsome man. She moved nearer, allowing him to gaze down the front of her dress.

"Do you know what it is like to wield absolute power over dozens of people?" she asked, her voice husky.

"You mean the peons who work the de Arguello land? That's nothing I've ever wanted. I hate slavery."

She wouldn't deny the peons' debts to their overlord put some of them in that virtual position. But she said, "The many are meant to serve the few."

"Not if I can help it."

How strange. "You are so soft and pure of heart, you, a gunfighter?"

"A former gunfighter," he said quickly. "I'm a casino floorman now."

She fluttered her hands again. "Still." He must be lying! She grew tired of this continual denial. She decided to offer what she hoped was the greatest reward of all. "You must think about the women, if your social position should change."

"Women?"

She thrust her breasts forward slightly, knowing he could see nearly everything but their very tips. Her nipples were fully outlined by the thin silk of her dress. She saw the spark of desire in his eyes, but also sensed some uneasiness. Was he afraid of her?

She attempted to put him at ease by smiling, speaking silkily, "As a *rico,* you could have whomever you want."

His glance flicked over her. "I can have plenty of women now."

"Not the good ones, Señor." Including herself, she implied. And even a lowly bastard mestizo should appreciate the offer she was making. "Not women who wear silk and smell of expensive soaps and perfumes, who keep their skin soft with lotions." She reached out to rake a finger slowly down his chest. "They are different."

He desired her, she knew it! She felt the thrill of victory, of promise, and raised her lips.

But then he brushed her hand away and stepped back. "I've had some expensive women. I didn't think they were that much different."

At first stunned, Ynez stood stock still. Then she flushed with anger and embarrassment. "You insult me, Señor!"

"You must want that land real bad if you're offering to sleep with me to get it."

Had her true motive been so transparent? Well, there was no use openly denying it.

"You are a pig! A man does not insult a woman so, even when he refuses her favors!" she cried, using social custom to excuse herself. In Hidalgo society, complicated flirtations, invitations, assignations and polite refusals were carried on with subtlety. "But what else should I have expected of a base-born peon?"

He did not look in the least insulted himself and he turned calmly when someone pounded loudly on the door. Ynez jerked her shawl up over her shoulders as Jones answered it.

"Sorry to bother you, Chaco." It was the red-headed woman from the front desk. She gazed at Ynez curiously. "But this Bible-thumper woman I know is outside yelling at the customers, calling them Satan, acting like she's plumb crazy. Never seen such a fuss! She's gonna embarrass somebody or get herself in trouble."

"I'll go talk to her, Belle."

"Don't think she's the sort who can see reason."

"Then I'll encourage her to leave . . . in a proper and reasonable way."

Not caring about crazy Anglo women or customers or Chaco Jones himself, Ynez brushed past both him and the woman named Belle, not bothering to wish them a good afternoon or evening. Her back straight, she pulled her shawl up over her mouth and chin, in case there was someone about who might recognize her.

Outside, on her way to her carriage, she saw the Bible-thumper. The woman's voice screeched furiously, calling upon God and the Angel of Death to deal a fatal blow to the Blue Sky, to the sinful men who frequented it.

Bitter and shamed, Ynez was certain she herself would smile if lightning should strike the place this very instant.

THE WIND CASTS NO SHADOW

* * *

Minna Tucker shrieked and wailed her anger and sorrow. The evil people in the Blue Sky brothel and casino had seduced her son. She'd followed Billie there and seen him enter, but she knew that her sweet baby boy would never have done so of his own accord.

"Devil!" she shouted, waving her fist at another horrid man approaching the den of iniquity. "You destroyer of the innocent, the little lambs of God!"

At the same time that man entered, another one came out. Tall and dark, he headed straight toward her, his stride and gaze menacing. Though he wasn't dressed like a savage, Minna knew he was one. She also knew his name was Chaco Jones. Billie had once pointed him out. She had no doubt that Jones had been setting his sights on her son's innocent soul then.

"Stay away from me, Satan!" She held up the cross she wore about her neck, trying to ward the fiend off.

"You should be moving along, lady. There's no church doings going on here."

"Satan!" she shrieked again, backing away from him. "I won't leave until you give me my Billie!"

"You know someone in there?" He glanced back at the building. "Well, you'll have to wait for him at home."

When he reached for her arm, she screamed to high heaven and backed up some more. "Don't touch me with your filthy hands!"

"Go on home and I won't have to touch you."

"Give me my Billie, Satan!"

"He'll be along later."

"Not later, now! I won't allow you to steal his soul!

To rip his heart out and replace it with a stone!"

Jones frowned. "You're crazy, lady. Haven't you got anyone else to take care of you?"

He knew she was alone! Her husband dead, having been shot down while doing his honest duty, Minna felt frightened for herself, as well as her son. But she couldn't do more for Billie now. She had to retreat. Backing away step by step, gathering her skirts, she summoned up all her righteous anger.

"God will smite you! He will send His minions to destroy you with tooth and claw! You will be torn apart and thrown into the maw of hell!"

Then she ran.

She raged—in the darkest hours of the night, she sped through the dirty streets, mindless, senseless with fury. Her feet dug into the sandy clay, her hair streamed in the wind.

Finally, panting, she fell to her knees in an alley behind a building from which a tinkling piano could be heard. She hated the sound that hurt her ears.

Growling deep in her throat, she swung her head back and forth, remembering the cadence of real animal rhythm. She spoke a few guttural words, tore at the clothing covering her heated flesh ... snarled and drew back her lips as the change began ...

... some time later, she was on the run again. She raised her face. The scent of her enemy carried on the wind.

He was nearby. How difficult to contain her excitement.

Snarling, she changed directions, leaping to the top of an adobe wall, running along it to speed her progress. A horse in the enclosure neighed in terror. A large dog whined and slunk under some bushes.

Still she ran on, after far better prey. Her muscles flexed as she leaped even higher to scale a rooftop. The town spread out about her, black shapes in the gray darkness. The air was alive with odors and scents. Yet she could easily locate her enemy.

Avoiding any needless, unwanted encounters, she kept to the rooftops, only slowing when the smell of her enemy filled her nostrils completely. Musky, sweet . . . and full of blood.

She circled, sniffing, snuffling, growling. He was here, right beneath her!

Gazing over the building's edge, she gauged her position and the second-story window some feet below. But there was a better way to unearth him.

The roof was old, cracked in several places and ready to give. Ravenous, lustful, furious, she dug, able to taste his throat already!

Chaco awoke sweating, uncomfortably aroused, deeply uneasy at the dream he'd had. He'd seen himself lying naked on the ground, a woman mounted on his belly, riding him for all she was worth. But then her eyes had begun to glow and her face had changed.

Not that he'd been certain of her identity in the first place. All he remembered was her searching lips, her sharp teeth, her streaming hair.

Scratch, scratch.

He sat up in the bed, suddenly aware of sifting earth coming down from the ceiling. "What the hell!"

In a second, he was on his feet, the Colt in his hand. He didn't even have time to light the kerosene lamp on the table. *Scratch, scratch, scratch.*

More earth filtered down, along with a part of a

latilla, the sticks laid between the ceiling's *vigas.* Was some damned animal trying to dig his way in?

"Hey, get out of here!" He raised the Colt.

Then he heard a low snarl and saw the glowing eyes peering through the widening hole in the ceiling.

Glowing eyes? The wolf creature!

Without thinking, he crouched, lapsing into Apache, "Get away from here, evil one! I am a spirit warrior, a *di-yin!*" And despite his trembling hands, he managed to pull the trigger.

As the Colt went off, the eyes flashed and the animal leaped back, yelping. The words of power had enabled him to wound it.

"Go, evil one!" Chaco shouted again.

And even though he heard no more growls, saw no more glowing eyes, he remained with gun raised for several more minutes, listening, looking.

Finally, stiff from the crouched posture, chilled from drying sweat, he stepped over to light the lamp, all the while sliding his gaze back and forth from that task to the ceiling.

No more sleeping tonight, he thought, skin crawling.

Instead, he'd gather his belongings so he could check out of the seedy old adobe hotel as soon as the sun rose. He would find another place to stay, a building with a good roof and more people around than an aged clerk who slept behind the desk in the foyer. The old man obviously hadn't even heard the gunshot, since he would have appeared by now.

Chaco got his clothes out of the dresser, thinking about the skin-walker. For he now believed she was real, not simply a figment of some underlying superstition. The hole in the ceiling attested to that. And she wanted him, had obviously followed him all the way from Lincoln County.

Why? Had he unknowingly offended an Indian who wanted revenge? Had some enemy put a supernatural price on his head?

There was nothing to do now except keep her at bay, at least until he could talk to a real medicine man.

8

A few days after he'd wounded the skin-walker, Chaco was still thinking about finding a real *di-yin*. The only problem being that his ties were with the Chiricahua, Apaches who roamed to the South and West, rather than the Jicarilla who lived near Santa Fe. Trying to catch up with the Chiricahua—one of the few tribes who hadn't made peace with the U.S. government—would take luck, not to mention days of riding. They were always on the move, traveling back and forth through the southwest, even disappearing over the Mexican border.

Besides, he didn't want to give up his new job. He enjoyed being a casino floorman and he liked the room he was now renting at the Blue Sky. Since he'd moved in, he'd had no more bad dreams, and there'd been no sign of the skin-walker. Hopefully, the last encounter had scared the witch away.

In a good mood, Chaco spent an hour or two every day simply relaxing on a bench in the Blue Sky's *placita*, sometimes talking to Adolfo or one of the other residents. He'd worked with the little Mexican at a real cow-punching job many years before. Adolfo was trustworthy and good-natured, if a little hot-headed.

Today, on a bench opposite Chaco, Adolfo showed Luz the long knife he carried inside his jacket. "See what it says? 'Do not draw me without cause, nor sheath me without honor.'"

"Ah, *bonita*." Luz reached for the weapon. "May I look at it more closely?"

"Better watch out or she'll wheedle that knife out of you," Chaco said. He realized Adolfo was obviously very taken with Luz.

Her eyes hardened. "I have plenty of knives of my own."

"She does, *compadre*," Adolfo told Chaco. "You ought to see her collection."

"I'm sure she can take care of herself." He'd noticed the young woman's strength and agility. She was slim, with firm muscles and wide shoulders, and she seemed very confident, as if she knew exactly what she wanted.

She wasn't the only one. Magdalena had surprised him when she'd stopped by his room late the night before. Tapping on his door, she'd casually offered a free sample of her wares. Though tempted, he'd turned her down, still haunted by the sexual dream of that glowing-eyed woman.

He'd definitely been under some sort of spell that night, had proven so the next day when he'd found a witch pouch in the pocket of his good black coat. Stuffed with poison powder, a snake's fang, and braided hairs, some of which had to have been his own, the packet had been meant both to bewitch him and to cause him harm.

What bothered him was that the witch had gotten close enough to slip the pouch into his pocket. Did that mean she was someone he knew? Was he rubbing shoulders with a skin-walker?

That suspicion made him carefully look over every woman he came into contact with. He didn't really think Magdalena had anything against him—though she hadn't seemed happy when he'd politely refused her favors a second time—but she knew more about *brujeria* than anyone else at the Blue Sky.

Including Frances Gannon. Now, in her case, he was dead certain *she* wasn't a witch.

Yesterday, she'd given him his first reading and writing lesson. She'd shown him the ABCs and how to spell a few simple words. At the same time, she'd kept staring at him when she thought he wasn't looking. He was pretty sure she was attracted to him, a fact that pleased him, considering he hadn't been able to get her out of his mind since he'd seen her in that red dress.

Frances Gannon was another reason he'd turned down Magdalena, though he had little if any chance of getting close to the casino owner. Even if she completely forgave him for killing her husband, Frances was a bit too fancy for a man like him to make a fool of himself over. Educated and well-spoken, she was as finely mannered as a Hidalgo woman, if far more open and decent-hearted than most of them. He'd bet *she* didn't believe in the many serving the few or that you could buy any man with the right price.

Quite a contrast to the arrogant, if beautiful, Doña Ynez. He wondered if de Arguello or one of the servants had suffered for the snit he'd caused by refusing her.

"Good morning, Magdalena." Luz's greeting brought him out of his musings.

Chaco scanned Magdalena's face for any sign of suppressed anger or furtiveness, seeing neither as the woman greeted everyone cordially and sat down beside Luz and Adolfo. But skin-walkers were known to have two faces.

Luz eyed the Indian blanket Magdalena had draped over one shoulder. "You have been out at the pueblo again?"

"My father's cousin gave me this. She also collected some eagle and hawk feathers for me." She drew a long, brown feather from beneath her blanket. "Pretty, yes? Unfortunately, I will not be able to visit the pueblo again for quite some time."

"Why not?" asked Luz. "Did you make someone angry?"

Magdalena shook her head. "The Indians fear a *diablera* is stalking them. If I go there, I might be in danger."

Chaco immediately focused on the word. "*Diablera?*"

"You heard about the murder?" asked Magdalena.

"Which murder?" There was a killing every once in a while, what with the army stationed in town and the railroad bringing in new people.

Magdalena looked solemn. "This was no gunfight or stabbing. A few weeks ago, a young Navajo man was found dead in an irrigation ditch. His throat had been torn out by an animal, while the other marks around him seemed to be human." Now that she had everyone's rapt attention, she lowered her voice to a hushed tone. "A footprint was left in the soil nearby. But worse, a hand print had been burned into his flesh!"

"A-i-y, *Dios!*" muttered Adolfo, his eyes round.

Chaco's skin crawled. Once again, he envisioned the wolf-creature. "A skin-walker." And the murder meant the witch obviously had other victims to stalk. He wasn't sure whether to be relieved or not. "Who was this man exactly?"

"His name?" Magdalena turned her steady, unsmiling gaze on him. "I only know that he was from the reservation north of here."

Chaco didn't see what he and the man would have in common, then, unless it was Indian blood. He stared at Magdalena.

"The Navajo's relatives are certain the murderer was a witch," she went on. "Everyone on the northern reservation is afraid."

Luz cut in, "But how does this concern the Pueblos who live closer to Santa Fe?"

"They lost a young man several years ago, a similar death. They are afraid, too." Magdalena added, "I only hope they do not begin suspecting everyone who acts in the least bit different—the reason I must stay away. I have heard of a pueblo south of here that reduced their village to five or six people."

"A purge." Chaco had also heard of that incident. "People go crazy and start thinking their neighbors caused a crop failure or somebody's death. They kill one another instead of listening to a wise person." A spiritual leader of some kind was part of every pueblo or tribe. "They need to have some sense talked into them. Not everyone is a *diablera*."

"What is this about witches?" Coming out of one of the doorways opening onto the *placita,* Frances approached.

Adolfo immediately leaped to his feet. Chaco wasn't good at social niceties, something Frances probably expected from a man. She glanced at him quickly before she took a seat at the opposite end of his bench.

Magdalena went into the whole tale about the pueblo and the murder again.

Frances looked horrified. "How terrible! Especially that innocent people may suffer at the hands of their own tribe. The Indians have problems enough with the U.S. government persecuting them."

She was taking the side of the Indians? That was certainly unusual for an Anglo woman.

"Do Anglos believe in witches?" Magdalena asked.

Behind the group, Chaco noticed Sophie entering the *placita*. She leaned against one of the little shade trees to listen.

"I certainly can't speak for everyone," said Frances, "but I haven't heard much about the subject until arriving here. There were the Salem witch trials, of course. The Puritans in Massachusetts tried and executed several people about a hundred years ago."

Sophie stirred and murmured, "Witchcraft is very much older than that."

"Except I don't think the Salem executions were really about witchcraft," Frances said. "Those people were victims of religious fanaticism."

"Perhaps the Puritans were ridding their group of people who followed the Old Religion." Sophie's voice was soft with French accent. "Indians said prayers to gods and made spells long before the Spanish ever came to New Mexico. People did the same in Europe before churches were ever built. And Africans brought voodoo to this country."

"Obviously, *you* believe in witches," Frances remarked.

"I have seen the proof," Sophie told her. "People who fall down dead when a voodoo queen casts an evil eye on them, witches who are possessed by gods and lift things twice their own size." She added, "The important question is not whether there are witches, but whether a witch is good or evil."

Just then, Belle came out to call the girls inside. They left, chattering among themselves.

Frances rose as well. "My book work awaits."

Though disappointed that she meant to leave so fast, Chaco couldn't think of an excuse that would keep her hanging around. "How about a riding lesson tomorrow?"

"Tomorrow would be fine."

"Around noon."

At least that would give him something to look forward to rather than spending his time brooding about some witch who might be after *his* skin.

Horseback riding wasn't as easy as it looked. Chaco claimed the sorrel mare he'd picked out was gentle, but Frances was having difficulties anyway. Not that the horse tried to run away with her. She merely couldn't get comfortable.

"Move farther up in the saddle," Chaco ordered as they walked their animals across a ridge outside the town. "And try to keep your hands light. You have to feel the horse's mouth."

Frances frowned. "Feel the animal's mouth?"

"Through the reins. For one thing, you need to gauge how hard to pull to get her to stop."

"You can't just say whoa?"

Chaco grinned. "Horses aren't dogs. They won't obey your voice. Where did you get that idea anyhow?"

"From carriage drivers." Who were always shouting the word. She didn't want to admit she hadn't paid much attention to what they were doing with the reins. "Are you making fun of me?" His little smirk annoyed her. "Don't forget this is my first time on a horse."

"I know. I didn't mean to make fun." He offered, "You can laugh at me when I'm trying to read."

"That would hardly be nice." As a teacher, she felt it her duty to be encouraging. "And it wouldn't be true." Chaco was quick and intelligent. "You're picking up reading and writing quite well."

In a way, however, she'd made fun of him the day she'd implied he was a big donkey. He'd been a good sport about that, so she should try to be less irritable now. Even if she couldn't help but feel that straddling a horse was slightly obscene. The split skirt she'd borrowed from Belle covered her adequately, but having her legs stretched so far apart felt distinctly unladylike. Not to mention suggestive.

"Most women travel by wagon or carriage back East," she told Chaco, making an excuse for her awkwardness. "But then, there are more roads."

"What about sidesaddles?"

"Women ride that way through the parks in Boston, though I've never tried it myself."

"Sounds kind of stupid to me," Chaco insisted. "How could you give the horse signals—or feel his mood—if you don't have your legs around him?"

"Maybe the animals are trained differently."

But he still didn't seem amenable to the idea. Frances noted the subtle way he quirked his mouth. Chaco *did* show emotion and reaction; she'd simply had to get used to his subtle manner.

She wondered if she'd ever be able to ride half as well as he did. In rhythm with the buckskin, he and his mount moved as one when he turned the horse onto a downhill trail. Disliking the ground falling away so abruptly, she stiffened when the sorrel mare followed. She didn't want to lose her balance and tumble off.

"Lean back in the saddle when you're going downhill," Chaco yelled, sounding amused.

Did he have eyes in the back of his head?

"And lean forward when you're going uphill," he went on. "You don't want to get the horse off-balance."

Heaven forbid! The animal would be even more likely to fall. Heart in her throat, Frances tried to relax a bit. A short piece later, the ground straightened and led into a blue-green copse of firs.

Chaco reined in and circled, then walked his mount beside her. "Are you getting sore yet?"

"Excuse me?" That certainly sounded lewd, and his meaningful glance at her rear made her want to blush.

"We can rest for awhile if you want."

"That sounds wonderful." Though she longed to master riding as much as she wanted to feel at ease around Chaco. "I only hope I can mount again."

"I'll give you another boost."

Meaning he'd have his hands on her leg again. No matter how she tried to steel herself, Frances was fully aware of each and every place he touched her. After dismounting, he helped her down out of the saddle. She felt the warmth of his hand at her waist where her short jacket rose to expose her blouse. Corsetless, she could count the imprint of each finger and a thrill shot up her spine. She tried to ignore it as she struggled to walk on land again.

"Whew! I am a bit sore."

"And you'll be stiff tonight."

"I'll soak in a warm bath."

She couldn't believe the images that conjured, unfortunately all involving Chaco, her suggestive state of mind probably the result of her short marriage. Having slept with a man had left her with certain appetites, and whether she liked it or not, she found Chaco particularly attractive. Even the memory of Nate's shooting couldn't douse her explicit thoughts about the man responsible, much to her shame.

"There's a nice view over here," said Chaco, tying the horses to some low branches.

He led her down a path through the trees and out onto a rocky overlook. Santa Fe lay in the wide valley below them, a great cluster of buildings surrounded by terra-cotta hills and the more distant loom of blue mountains. Smoke rose from several chimneys, the breeze bringing the scent of burning pinon logs.

Frances could smell fresh pinon where she stood now, a greener, sharper odor. She sat down on a big boulder, while Chaco eased himself down on a log some feet away.

"You're doing pretty well for your first time."

"Are you trying to encourage me?"

"Telling the truth." He smiled, the skin crinkling about his eyes.

The expression softened his face, but also made him look a little older. Frances guessed he was in his mid-thirties, though it shouldn't matter to her. Chaco intrigued her, her interest going beyond the wild and exotic cast of his Indian and Spanish features. He exuded quiet strength and intelligence that had nothing to do with book learning. He was so innately competent, so discerning, so lacking in fear, she could understand why people had hired him to guard them and why troublemakers feared him.

"So how do you like New Mexico Territory?" he asked.

She'd grown so used to his taciturn personality,

Frances was always surprised when he initiated conversation. She gazed down at Santa Fe, its zigzag of red-brown dirt roads a crude map.

"It's a fascinating place. The bright sunlight is beautiful and so is the clear blue sky. And I love the mountains surrounding us."

"You can reach those mountains in a few hours' ride."

"I'm looking forward to being able to do that."

"We'll take a day and head for the Sangre de Cristos Mountains whenever you're ready."

A whole day in his company? Not certain that would be wise, she raised her brows.

"If that's all right, with work and all."

At least he wasn't forgetting she was his employer. She needed to remember that as well, to keep some sort of upper hand. And while she wanted to put the past behind her, she had to remember she was in mourning.

"We'll see."

She took a deep breath, savoring the fresh air as she listened to the heavy branches soughing in the wind.

"Do you like living at the Blue Sky?" he asked.

"I had to do some adjusting, get used to the idea of the Gentlemen's Club."

"You don't usually find schoolteachers in that kind of place." Barely hesitating, he inquired, "How did you and . . . Mr. Gannon get together anyway?"

He was certainly being direct. And casual about the man he'd killed, accident or no.

"Nate wasn't exactly honest with me," she said a little stiffly. "He told me he owned a hotel and a restaurant in Santa Fe."

"I see."

"I was startled when I met Belle." Not to mention stunned by having to deal with Nate's untimely end the very same day. "And I admit I was shocked when I found out about the Blue Sky. But I had nowhere else to stay." She added, "I've come to realize that Belle's ladies are doing what they believe they must to earn a living. But I hope that situation will change as did yours. Did you like being a gunfighter?"

"It paid better than cow-punching."

"So you also needed to earn a living." She would hate to think the violence had attracted him. He'd claimed he'd never shot anyone unless he had to.

"I got plenty tired of the job after a while. I don't mind watching someone's back, but all out war is another story."

"Are you talking about Lincoln County?" She'd heard of the unrest there.

He nodded. "A lot of blood is being shed down south." He stared down at the valley, his profile sharp against the sky. "The men who were trading shots with me in Galisteo Junction were some of The Boys, one of the gangs from Lincoln County."

She hadn't even thought about the reason for the gunfight.

"I quit the Double-Bar, the job I had, after that happened."

And after he'd shot Nate.

Was Chaco implying that the incident had affected him so deeply that he'd reevaluated his life? He wasn't the sort of man to say so outright, but that thought somehow made Frances feel better. A little of the weight she'd been carrying around lifted from her heart.

"Violence seems to be more acceptable here than out East," she said. "I don't like that aspect of the West."

"The mix of people . . . all the change going on . . . when the wind switches directions too many times, it brings up storms."

As they sat above Santa Fe, Frances spotted a cavalry unit riding down from the hills. The westerly sun glinted from shiny objects—buckles, epaulets, swords, rifles.

"Are they coming back from maneuvers?"

"Probably, or else they've been chasing Indians back onto the reservation."

The mention of Indians being treated like criminals brought up a whole host of unwelcome memories. "Do the Indians escape a lot?"

"Once in a while. They're getting used to being penned up."

"How awful." She shook her head in sympathy. "At least they're living on the land they grew up on." Not being shipped away like the Indians she remembered from her childhood. "If that's any consolation."

"The Chiricahua Apaches southwest of here are still a problem," Chaco said. "They haven't given up their freedom yet. They can cover a lot of territory if they want to and they raid *ranchos* every once in a while."

"Isn't Geronimo a Chiricahua?" She'd heard of the great chief, even back East. "Everyone is frightened of him."

"With good reason. He's been on the warpath ever since the Mexican Army killed his family." He looked straight at her. "Real name's Goyahkla, and he's my uncle."

Her eyes widened. So Chaco descended from the wildest and wiliest group of Apaches. Had he inherited his toughness and fierce self-possession from them?

"Have you ever met him?" she asked.

"Coupla times. When I was a boy, my mother used to take me to the Chiricahua camps in the summer. We traveled south in 1851, not long after my uncle's family was massacred. While he mourned beside a river for his mother and wife and three children, he heard a voice call 'Goyahkla' four times—four's a magic number to an Apache—and the voice said he would never be killed by a bullet."

Not exactly knowing what to think about people who heard voices, she tactfully asked, "He had a vision?"

"Something like that."

She noted Chaco's expression was rapt, faraway. "And you believe it, I see."

"Why not? I've had a few visions myself." He explained, "They were dreams, actually, or feelings that something was going to happen."

"Premonitions?" She could accept that. Again, as with Ruby when they'd discussed Magdalena's predictions, she asked, "Did they come true?"

"Yes." The answer was decisive, unequivocal.

Which fascinated Frances even more. Chaco had abiding faith in his own intuition. That probably also added to his aura of strength.

"You haven't had visions or dreams yourself?" he asked, turning to look at her.

She shook her head. "Even if I did, I'm afraid I lack the faith to believe in them."

"Why?"

"My father was a minister—"

"A type of holy man."

"Supposedly." She went on hurriedly, "But he was very overbearing and I didn't agree with all of his ideas. I thought some of the church's rules and attitudes were more harmful than good and said so. After my honesty created a rift with my own father, I had trouble believing in anything."

"What were these ideas you didn't agree with?"

"Well, the excessive strictness of following every rule for its own sake, for one. It didn't seem like anyone should be joyful or the least bit spontaneous. I also didn't agree with the attitude toward some people, like women . . . or Indians."

Chaco nodded. "Yesterday, you said you thought the government persecuted Indians."

How well she remembered. Scenes from her childhood often haunted her at unexpected times.

"My father served in a reserve camp when I was a child. The government was shipping Indians out West away from their homes. A terrible situation. And my father and other missionaries thought the Indians deserved to be treated no better than cattle because they weren't Christian."

"And they weren't white."

She sighed. "Many thought Indians to be evil. And I knew it wasn't true even as a child. There were good and bad among them, as with any other people." A lump grew in her throat. "One family befriended me. I used to play with the children. They were torn away from their mother, so they could be sent to missionary school, where they'd adopt 'good' rules for living." She cleared her throat, wondering once again what had happened to her little friends. "Their mother was never the same again. She sat in the same place every day and mourned. Finally, she died. I think it was from a broken heart."

Chaco's eyes pierced her as if he were trying to look into her very soul. "You have a kind heart."

"I'm only human."

"But some humans are kind and some aren't."

"The missionaries were supposed to be kind, but they wanted to preach to the Indians and make them into something they weren't rather than try to understand them. They didn't care about anyone's feelings. Not even when a man killed himself rather than be taken away from his homeland." She'd seen him lying in a pool of blood. "For the missionaries, it was only one less Indian."

"They believed they were dealing with enemies. The Indians were competing for the same land as the whites."

She hadn't thought of it in such practical terms. "This is a huge country. Can't everyone live in peace?"

"Could you live in peace with the Chiricahua, who would steal your horses and butcher your cattle when they needed to?"

Frances was startled. "Are you suggesting I consider your own relatives my enemies?"

He shook his head. "It's just so easy for people to become enemies in the first place. They fight over land and food and water and then find excuses—pick on the differences between them—to justify themselves."

"Like race and religion." She shook her head sadly.

"True." Then he smiled at her so warmly, he chased away her memories. "Maybe you and your good heart belong here in New Mexico Territory with all its differences."

A bit embarrassed, she fiddled with a button on her sleeve. "I'm beginning to think my future is here," she admitted. "Though I'm no saint."

"But you're a good person, someone who cares about others." As if he realized he'd made her uncomfortable, Chaco rose and glanced toward the horses. "Have you rested enough? Shall we ride again?"

Frances gladly followed him back through the trees.

As the sun faded, the shade beneath the branches deepened into shadow. But she couldn't get her mind off some of the more unusual differences in beliefs—like having visions and fearing witches.

"Do you believe in the *diablera* the girls were talking about yesterday?" she asked.

Chaco nodded. "All witches aren't bad, though. The Apache believe evil comes from a person letting hatred or anger or envy eat them up from inside."

"You sound as if you speak from personal experience." When he didn't answer, she asked, "Would you know a witch when you saw her?"

"Maybe, maybe not. She can have two faces, one for day and one for night. It might take some time to see through the false face. A *di-yin* would be better at it. That's a medicine man or shaman," he explained. "And that's what he trains for, to see below the surface. Goyahkla is a *di-yin*."

She frowned. "Yet he's bent on revenge. He's on the warpath." Which surely meant he wasn't a good man.

"He's fighting the enemies of his family and his people, not personal enemies. And he knows he'll have to pay a big price for it in the end." Chaco sounded fatalistic. "A bullet might not take him, but he'll probably suffer something a lot worse."

What a conversation. Though Frances felt a bit overwhelmed, she'd also gotten to know Chaco on a much deeper level. She sensed he'd seen and experienced terrible things, far more so than she. He was a mix of the battling cultures of New Mexico Territory, yet he somehow remained centered, secure in his own identity. He was no idealist, yet she believed he was a decent man.

She had been especially touched by his insisting

that she was a good-hearted person. He must possess some goodness himself, if he could appreciate the quality in someone else.

He untied the sorrel mare and slipped the reins up over her neck. "Let's get you back in the saddle."

Then he tried to give Frances a leg up, but she had trouble, even when she grasped the mare's mane.

"This horse is too big!" she groused.

He laughed and took hold of her waist. Once again, she felt the warmth of each and every finger. Distracted, she let her foot slip out of the stirrup as the mare stepped forward. She fell back against Chaco, making him stumble.

"Sorry!" Turning in his arms, she found herself face-to-face with him.

His smile faded to be replaced by a much more serious expression. He let her slip down farther, her body whispering against his and reacting in kind. She caught her breath at the intense sensations spiraling through her. For a moment—all differences forgotten—the world stood still.

Keeping his arms about her, he lowered his head, his eyes smoky. Then he angled his mouth over hers and kissed her deep and hungrily. She opened her mouth to his delving tongue and wrapped her arms about his neck. She could feel his heart thudding hard through the solid wall of his chest. Part of her wanted to protest—thought she *should* protest—but he made her forget everything but the path of his fingers as he slipped a hand beneath her jacket and splayed it across her back.

Arching, she pressed herself against him, her breasts flattening, nipples hardening. He slid his hand farther down her back, anchoring her hips. The hard proof of his desire pushed against her belly. Heat spread outward from her middle, making her knees weak.

Chaco murmured something against her mouth and turned her to cup her breast, which fit his hand perfectly. He teased the aching crest with his thumb, then began undoing the buttons of her blouse.

When the cool air laved her heated skin, Frances suddenly stiffened in shock as she realized where this was going. "Stop!" Her hand shook as it caught his.

For a moment, they both stood there, breathing heavily. She could hardly meet his eyes. She was shocked not only at him, but at herself.

How could she be so loose and with the man who had ended Nate's life?

Caution warred with passion in Chaco's eyes as he said, "There's nothing wrong with two people wanting each other, Frankie."

His calling her by the name Belle had given her incensed Frances further. "There is when one of those people killed the other's husband."

He stiffened and backed off. "I thought you believed that was an accident."

"Maybe I do, but that doesn't bring Nate back, does it?" Tears sprang to her eyes and Frances was ashamed to realize they were more for herself than the dead man she hadn't really known. Nate's lies had diminished the burgeoning feelings she'd had for him, but even now she foolishly longed for the dream he'd offered her. "And it doesn't change the fact that you were on that street to kill someone."

"To protect another man!"

"With a *gun*."

Chaco's tone turned cold. "In the West, guns are part of life."

"And part of death!"

"And death," he echoed. "If you can't accept

that, maybe you don't belong here, after all. Maybe you should just go back East where people are more civilized."

The softness she'd seen in Chaco moments before had vanished in an instant, as quickly as had her dreams. Or maybe she'd seen what she'd wanted to see as she had with Nate. More wishful thinking on her part.

"Maybe I will leave just as soon as Belle has the cash to buy me out!" she said angrily.

The problem was, Frances didn't know where she would go. She didn't seem to belong anywhere.

9

As they headed back to Santa Fe, Chaco's thoughts were grim. Though Frances had returned his passion for a moment out on the trail, she'd obviously lost her head and had taken no time in regretting her actions. She still blamed him for her husband's death. He guessed she was right in doing so, even though he'd lost some respect for the dead man after learning Nate Gannon hadn't had the decency to be honest with his bride. At least he had that in his own favor, Chaco thought—honesty, and an aversion to making himself out to be something he wasn't.

For all the good it did him.

He'd thought that might count for something to a woman like Frances. That and the fact that he'd turned his back on the only way of life he'd known since his mother had died. Well, he'd been wrong.

Chaco could tell Frances was still nerved up about their encounter. While she didn't speak to him directly, she spent plenty of time muttering to herself or her horse under her breath as they rode along.

When he helped her dismount at the Blue Sky, he let his hands linger at her waist. She gave him a look that might have frozen a lesser man and stepped sharply away. He couldn't help but inhale her scent and admire the shiny gold-brown hair that tumbled about her shoulders.

"Is this mare yours?" she asked, her words stiff. "Will I have access to her, so I can practice?"

"Sure, I borrowed the horse from a friend but he doesn't need her for a while. She'll be in the stable right here." He indicated the building in back of the Blue Sky, where Belle kept her horses and carriage.

"Wonderful, maybe I can ride up and down the street a few times every day."

That made him remember how nice her rounded bottom had looked in the saddle. "You'll be ready for the mountains in no time."

Too bad she would never be ready for him.

Not that his attraction was limited to the physical. As they walked toward the back door of the Blue Sky, he thought her heart and her spirit were as beautiful as her face. If he told her the complete truth, the way he was feeling about her, she would probably be outraged. He'd never had his guts tied up over a woman before, not like this. On one hand, he wanted to kiss her, to bed her, to shelter her from danger. On the other, he wanted to back away.

The last was sounding better and better.

What a mistake he'd made cozying up to her. His connection with his boss was quickly turning into something serious. For him. Obviously not for her.

Frances meant to leave Santa Fe eventually. Chaco wondered if he couldn't help her along a bit. The sooner she was out of his life the better. Then he wouldn't go around mooning like some love-struck pup, wouldn't make a fool of himself any more than he had.

Wondering exactly how to go about it, he followed Frances inside, but soon forgot about everything except the scene in the hallway. Belle had Sophie and Avandera cornered, the Creole sheltering the frightened young woman.

"Stupid fool!" Belle raged as Avandera wept. "How the hell are we gonna make any money if you give your wares away free?"

"Stop shouting at her," Sophie said. "Can't you see you're scaring her?"

"Get away from her, Sophie, this ain't none of your business!"

Frances flinched, obviously upset by the argument. But when she opened her mouth to interfere, Chaco put a hand on her arm and gave her a warning look. With the mood Belle was in, they'd be better off staying quiet. The madam was seeing-red furious.

"Please, Señora Janks," moaned Avandera. "I am sorry. I will sell whatever I have and repay you."

"You ain't got nothing worth more'n two dollars!"

With a screech of fury, Belle grabbed a spittoon off the floor and flung it at the women. It crashed into the wall, putting a crack in the plaster and splattering them with streams of discolored juice and wads of tobacco.

"Are you crazy?" Sophie yelled, wiping some of the stuff from her cheek. "What is wrong with you, Belle? Avandera is young! She thought she was in love. This is no crime."

Belle was clutching her shoulder. "Damn it! Damn you! Now I sprained my arm! No excuses. I'm running a business, not a matchmaking society!"

Avandera sobbed. "I was so lonely. I only wanted someone of my own."

"So you sleep with a shepherd on my time, a man who don't have a cent?" Rubbing her shoulder, Belle shook her head. "Stupid fool!"

"Poor girl," breathed Frances, her expression sympathetic.

Although she barely whispered, she caught Belle's attention. Her expression horrified, the madam gazed from her to Chaco before she turned back to Avandera and Sophie.

"Don't ever make such a mistake again, I'm warning you." With that she strode away, her skirts swishing as she disappeared around a corner.

Her arm around Avandera's shoulders, Sophie led the sobbing young woman away toward the stairs.

Frances sighed. "Why can't Avandera get married if she wants to?"

"Maybe she can," said Chaco. "I don't think that's the real problem. Avandera doesn't know what she wants. She's unhappy." And probably lonely, something he could understand.

They headed for the front desk where Belle was waiting, looking like she was forcing herself to swallow her anger.

Her voice low, the redhead addressed Frances. "Sorry you had to see that, Frankie, honey. I don't usually haul off and lose my temper, but I been having a hell of a time lately."

"Not making enough money?" Frances asked.

"The Gentlemen's Club is doing fine. It's Louisa who's got me on edge." She tapped her fingers on the desk. "I shouldn't take it out on somebody else, I know."

Frances seemed concerned. "Is Louisa all right?"

"Ain't sure." Belle gave Chaco a sharp look. "I need to talk to someone about her."

Frances immediately offered, "I'm available. I told you I would be."

Seeing the two women would rather be alone, Chaco ambled away in the direction of his room. "I'll be going."

Even so, Belle gave him another narrow-eyed look, as if she didn't like him.

Which got him to thinking. The madam had lived with a Comanche and could know something about Indian magic, as well as *brujeria*. She also had a ferocious temper. He'd once heard a rumor about her carving up a man in Texas and now he wondered if it was true. But surely Belle wasn't angry or vengeful enough to take up skin-walking, even if she held Nathan Gannon's death against him. She'd never said one word about the shooting.

Still, Chaco had good reason to be suspicious about any woman who might mean him harm. Rather than mooning over Frances, he should be watching his back.

Her shoulder hurt long after she had extracted the bullet. Every day, she cursed her enemy the first moment she woke up and the last moment before she closed her eyes to sleep. How dare he cause her pain?

Yet to her deep and abiding horror, he seemed to be gaining in strength. She had not been able to obtain any advantage over him. Even the love spell she had created had failed. How had this happened? What was his secret?

She was beside herself with fury.

She would find comfort in appropriate prey. She settled for a Jicarilla youth half-drunk on corn beer. Seducing him with her eyes, with her words, promising to lie with him, she took him to some open land outside of town.

"Come!" she ordered, dragging him by the hair toward the blanket she had thrown on the ground.

No doubt used to the man having the upper hand, he grunted and cursed her in Apache. But when he pushed at her roughly, she slapped him hard across the face.

"Barbarian!" she hissed in his own language, pleased that a sharp nail had left a trail of blood down his cheek.

He looked surprised, then angry. Good!

"Come, attack me!" she taunted.

She ripped off her clothing. The sun was sinking but enough light remained to display herself. His anger faded into lust. He staggered toward her and launched himself, knocking her to the ground. Falling hard, she quickly regained her breath and slapped him again. But before he could retaliate, she slid her hand beneath his loincloth and grasped his engorged penis.

"So strong, so young!" she purred.

He made an animalistic sound, spread her legs and thrust into her so hard, she felt she was being pounded into the earth. She gloried in it, arching her back, writhing in ecstasy as he rocked her back and forth. Holding his scrotum with one hand, she used the other to shred the back of his shirt. She sank her nails into his flesh in both places. When he cried out, it was with intense pain, as well as pleasure.

As he sank down in exhaustion, she continued to writhe, the heat rising in her body. A growl began deep in her throat and her limbs thrashed with renewed energy.

"Whore!" he muttered. "I am a married man."

Her lips curled into a feral grin. "Married? Then I must mark you."

Just as stern Apaches marked their adulterous women. Before he could move an inch, she jerked forward and sank her teeth into his nose, her sharp teeth biting off the fleshy tip.

He yelped in pain as his blood spurted over her face. Liking the salty, coppery taste, she sucked on the piece of flesh before spitting it back at him. Then she used her increasing strength to throw him off her.

He lay on the ground, screaming. "Witch!"

"Ah, so you know who I am."

She murmured her secret words and rolled to her knees. Her head lolled and she pricked her ears. Her hearing amplified, she was aware of the catch in his breath, the sound of his terrified heart, the hush of twilight's birds and insects as they sensed the predator in their midst.

Eyes wide with terror, the Jicarilla scrambled to his feet and started to run, his very hysteria thrilling her. She loved the chase! Flexing her muscles, she pursued him as he tore back toward the town. Not that he had any chance of escaping her. She played with him for a while, then sped up, weaving from one side to the other, relishing the acrid smell of fear as she felled him.

"Yah—h!"

He rolled over, hands thrashing at her ineffectually, his face a mask of horror as she went for his throat.

* * *

Frances went to see Louisa without bothering to change out of her dusty riding clothes. When Belle had admitted that she didn't know whether her daughter would even be there, not after the terrible argument they'd had earlier in the day, Frances had been worried.

But the girl was moping about the house, thank goodness, not riding for the mountains with all her belongings loaded on a pack animal.

Louisa lay on her bed in a messy attic room strewn with clothing, books, blankets, saddles and bridles.

"Frances!" As soon as she caught sight of her visitor, Louisa jumped up and smiled. "What are you doing here? It's been so long! I've missed you."

"I've missed you, too." She hugged the girl, thinking she looked as pretty and lively as ever. It was hard to believe her mother thought Louisa surly and troubled.

Then the sixteen-year-old drew back to gaze at the split skirt. "Have you been riding?" When Frances nodded, she pulled a face. "Drat, I wanted to teach you!"

"I know. I'm sorry. I had to make a bargain with someone, trade riding lessons for something else." Not wanting to mention Chaco, however, or the fact that he was illiterate, she didn't go into it. "Your mother told me the two of you haven't been getting along."

"Did she send you here?" Louisa's mood swiftly changed to hostile.

"I came of my own accord. I'm concerned about you."

"I haven't done anything wrong."

"I didn't think you had." And she meant that sincerely. "You've never been the sort of girl who seemed man-crazy." Like some of the students at Miss Llewellyn's, the kind who'd rather giggle about boys than study.

"Ma mentioned Eusebio Velarde?"

"That you were entertaining him in the barn."

Louisa's dark eyes flashed. "We were only talking. She doesn't have to worry. I'd break a post over his head if he tried to touch me!"

"Then why were you out in the barn?" Belle hadn't gone into details, only that she was very upset over the incident. "Sounds like you were trying to hide something."

"Of course, I was trying to hide." Louisa raised her brows. "Ma wouldn't want me talking to a strange man. She's so afraid I'll run off with somebody—like she did when she was thirteen."

"Belle ran off with your father when she was younger than you?"

Louisa shook her head. "My father was her second husband." She sighed and threw some clothing off a chair. "You might as well sit down, make yourself comfortable." The girl plopped back down on the bed. "Ma's first husband was a horrible man who beat her up all the time. She tried to run away but he kept catching her. Finally, she went crazy."

Frances was startled. "Belle? Insane?"

"Whenever she thinks about it now, she gets a little crazy all over again."

She couldn't help but envision the scene at the brothel and remembered Sophie asking Belle if she was crazy. Uneasily, she asked, "What happened to your mother's first husband?"

"He was murdered. Ma doesn't know who did it. She just woke up after a year or so and she wasn't in Texas anymore and he was dead."

"How strange. Where did she wake up?"

"Louisiana. But she went back to Texas again. She lived there for a few years before the Comanches captured her. My father, Red Knife, offered to marry her, though. She said he was a much better husband."

What an unusual life Belle had led, Frances mused, watching Louisa toy with the necklace she wore, a large claw on a leather thong, decorated with bits of natural stone and tiny feathers.

"I wish I'd been able to see what living in an Indian camp was like," Louisa said. "Ma had to leave after Red Knife was killed—some posse was looking for Comanche horse thieves."

"An Indian camp could have been a sad existence," Frances pointed out.

"I'm probably better off the way I am," Louisa agreed. "I don't intend to have a sad life in the future either, not if I can help it. Ma's always worrying about that but she doesn't have to."

"Well, you can see why she would worry, after all she's been through. She wants you to have better opportunities."

Louisa tightened her mouth. "I'm never going to work in her profession . . . or let some man beat me. I'd rather dress in trousers and carry a gun like Calamity Jane."

Frances had heard of the notorious woman, having read articles about her in Boston newspapers some years before. "I don't think you have to go that far." Being notorious wouldn't make Louisa happy. "And I hope you won't let your mother's life turn you against men. Not all are brutes. I believe you can find someone to marry, a man who really loves you—"

"I know," Louisa cut her off. "I wasn't saying I didn't like men. But I don't want to get married until

I'm much, much older. And I'm not going to sleep with anybody and get pregnant, so that I have to get married, either."

Frances was surprised to hear such words coming from a sixteen-year-old's mouth. She hadn't been so wise herself at twenty-one. "At least you seem to be very . . . knowledgeable."

"I know all about how babies get started. And I'm also aware of the difference between flirting and sleeping with a man." She gazed at Frances. "I was only flirting with Eusebio, you know. Why not? It's so boring around here. I had this friend who lived down the street but she got married. At fifteen!" She looked disgusted. "What am I supposed to do with myself? Everyone's gone."

Including Nate, whom Louisa used to confide in. Frances felt both sad about that and guilty that she hadn't been thinking about the girl. "I could come see you more often."

"That would be nice."

"And you said you wanted to ride your horses."

"I have been riding them, every day. But I'd also like someone to talk to." Louisa played with the unusual necklace again.

"What is that? A claw?"

"Uh, huh, a bear claw." The girl leaned forward and held the necklace out for Frances to see more closely. "It's supposed to be an Indian charm against evil. It belonged to my Pa."

"How interesting." Frances examined it, wondering how to bring up the topic of education, something she'd promised Belle. She already thought she could reassure the woman about Louisa and men. Perhaps Belle might relax her attitude a little and her daughter wouldn't have to hide her friendships. "If you're so bored, you might try some reading."

"I've read all the books that I own."

"Then you could borrow some of mine."

"I'd rather be outside. I want to raise horses someday, not be a teacher like you. Not that there's anything wrong with teaching."

"You will always have more opportunities if you have an education."

"I'm not leaving New Mexico Territory again." Expression stubborn, Louisa rose to look out the window. "I love it here."

"But you're bored. What if you could go to school right here in Santa Fe?"

Louisa turned, her expression horrified. "With the Sisters of Loretto? Nuns?"

"They might not be so terrible. And their lives aren't that different from the teachers at Miss Llewellyn's." She herself had led a nunlike existence.

"Is this your idea or Ma's?"

Belle had brought up the subject, but Frances thought Louisa would be more receptive if she didn't admit that. "We both talked about it." She urged, "Won't you at least consider the possibility? You don't have to make a decision right now."

"I can't go to school for awhile anyway, not until I replaster the walls and paint them. I owe Ma some money."

At least Louisa wasn't saying no. And she was trying to be responsible about the money she'd taken. Belle ought to be happy that she'd made some progress, Frances thought, smiling.

"I heard that you bought a horse."

Louisa's face lit up. "A real beauty. Want to see him before it gets too dark?"

"Of course."

The girl led her out the back way, past a big cottonwood tree and into the fenced pasture. Frances's gaze was immediately drawn to the long-legged bay who was prancing and snorting. The smaller horses in the enclosure, the paint and the dark-colored one, also seemed nervous. They rolled their eyes, showing the whites.

"Defiant!" called Louisa. "Come here, you big baby!" When he didn't respond, she glanced about. "I bet there's some coyotes around here. They can smell them."

"Will they attack the horses?" Frances also felt nervous, though she wasn't sure why. Maybe all that talk of premonitions earlier . . .

"A full-grown horse can stomp a coyote. But I'd better warn Señora Rodriquez, tell her to make sure she's cooped up all her chickens."

Before the girl did so, she accompanied Frances out to Belle's borrowed carriage parked in front of the house. Frances hugged Louisa a second time.

"Defiant is beautiful, truly elegant."

"Isn't he? You can ride him the next time you visit."

Frances laughed. "I only hope I'll be ready for that." The horse was so tall.

"You *are* visiting me again soon, aren't you?"

"I promise—next week."

Frances vowed she would make the time to do so, wanting another chance to work on Louisa. Not that she didn't also enjoy the girl's company. Louisa waved as the carriage drove away, the driver cursing as one of the matched set of grays reared and snorted. He snapped the reins and pulled until the horses settled down.

"Coyotes?" asked Frances.

The driver turned. "*Que,* Señora?"

"Never mind."

The carriage lurched over some ruts, then rolled on more smoothly. Frances gazed out at the wild land beyond the town's edge, desert gray with dusk and sprinkled with black, shadowy junipers. A few stars pricked the darkening sky overhead. Two tiny lights also flickered in a ragged copse of chamisa. Curiosity aroused, Frances stared, then caught her breath sharply as the flickering lights suddenly became glittering eyes. A large animal with matted fur and huge jaws emerged from the chamisa and stared directly back at her.

A coyote? A wolf?

Frances shivered, afraid. "Driver? Señor?"

By the time she was able to get the man's attention, the creature had disappeared.

Safely inside the lobby of the Blue Sky, Frances wondered if the wolf had been a figment of her imagination. The driver had certainly acted like she was hysterical when she'd gotten wild-eyed and insisted he stop the carriage to look out into the desert.

He must have also thought it odd when she needed so much help getting out of the conveyance a few minutes ago.

Heightened emotion and physical exertion had caught up with her. Tired and sore, Frances wanted nothing more than to go upstairs and collapse. But first she had to find Belle. When the clerk on duty said the madam was busy, she felt relieved.

"Can you give her a message for me? Tell her that her daughter is safe at home and in good spirits."

"Sure, I'll tell her, Mrs. Gannon."

"And could you get someone to heat water for my bathtub? Right away?"

Frances then headed upstairs. Soon, she'd be able to soak and relax in a warm tub, then snuggle into her feather bed. Maybe she wouldn't even talk to Belle until the next day. Unlocking the door of her bedroom, she took off her jacket and sank onto a chair, not knowing if she had enough energy to pull her boots off, even using a bootjack.

That's when she heard the splashing sounds coming from the adjoining room, whose connecting door stood ajar.

"Juanita? Rosa?" Were they already filling the tub? Frances struggled to her feet and went to investigate, freezing at the sight before her. "Chaco!"

Immersed in soapy water, his hair wet and slicked back, he didn't even have the decency to look embarrassed.

"This is my bathtub!"

His eyebrows shot up. "It has a door to the hall."

"Which should have been locked. The other door opens into my bedroom." Which he certainly knew, after carrying her there the night she'd been smacked in the jaw. She felt particularly uncomfortable after what had happened between them today. "Who said you could come in here?"

"No one. I asked to have the tub filled."

"Well, you'll have to get out."

A strange glint lit his eyes as he asked, "Right now?"

Before she could answer, he stood up, rivulets of water running down his torso. Stunned, she let her eyes drift over the muscular chest, the line of dark hair that swirled across it and inexorably downward...

She swallowed, and her face grew hot.

"I—I didn't mean get out this very moment! You're naked!"

"That's the way I always take a bath."

She turned away, desperately grabbing for a towel in the cabinet and throwing it at him. "Here!"

Still standing in the middle of the tub, he began drying his face and hair, leaving the rest of him fully exposed. What in the world was wrong with him?

"Oh!" Seeing no other course, she retreated into the bedroom. But she continued talking. "You knew I was going to take a bath tonight! I said so."

"I thought you would do it later." His voice came from the other room, along with louder splashing that meant he was finally getting out of the tub. "Adolfo told me you went to Belle's house."

"Still, the bathtub isn't public property."

He came to the connecting door with the towel draped about his middle. "You don't share it, huh?"

"Share it?"

He was suggesting they bathe together? She imagined her wet skin sliding over his, their limbs intertwining, and was appalled. No doubt he thought she was easy because of the wanton way she'd responded to his kiss. She'd thought she'd set him straight, but it seemed he didn't have the decency to take no for an answer.

Furious, she locked gazes with him. "I may have kissed you, but I didn't promise you any liberties. Quite the contrary. You can't traipse into my rooms, flaunt yourself naked and say whatever you want to me!" She glanced at the bed. "Next thing, you'll be—"

He raised his brows, obviously catching her drift. But he asked, "I'll be what?"

"Never mind! Good night!" Stepping forward, she slammed the door in his face and locked it.

Then she threw herself on the bed, clothes, boots

and all. As happened far too frequently, Chaco had managed to get to her. She had to remind herself that she didn't want to get involved with him, had to remind herself that, if it weren't for Chaco, Nate would be sharing her bed.

Only thing was, she could hardly conjure up Nate's image in her mind anymore. She kept seeing Chaco instead.

A shiver ran through her. And an unbidden thought, one that Frances recognized as a premonition of sorts. She was properly spooked.

Getting any closer to Chaco Jones would be dangerous not only to her emotions but to her physical well-being.

10

There were witches everywhere—she was certain of it.

Minna Tucker huddled in the darkened church, praying she wouldn't run into any. She'd begun making daily visits to the plain, almost forbidding sanctuary since finding the Navajo who'd gone and gotten himself killed on her property. Not that she cared about there being one less Indian around. Rather two, she reminded herself. His throat ripped out in addition to having other—some unspeakable—injuries, an Apache had been found lifeless and bucknaked near that harlot Belle Janks' house the day before.

Or had it been two days now?

Minna tried concentrating but couldn't remember. That made her nervous. Too many faces and voices had been crowding her mind lately, and she was having trouble separating dream from reality.

Renewed nerves started up the cursed cough, the jarring motion making her already muddled head feel like it was ready to explode, shooting a hot pain through her already aching shoulder. Gasping for air, she sneaked a look around. Certain she was alone, she slipped a small vial from the pocket of her voluminous skirts, uncorked it and took a swig. The tickle settled and the ache receded—praise the Lord for her patent medicine. She didn't know what she would do without it. Her coughing spells had gotten worse since she'd started worrying over Billie's immortal soul.

He'd finally come home the day after she'd followed him to the Blue Sky, properly penitent that he'd allowed the fallen women there to bewitch him into having sex with them.

She took another swig. Some of those whores were at least part Indian as was that Satan, Chaco Jones, who'd kept her from saving her only son. No doubt one of those Indian witches had cursed her boy with the dreaded appetite. Shamefaced after she'd made him kneel and pray for the Lord's forgiveness, Billie had said he hoped he wouldn't fall from grace again . . . but admitted he had no control over his urges. How disgusting.

What was a mother to do?

Minna was feeling more and more out of control these days. Unable to control her boy. Unable to control her memory. Unable to say exactly why or when she'd taken to leaving her bed at night and wandering who knew where. One morning, she'd come to her senses in her front yard at dawn. Her nightgown had been soaked with blood and it wasn't even her time. She'd burned the thing in the fire before making breakfast.

Certain that her blowsy neighbor, as well as Belle Janks, had been gossiping about her, saying she was crazy, Minna was worried that someone might believe painted harlots, might think that *she,* a good Christian woman, was capable of killing those savages just because they had no souls.

She raised the vial to her lips and let the soothing liquid splash back against her throat before corking and secreting the medicine. Her supply was running low. She'd have to send Billie for more before she ran out.

Tottering to the door, Minna squinted against the brilliant afternoon sun and left the church. As she navigated the crude dirt street, her legs were wobbly and her head felt like it was plumb stuffed with cotton. But her eyes were still sharp. They didn't miss the carriage careening around a narrow corner just as she reached the crossing. She jumped out of the way and was outraged at seeing who sat behind the team. Belle's little half-breed was laughing with a young Spaniard.

Minna screeched, "How dare you try to run down a God-fearing woman!" She clutched the cross dangling from a chain about her neck and held it out to protect herself against evil. "Children of Satan!"

"Old biddy!" Louisa Janks yelled in return.

Scowling, the half-breed grabbed at the heathen necklace she wore—an animal claw of some sort—and dared to hold it out in the same fashion as Minna did her cross.

The carriage sped down the street.

Minna nearly fainted of fright.

A strong hand under her arm steadied her. "Ma'am, you all right?" asked a mustached, middle-aged man.

"Yes, thank you," she said breathlessly. She couldn't

tell him the girl had given her the evil eye, perhaps cursed her. "I merely twisted my ankle on the street."

"Do you need help getting home?"

He was a fine-looking Christian man. Minna hadn't had much male company other than her boy since her husband had been shot down by a cold-blooded gunman while doing his job for the railroad, leaving her and Billie to fend for themselves. Ezekiel had often been cantankerous, but she'd felt safer with him around. "If you would be so kind," she said, offering the stranger a tentative smile. "And I hope you'll let me show you my appreciation . . . with some coffee and homemade pie." Billie was working at the general store this afternoon and wouldn't be home till supper time.

The man's mustache curled and a gleam entered his eyes. "Don't mind if I do."

Still clutching her cross with one hand, his arm with the other, Minna set off, relieved that she wouldn't be going home alone, for it was all coming clear to her now. She wasn't safe in her neighborhood, maybe not in her own house.

Two bodies, both found nearby, both since the half-breed came home, tail between her legs, from that fancy school back East.

Louisa Janks was a witch—maybe the one who'd killed those savages—and now she knew that Minna recognized her for what she was.

Knowing she wouldn't feel safe until something was done about the little heathen, she asked her companion, "Have you heard about the recent terrible murders?" and was gratified when he appeared to be eager to hear what she had to say.

* * *

"You'll have to move faster if you don't want me to lose you," Chaco called back to Frances as his own mount swept him up the craggy hillside and dodged a patch of tall cholla.

"Maybe that's your intention," Frances groused, barely avoiding the nasty-looking cactus.

What in the world was wrong with him? He wasn't at all the considerate companion he'd been last time. He was pushing her as hard as any experienced rider.

"We could go back. Just say the word."

"No!"

Frances dug her heels into her mount's sides, then was startled when the mare shot forward with more speed than she'd counted on. Swaying in the saddle, she clung to the horn for dear life. More cholla below! Catching up to Chaco, her heart sank as she realized that her bottom was bouncing emphatically against the leather. An hour's ride out of Santa Fe and she was only marginally sore. So much for the hope that she'd stay that way.

Chaco glanced over his shoulder. "That's better."

She swore his fleeting grin was due to her obvious discomfort, but he quickly turned his attention forward and lapsed back into silence. He seemed as intent on continuing without stopping as he was with not talking to her unless he absolutely had to. Frances suspected he was trying to make her complain. Maybe even to give up and demand he take her back. But why?

The answer was obvious, of course. He'd been acting oddly with her since the kiss, by turns deeply troubled . . . overly charming . . . and downright antagonistic. Not wanting to dwell on the incident that still kept her tossing and turning nights, Frances put her mind to her surroundings.

They'd ridden northwest from Santa Fe through rolling hills, the highest of which were graced with stands of ponderosa pine and Gambel oak. The dirt roads had grown redder with the miles, the color a brilliant contrast with the greens of juniper and sagebrush and pinon. For a while, they'd followed a stream lined with cottonwoods, box elder and buckthorn, but now they were back in drier country. Ahead, the land changed dramatically, pale mesas looming so close she felt she could touch them. Of course, that was a mere illusion, for the flat-topped cliffs were still quite a long distance away.

She had to admit the land was rugged, hard and yet stunning. Such vistas nearly took her breath away.

As did Chaco. He was dressed as she'd first seen him—his clothes black, his long hair loose, his face stubbled with beard, his gun belt slung low over his hips—almost as if he'd wanted to remind her of that fateful day.

Urging her mare faster yet, she came alongside Chaco while doing her best to keep her seat. He raised his eyebrows, but said nothing.

Flustered, wondering why she felt this need to confront him, she stiffly said, "I've been practicing, you know."

His glance swiped her rear, which was still bouncing in the saddle. "Really?"

Irritated that he didn't seem as if he wanted to believe her, she said, "Several times. I rode around town. Not at a *gallop*, of course."

"We're not galloping. Yet."

Maybe she should have kept her mouth shut. Now he'd be sure to push her faster, just to make her miserable, no doubt. He was punishing her, that's what he was doing. And all because *he'd* made inappropriate advances that *she'd* been weak enough to indulge in for a moment before coming to her senses. About to light into him, she was stopped by a piercing whistle and the sound of hoof beats from behind.

Frances whipped around in the saddle, then gasped, "Oh, no!" when she felt herself falling.

Chaco swooped down on her and slid an arm around her waist. Agitated by his touch, she tried fighting him. She might as well have saved her energy. Her heart bumped against her ribs as he pulled her upright and steadied her, not letting go until she regained both her humor and her sense of balance. She tried not to take the contact personally . . . but her body's reaction to him certainly was. He slowed both horses and turned them to face their pursuers. Staring at a moving cloud of dust some distance behind, he narrowed his gaze speculatively.

Several riders were on their trail.

"I don't like this," Chaco muttered, removing his hat and waving it at them.

Neither did she. A fluttering feeling attacked her insides. "My premonition." When he gave her a puzzled look, she explained, "The other day, I had this odd sense that something was not right . . . dangerous." But omitted the portent that he was the instigator who involved her, too.

The riders were nearly upon them. Frances recognized a couple of the men, starting with Adolfo at the head of the pack. One of the riders was significantly slighter than the others, had definitely unmanly curves and bared brown legs. When they drew closer, Frances recognized the other woman. Luz. She was riding with her skirts hitched up.

"What the hell's going on?" Chaco shouted against

the neighing and snorting of protesting horses that were now swarming around them.

"Problems, *compadre*," Adolfo said. "Apache raids!"

"Indians on the warpath?" Heart in her throat, Frances took a deep breath. "Are you certain?"

"Magdalena heard about it from her cousin, who came into town this morning for supplies," Luz said.

Adolfo added, "The Jicarillas want to avenge the death of their clansman. They're after the *diablera* responsible . . . and God help anyone in their way."

A chill shot through Frances as the premonition of danger returned, stronger than the first time. "How would they know where to look for this supposed witch?"

"A shaman has told them where to go," Adolfo said.

Though she knew she shouldn't be shocked after the things she'd seen as a child, Frances shook her head. "A holy man agreeing to murder."

"Not murder," Luz protested. "Justice."

"As long as they only get the witch," Chaco said, sounding worried himself.

"Exactly," Adolfo agreed. "The Apache believe the *diablera* is hiding nearby somewhere in this area. Nothing and no one will stop them from finding her if they have to sweep through all the way to Santa Fe. We're riding to warn our people. My family is in Niza, a small mountain town a few miles north of here. Javier and Tobias have people in the next village west."

"Both close to the de Arguello spread," Chaco muttered, following the statement with a low curse.

Startled, Frances noted a curious if fleeting expression cross his features before a hard mask slipped in place. Did he have friends on this ranch? He'd worked on a place south of Santa Fe, but she supposed that didn't mean he couldn't know people in other parts of the Territory.

"The Apache are the army's sore spot, especially the Chiricahua." Chaco seemed to be talking to himself as well as the rest of them. "If anything happens to the villages or ranches, the government will dispatch entire regiments . . . and they won't distinguish between bands. We'll be looking at a massacre across the Territory." He shook his head. "We have to stop this from starting. I'm going with you." He looked to Adolfo's three male companions. "Can one of you escort Mrs. Gannon back to Santa Fe?"

"Sure—" the Anglo named Lauter began, only to be cut off by Frances.

"I'm not going back to Santa Fe." The words were out of her mouth before she had time to think about them.

Chaco looked grim. "You can't wait around here alone. I don't know when I'll be back."

"I'm not staying here, either." For a moment, the world narrowed to the two of them. Her heart was pumping. Hard. She fought the fear that tried to claim her. If danger lay ahead, then it was for all, and she would not be so poor spirited as to let the rest of them venture forth alone. "I'm going with you."

"Don't be ridiculous. A woman—"

"Luz is a woman."

"Luz can handle herself."

Frances glanced at the wild-looking Mexican woman, who had a rifle strapped to her saddle, a knife to her exposed thigh. Indeed, Luz looked as if she were part of this rugged country. As Frances wanted to be, if in a more genteel way.

"We all have our different strengths," she said. "I

may not know how to use a weapon, but maybe I can combat fear with words." She noted Luz appeared surprised. And approving. Frances locked gazes with Chaco, who once again seemed as hard a man as any she'd ever encountered. "The idea is to prevent bloodshed, isn't it?"

"Yes, but—"

"Then I'm going."

She hadn't been able to stop the atrocities she'd seen as a child, but now she was an adult. Surely her intelligence counted for something.

"No one's going to mollycoddle you," Chaco growled. "We'll have to ride hard."

"Baptism by fire. I've had some experience." Having been thrown out into the street by her own father for challenging him. "What are we waiting for?"

Brave words—Frances wouldn't let Chaco see her fear.

Scowling at her, he quickly took the lead from Adolfo and set a far faster pace than she was used to, though the ride seemed a bit smoother. Even so, she fell behind, and if he noticed, he didn't show any mercy. Luz, however, was another story. She dropped back until she rode side by side with Frances.

"Why are you doing this?" the woman asked. "You could be safe back in Santa Fe. You're not one of us. You have nothing at stake."

"You're wrong, Luz. The rest of my life is at stake. I don't want to be outside looking in."

For that's how she'd felt most of her life. As if she didn't belong. That seemed to satisfy Luz, who nodded and concentrated on what lay ahead.

But Frances was curious, too. "What about you, Luz? You have family in Niza?"

Luz shook her head. "Adolfo might get himself

killed without someone like me to watch his back."

Frances gave the other woman a swift look of surprise. If she expected to see some softening, she was disappointed. Luz was tough and didn't let down her guard. Yet her simple response had revealed a lot. Though she did everything in her power to appear unaffected, Luz obviously returned Adolfo's feelings for her.

As they came within sight of a bunch of ratty little buildings that she guessed passed for a village, Chaco raised a hand and slowed his mount, then waited for everyone to catch up. Thinking how readily the others had accepted him as their leader, Frances took a good, long look at him. Tall and straight in the saddle, he appeared confident, fierce and even dangerous, and yet she neither held him in awe nor feared him. She wondered if—like Luz did for Adolfo—she had feelings for Chaco Jones that she didn't want to face.

The thought unsettled her.

And made her wonder if her premonition didn't have more to do with her getting personally involved with the man than any danger he could lead her into.

With the villagers prepared to defend themselves if necessary, Chaco led the small band onto de Arguello property, telling himself he was merely acting like a human being rather than a worried son. The spread stood between the Apache and the villages they'd just left.

They moved as one, their tiring mounts fast eating the distance to the *estancia.* Red dust swirled around them, alerting a guard who fired a warning shot over their heads from a nest of rocks barely within sight of the house. Realizing the man meant business—and that no guard had been stationed there last time—Chaco brought the riders to a swift halt.

"I'm here to see Don Armando de Arguello!" he shouted in Spanish. "Chaco Jones—I was here a coupla weeks ago!"

"I remember!" the guard yelled. "Go on through!"

Checking back on the others, making certain Frances was still in the saddle, hardening himself to the exhaustion he saw etched on her face, the discomfort in her body, Chaco started off at a less frantic pace, his instincts on the alert. The guard wasn't alone and there were others stationed in various strategic places around the walled house, which today reminded him of a garrison. Other men, Mexican peasant and mestizo workers, were lined up around the stable area, some of them armed, all of them agitated and talking low among themselves.

As they drew closer, an uncomfortable feeling made Chaco's neck hair bristle.

The distasteful sensation was stronger this time than last.

Adolfo pulled his horse alongside him. "What do you think, *compadre?*"

"I'm thinking there'll be trouble here today."

Surely the reason his senses sharpened. He could smell danger, and he swore the place reeked of it.

"Then maybe we'd better hurry," Adolfo said.

Chaco dismounted near the stables and asked Tobias to take care of the horses. He didn't pause to see who else would stay behind, who would follow as he entered the *placita*.

The open area was empty. Silent. The very air was still. The flesh of his back rose. This time he wouldn't wait for a maid to answer the door or for Ynez to find the old man. He threw open the door and swept into the house without warning—aware of Adolfo and Luz and Frances following more tentatively—and made his way blindly along the maze of corridors until he heard raised male voices.

A familiar one was barking orders.

Chaco burst in on de Arguello, who was delivering strategy to his men. The inner, windowless room was filled with racks of weapons and cases of ammunition. Enough, he thought, to stock a garrison. One of the men was muscling a Gatling gun from a crate in the corner. Hell, they could wipe out a whole tribe in minutes with one of those.

Seeing Chaco gave the old man pause. His eyes widened for a moment. Then he sharply demanded, "What is this intrusion?" in Spanish.

Purposely answering in English, Chaco grit out, "I came to warn you about a possible Apache attack, but I see that my concern's not necessary." And obviously unwelcome.

He was intent on leaving, about to herd the others back into the corridor, when de Arguello said in English, "Chaco, stay and fight side by side with me as it should be."

As father and son? The plea infuriated Chaco. Heat flared through him as he whipped around and took a few steps toward the old man, vaguely aware of someone following close behind.

"I'm sick of fighting."

De Arguello's expression was that of a seasoned veteran when he said, "A man must protect what is his."

"I have no claim here."

"A man must go after the enemy before the enemy attacks first, vanquish him before he can retaliate."

Wondering if that was how his mother had become de Arguello's sex slave, Chaco seethed.

Frances suddenly stepped around him and faced down the old man who would be his father. "You plan to spill blood even if needless violence can be prevented?"

The Hidalgo pulled himself taller and locked gazes with his son. "Who is this insolent Anglo, who speaks so freely when her opinion is not asked?"

"A friend."

Refusing to acknowledge Frances—a mere woman, after all, Chaco thought—de Arguello said, "Then tell your friend the Apache are on a witch hunt. They will burn us out if we do not kill them first."

But Frances wasn't intimidated. "Have you ever tried talking before fighting?"

"Tell her—"

"If you have something to say, then say it to *me!*"

Amazed by her determination to be heard, Chaco stood silent and waited for the confrontation to play out. De Arguello looked apoplectic. His face was flushed and his mouth worked silently. But stronger vibrations racked the room, making Chaco turn toward the door and look past Adolfo and Luz to where Ynez stood, her dark eyes fastened on him.

"War is for men," de Arguello was saying as his young wife silently drifted into the room. "Women have no place in—"

Frances cut him off. "If you think your spilling blood won't bring a worse revenge down on you, then you're an arrogant fool."

"You do not speak to my husband so!" Ynez hissed, grabbing Frances by the arm to whip her around, then jumping back when Frances scowled at her, as if she were afraid of the Anglo woman. "Don Armando is a good man, and we are the ones threatened." She hugged herself and nervously rubbed at her shoulder.

"If he wants to kill the savages before they can harm us, who are you to stop him?"

"The voice of reason, I hope." Dismissing Ynez, Frances turned back to de Arguello. "Please, think. Peace is so fragile. And who is to say who will live, who will die? Are *you* ready to go to your maker?"

The question startled Chaco—for hadn't Frances told him she'd lost her own faith?—and made the old man pause.

"If I do not act, then who will stop the witch hunt?" the Hidalgo finally asked her directly.

"If I spoke their language, I would try," Frances said fervently. "Is there no one among you who can do so?"

She gazed around the room, her stare touching every man. Most shook their heads or shrugged. A few looked away. Mestizos, maybe some part Apache themselves. Chaco figured they probably could parlay with the Jicarilla, but were afraid for their own scalps.

Then she caught him with those big, pleading eyes.

Hell and damnation, he wasn't any hero—far from it! And he wasn't much good with words.

About to tell her that, Chaco couldn't force the denial from his mouth. Not when she acted so brave herself. And not when she was looking at him like that, like he was the only man in the world she could count on.

He felt himself weaken.

Maybe he could find the band. He'd learned to track when his mother had taken him to the camps of her relatives. And though his ancestors were Chiricahua, he could speak several Apache dialects, including that of the Jicarilla. If he used his head, he might be able to reach the shaman, who could then influence the others to turn back and keep the fragile peace—he glanced around the room and took in the arsenal—and their lives.

"All right," he growled. "I'll do it." And pray he would live and not regret the decision. Frances's immediate smile cut through him and Chaco shifted his gaze to de Arguello. "If you'll call off your men."

The Hidalgo didn't answer immediately. He studied Chaco as if estimating his worth. Chaco's gaze didn't waver, and he was almost surprised when the white head dipped in agreement.

"I shall not send my men out. But we will prepare for trouble should it seek us."

He signaled his men who picked up guns and ammunition and carried them out of the room. Even Ynez seemed intent on showing her support for her husband. Giving Chaco a cold stare, she moved to a gun rack where she awkwardly lifted down a rifle one-handed and then almost dropped it, catching the weapon before it hit the floor. She winced, as if she'd hurt herself, but quickly masked her discomfort.

"God go with you, my son," de Arguello said, guiding his wife out of the room.

Chaco had to clench his jaw so he wouldn't utter a curse in return. He only hoped the old man didn't think he was acting like some heroic fool for him.

As if she sensed his inner turmoil, Frances touched Chaco's arm. "You can do this."

Gazing at her, reading the faith in him in her eyes, he nearly believed it. "You're the one good with words."

"Then I'll come and—"

"No! No telling what might go on out there. You'll be safer here." And if something happened to her, he would never forgive himself.

On returning to the horses, Adolfo also volunteered

to ride out with him, but Chaco refused this offer, as well, telling him to take care of the women. Luz gave him a filthy look . . . then removed a small leather pouch from around her neck and offered it to him.

"For protection."

Remembering the skin-walker was a woman, that she had already planted some of her witchery on him, Chaco hesitated. He looked deep into Luz's eyes and saw only concern and an edgy pride. She would be insulted—and hurt—if he refused her.

"Thanks," he said, taking the pouch and slipping it into a pocket. "I can use all the luck I can get."

A chalky-faced Frances watched him mount. "This will work," she said softly. "It must."

In her face, Chaco read something more than simple concern of one human being for another. She reached up and covered one of his hands with hers, shooting a rush of warmth up his arm and straight to his heart.

As he turned away, he swore he heard her echo de Arguello's words. "May God go with you."

Chaco might wish it, too, if only he knew whose God to pray to.

He set off at an easy lope, quickly putting distance between him and the others, passing the sentries with a wave. But he hadn't gotten far when a gut-level warning kicked in. Still within sight of the *estancia*, he knew his back wasn't the only part of him being watched.

The very hills had eyes.

Slowing his horse to a walk, he threw back his hat, letting loose the shoulder-length black hair that was his legacy from his Indian ancestors. He shouted a greeting in Apache. "I come in peace to share the wisdom of your leader."

Though he could see nothing but rocks and cactus,

sagebrush and a few cottonwood trees, he had no doubt Jicarilla warriors surrounded him. The question was how many. And how long before they attacked.

Chaco reined in his mount. Raising one hand, he slowly drew his rifle from its sheath with the other, careful to keep his actions slow and unthreatening. He hoisted the weapon above his head. Clasping the barrel with his free hand, he held the rifle high.

"I, too, seek the *diablera* who walks as a woman by day and on the legs of a wolf by night."

In answer, a *thwang* reverberated over his head and between his raised arms, almost making Chaco bolt for cover. An arrow, its tip undoubtedly treated with poison concocted from blood and venom aged in putrefying animal extracts, fell harmlessly behind him. But he'd felt the whisper of its power, too close for comfort.

Sweat rolled down his back.

Gritting his teeth, knowing they would have killed him if that had been their intent, Chaco waited, still and silent on his mount. Fine-tuned with his surroundings, he caught a soft snort and a brush of hoof against loose rock. A moment later, the high desert sprouted life: nearly a dozen braves surrounded him. All were armed, not only with traditional bows and arrows, war clubs and decorated buffalo-hide war shields, but with the white man's rifles, as well.

He and the others hadn't arrived on de Arguello land too soon, Chaco realized. Another hour and who knew what they might have found. And if he couldn't present a convincing argument against it, blood would run, starting with his own.

"Who are you that speaks our tongue?" one of them finally asked.

Chaco stared at the warrior, dressed in a combination

of white man's cloth pants and shirt and the traditional Apache buckskin breechcloth and knee-high moccasins. While many of the others were bareheaded but for a thick band circling their foreheads and holding back their long, loose hair, this one wore a buckskin headdress, beaded and decorated with antelope horns. Only seasoned warriors were allowed the highly individualized war caps, so Chaco addressed him directly.

"I am Apache."

"You are not one of us."

"My mother was Chiricahua," Chaco added, hoping that the particular band these men belonged to had no active feud with her people. Slowly, he lowered his arms but continued to hold the rifle before him balanced against the saddle horn in a nonthreatening manner. "And the *diablera* who is your enemy is my enemy." Knowing this was the man to convince, Chaco said, "Our minds are as one—"

"No! Your Apache blood runs thin. You live among the White Eyes. You seek to protect them."

"I do not want to see blood shed—this is true."

"If they give up the witch," the war leader said, "no blood will be spilled but hers."

"They do not know her." And even if they did, white men would not give over one of their own to men they considered to be savages.

"You know this evil woman?"

"Not in her human form," Chaco admitted. "Not yet. But I will." He shuddered even thinking about it—though he might not know the reason, he was certain she wasn't done with him yet. "She has sought me when she skin-walks."

"I am no fool!" the war leader thundered. "Your throat is still whole."

"Because I wounded her with a bullet."

To show his disbelief of and contempt for Chaco's claim, the other man spat on the ground.

Desperate to convince him that he was telling the truth—that he had the ability to sense and therefore protect himself against such evil—Chaco admitted, "Some say I am *di-yin*."

That got the man's attention. His eyes narrowed and his black gaze penetrated Chaco, who almost felt as if the warrior were inside his skin, peering around, gauging the purity of his heart.

Chaco went on. "Perhaps you have heard of Goyahkla . . . the white man calls him Geronimo. He and my mother shared the same father."

The admission set off a reaction around him, the braves talking among themselves. Chaco sat still and silent, his gaze flying over each and every one of them, calculating which were the fiercest warriors.

Just in case . . .

Then the war leader urged his mount forward and all speculation ceased. Chaco kept his eyes on the weathered face, watching for any betrayal of the man's thoughts. He could read nothing. Could only sense that the other man was fair. And smart. Still, by the time the Indian pony stopped a few feet away, Chaco was covered in a light sweat.

The warrior kept him in suspense for a moment longer. Still testing. Probing with impenetrable black eyes. Making up his mind. Finally, he nodded and backed the pony off just enough to give Chaco breathing room.

"What do you want from us?" he asked.

Though he felt like sagging in relief, Chaco knew he could not show a moment's weakness. "Keep the peace. That will be best for everyone, white and Apache."

"We must avenge our own."

"But only one person was responsible for the death."

"And she lives among the White Eyes. We must do what is necessary to destroy her."

Chaco thought quickly. "Maybe this is what she wants—your breaking the peace, being responsible for killing innocent people to get to her. Then the white man's government will send their soldiers for more revenge. Apache will be massacred. The bloodshed will go on and on, and all because of one evil woman who is not worth a single life."

Chaco could tell the warrior was considering his words seriously. For a man who mostly kept his thoughts to himself, he figured he'd done all right. Good enough to make Frances proud? he wondered.

"Your words are wise," the leader finally said. "But the witch cannot go unpunished."

"She won't," Chaco assured him too quickly, figuring someone was bound to be strong enough to fight her, perhaps even to kill her.

"*You* will see that she receives justice? That she doesn't seduce more Apache with her evil ways?"

The sweat started up again, slipping and sliding beneath his shirt. While Chaco knew the skin-walker hadn't finished with him, he hadn't thought in terms of being personally responsible for her. But that's exactly what the wily fox was suggesting.

"I can't promise anything . . ." Chaco let his denial trail off when he noted the hardening of the other man's expression. ". . . but that I will try."

The moment the words were out of his mouth, Chaco felt as if he had condemned himself to the white man's hell. The *diablera* would be a formidable enemy, one he was not trained to fight. He'd made a living with his gun, had killed more men over the years than he wanted to think about. His possible death to save other lives now . . . to keep Frances Gannon safe . . .

Honest with himself, Chaco figured maybe it wasn't such a bad trade.

11

It was all that Frances could do to restrain herself when Chaco rode up to the stable area looking as unscathed as he had when he'd left. Though he'd been gone less than an hour, she was fraught with tension; her nerves were ready to snap. Tempted to throw herself at him when he dismounted from the buckskin—and no doubt make a fool of herself—she stood back while the others gathered around him eagerly.

"Good to see you alive and still the owner of all that pretty hair, *compadre*," Adolfo said heartily.

One arm around Luz's waist, he gave her a big squeeze. She didn't object.

Obviously disliking the Mexican's jest, Don Armando scowled down at him. "What happened?"

His expression grimmer than Frances had ever seen it, Chaco said, "They agreed to wait."

"Wait for what?" the elderly man asked.

"For the witch to be brought to justice. Until the next new moon."

"Less than two weeks away," Luz said.

"As long as no other of their clan dies by her magic before then. Otherwise . . ."

He didn't have to finish. Frances shivered. She could imagine the horrors in store for innocent people, white and red alike. And now that she looked closer, there was something about Chaco that made her doubly uneasy. Certainly, he was troubled over the situation as they all were, but she sensed something far more personal tormented him.

Chaco met her gaze, his spooky gray eyes hollow. "We ought to get back to Santa Fe."

"Yes, that would be best," Frances agreed, though she wasn't exactly looking forward to getting on a horse again. She didn't want to think about how long she would be stuck in the saddle.

"First you must eat," Don Armando protested.

"Maybe something for the trail." Chaco again looked at Frances. "We can eat when we rest."

A surprising declaration since he hadn't seen fit to go easy on her earlier.

The ranch owner imperiously gestured to his young wife. "Doña Ynez, gather together food for our guests."

Frances noticed the woman was not made happy by the demand. But her resentful expression quickly faded to be replaced by the compliant smile of a good Spanish wife as she scurried to do her husband's bidding.

"Luz and I will eat with my family," Adolfo said. "We're going back to let them know what happened."

Luz disentangled herself from his possessive arm and moved closer to Frances. "Would you give Belle a message?" she asked in a low voice. "Tell her we'll be staying the night with Adolfo's people, and that we won't be back at the Blue Sky until sometime tomorrow."

A wide-eyed Frances agreed. In a few short days, Luz had gone from protesting Adolfo's attention to spending the night with him. Was love always so unpredictable? Remembering Belle's reaction to Avandera and the shepherd, Frances wasn't looking forward to passing on this news, but personally, she was happy for Luz. Maybe a life other than selling herself would be possible for at least one of Belle's girls, after all.

The couple left immediately, and the three other riders, anxious to get back to Santa Fe as soon as possible, headed out with them.

"Before you go," Don Armando said to Chaco, "I have something for you."

Frances was startled when Chaco vehemently said, "I told you before I don't want anything of yours!"

When they'd first arrived, she'd gotten the idea the two men were acquainted but disliked each other. Now it seemed the association wasn't that simple.

"Your mother made this." The elderly man's expression was sad as he pulled his hand from a pocket, withdrawing a strip of hide decorated with a beaded design. "I did love Oneida, but society's attitudes were such that we could not be man and wife. I am truly sorry about everything she suffered, Chaco. And you. She gave me this token before she left. It is all I have had to remember her by."

Don Armando held out the strip of beadwork. Chaco stared a moment, seemed reluctant to take it from him, then did so with a curt nod.

As she watched the two men, Frances got an

uncomfortable feeling that made her turn to find Ynez standing in the doorway, clutching a bulging leather pouch. Fixed on Chaco, her dark eyes were filled with complex emotions, one of which Frances recognized as pure hatred.

Because her husband had once loved Chaco's mother?

The two men were staring at each other, both appearing ill at ease. Clearing his throat, Don Armando was the first to look away, grumbling, "Where is that woman with the food?"

"I am here, Husband."

As she stepped forward with the offering, Ynez had never looked lovelier. Or happier. She smiled radiantly at both men. And if she hadn't made up her mind about Don Armando's wife before, Frances now was certain she disliked and distrusted the two-faced woman.

They took their leave. Both men were sober. Unemotional. Almost like strangers. Yet Frances felt the underlying tension between them. Filled with questions for Chaco, she nevertheless waited until they were a good ways out on the trail, setting a steady pace back to Santa Fe, before she broached what she was certain was a sensitive issue.

"Don Armando . . . your mother loved him?"

"If she did, she was a foolish young woman."

"He loved her."

"So he says."

"He sounded sincere." Frances only hoped her thinking so would make Chaco feel better. "And he kept the beadwork she gave him."

"Probably forgot about it until now."

"Then what reminded him?" she asked, even knowing the answer. "You?"

"Yeah. I'm something the old man all of a sudden can't forget."

Reluctant to intrude on his privacy, Frances couldn't help herself. "His son."

Chaco gave her a wild look and his horse a sharp kick. The buckskin took off and her own mare followed close behind. Frances clenched her jaw and hung on for the short time it took him to get his temper in check.

He slowed with a mumbled, "Sorry. Shouldn't take my problems out on you."

"Want to talk about it?"

He shook his head. "Not now."

That left the future open. And Frances feeling as if she had something to look forward to. Why should she care whether or not Chaco Jones was willing to tell her how he felt about his father? Because she cared about him. Because she was falling in love. Not the kind of love she'd had for Nate who'd filled her with gratitude and a sense of adventure and a false future to look forward to.

But the kind of love that came from knowing a man inside.

From respecting him.

The realization took away her breath. She respected the man responsible for her husband's death more than she respected the dead man. Nate had deceived her, if not maliciously, then to protect himself. And while Chaco was rarely open about himself, she knew she could trust anything he told her.

"Just keep something in mind," Frances advised him. "I'm sure you have reason to distrust Don Armando. Maybe to hate him. But he made the first move. You have a chance to settle things with him, make your peace." She thought of her own uncompromising father and of her meek mother who wouldn't stand up to her own husband. "Some of us may never have that opportunity."

His gaze scorched her. Cheeks flaming, she shifted, trying to find a more comfortable seat. Instead she found more sore spots.

"You look miserable." Chaco sighed and reined in his horse. "Let's get down and walk a while, stretch our legs, maybe sample those vittles."

Dismounting, he quickly moved to help her, though Frances beat him to it and got off on her own. She tottered a few steps as the stiffness in her legs and back eased, then found a more comfortable rhythm.

"Another apology." Taking her sorrel's reins from her, Chaco led both horses as they walked. "Maybe I shouldn't have been so hard on you, going at the pace I did."

"And perhaps I should have returned to Santa Fe like you wanted me to."

"If you had, things might of turned out different. Lots of people might be dead."

She gave him a look of amazement. "I didn't do anything."

"I wouldn't have powwowed with the war leader if you hadn't shamed me into it."

"You would have done something." She truly believed that.

"With a gun, maybe. Words are *your* weapon of choice, remember?"

He grinned at her, but the light demeanor was all surface, mocking. Once more, Frances sensed something very, very wrong. She tried to mind her own business, but the reflection of Chaco's inner turmoil didn't fade, and finally, she had to know.

She stopped short, demanding, "What is it that's

bothering you?" When Chaco stopped and gave *her* a curious look, she insisted, "Tell me. I felt something was terribly wrong the moment you returned."

"Another premonition?" he asked in a too-tight voice.

"Perhaps." Or perhaps a bond was growing between them as fast as her feelings. "Tell me."

The grin gone, he said, "Let's eat."

He led the horses over to a lone buckthorn tree where he secured the reins on a branch, removed his saddle roll and spread the blanket on the dusty red earth in its shade. He dropped the food pouch and water canteen at its center.

She waited until they were seated and he was foraging through the bag before again asking, "Tell me what's bothering you. Please."

Mumbling what sounded like an Apache curse, Chaco finally said, "I had to agree to seek out the witch and bring her to justice."

"Personally?"

He nodded. "The war leader's a wily one. I couldn't exactly refuse."

She was appalled. "But isn't that the job of the lawmen in Santa Fe?"

"How many white men do you know who believe in skin-walkers?"

"Skin-walkers?" Frances frowned at the odd sounding word. "Another name for a witch?"

He laid the food on the blanket between them. "A special kind of evil. A human being who can take the form of an animal. The reason those men had their throats torn out. No dog did that."

"You're right—about not many believing it." She wasn't sure she could, either.

"The skin-walker exists."

"How do you know for certain?"

"Saw it with my own eyes. A wolf. Came after me twice now. It'll come again."

A wolf? The flesh along her spine crawled and Frances had trouble catching her breath. Hadn't she decided she could trust anything Chaco told her? If so, then she had to believe. Or at least trust that *he* did. She'd seen that wolf near Belle's place, and then the Apache had been found . . .

"How will you find her and . . . and deal with her?"

"That's the problem. I don't have a clue. There's an old Apache saying that the wind casts no shadow."

Puzzled, she frowned. "I don't understand."

"The *diablera* is like the wind—she comes and goes at will, breathes down our necks, leaves destruction behind, but never a trail. And it's not like I can call her up out of hiding, make her show her true face."

Another reference to multiple faces. Frances remembered Ynez's duplicity.

Chaco unfolded a cloth holding four stuffed-and-rolled tortillas. They each took one. Ravenous, Frances bit into hers without caution. Added to cheese and meat were peppers hot enough to sear her stomach and make her sweat. Gasping and wild-eyed, she grabbed for the canteen, uncorked it and took several long swallows until Chaco anchored a hand on the bottom and stopped her.

"Whoa! That's got to last until we get back to Santa Fe."

"I'm breathing fire!"

She wondered if Ynez hadn't meant for the food to be so hot out of spite.

Chaco didn't seem concerned. He took the tortilla from her, unwrapped the thin bread and picked out the peppers, tossing them into the brush.

"Now try it," he said, rerolling and handing the tortilla back to her. "It'll still be spicy, but I bet you can handle it."

"I don't know . . ."

"I do. So far you've handled all the cards dealt you pretty well, especially the bad ones."

Avoiding the appreciative expression in his eyes, she took the food from him and tried again. He was correct. While spicier than she was used to, the filled tortilla was edible. Swallowing, she glanced at Chaco, who was grinning at her, looking like he was enjoying himself. Then he took a big bite of his own ration, whooped aloud and smacked his lips.

"Mm, good!" he said, stuffing his mouth with more.

Frances laughed at his enthusiastic appreciation and continued eating herself. Though the atmosphere had lightened, the situation hadn't changed.

Chaco—or someone—had to find this supposed *diablera*. Then what? If this woman really had evil powers, whoever faced her down could be in more danger than if looking into the barrel of a loaded gun.

"You love to court danger, don't you?"

Louisa whipped around in her saddle, Defiant doing a nervous dance beneath her. "Oh, it's you." The pretty toy soldier who hadn't been able to best this magnificent beast. Quiet hands and legs finally settled the gelding down. Noting Lieutenant Samuel Strong's handsome features were once more pulled into a disapproving expression because of her, she asked, "What's your problem today?"

His signal so subtle she didn't catch it, he moved his mount up to ride beside her. She didn't object.

With no one to entertain her, she was still bored, the reason she'd sneaked off to meet Eusebio for that carriage ride. Not that she would see *him* again. To her fury, the weasel had propositioned her. And when she'd set him straight, he'd called her a teasing bitch of a breed, who ought to be honored by his interest. And who needed to be taught a lesson. Louisa had taught *him* one—she wondered if he was walking normally yet—and had sent him on his way.

"You shouldn't be riding alone," Strong told her.

Before he could inquire about her parents again, Louisa said, "I'm not alone anymore." For good measure, she smiled and batted her eyelashes at him.

He narrowed his gaze at her. "How old are you?"

"Nineteen," she promptly lied. "On my next birthday," she added to sound more convincing. "How old are you? Twenty-one?"

"Twenty-three!"

She'd touched a nerve. No doubt many of the men under him were far older. "So where do you want to ride?"

She'd been out in the hills and was on her way home, but she wasn't especially anxious to get there.

He looked down his aquiline nose at her. "I can't escort you. I was on the way back to the fort—"

"On duty?"

"Not officially. But I have some paperwork to catch up on."

"Relax. This is the West. We take things as they come here."

"So I've noticed."

Louisa noticed he didn't sound thrilled. "Don't you get tired of being so serious all the time?"

"I have a serious job. Responsibilities."

"What do you do for fun?"

He looked at her as if the word were foreign to him. Then he said, "Ride, mostly."

She believed it. He sat on his horse like a professional—which as a lieutenant in the United States Cavalry, he was. Even so, she couldn't help baiting him. "Think you're good?"

"I know I am . . . despite what you may have heard about my compatibility with Defiant."

"Good. Then how about a race?"

He looked as if he were appalled. "No!"

"Why not? Afraid you'll lose?"

"My racing a young lady would be inappropriate."

"Pooh!" Louisa scanned the horizon and pointed to a small knoll. "See that rocky place up the road a piece." Which was practically on the edge of the Janks property. She leaned in close to him. "First one there's the better rider."

"I'm not racing a—"

But she'd already reached out to whomp his chestnut gelding on the rump. With a surge of muscle and an indignant squeal, the horse bolted. Laughing, she lightly dug her heels into Defiant's sides. The larger bay took off immediately. She shifted her weight so that she was practically standing in the stirrups and leaning forward.

"Little fool, you're going to break your neck!" Strong yelled as he glanced back at her.

"Or break *yours*."

Strong gave her a filthy look and then suddenly his expression changed. He clenched his jaw and looked straight ahead, and Louisa knew he was into the race against his better judgment.

Her amused laughter sang over the high desert as Defiant drew alongside him.

Neck and neck, the horses flew down the dirt road,

enveloping themselves and their riders with red dust. Louisa held her breath and squinted her eyes against the dry particles. Gently, she squeezed her legs and was gratified when Defiant gave her an answering burst of speed. The chestnut was right there on the trigger to challenge her. And from what Louisa could see, Strong wasn't doing anything obvious to make his mount work so hard. Hands and legs steady, leaning forward in the saddle, he and his horse were a single unit. Her competitive spirit forgotten for a moment, Louisa couldn't help admiring Lieutenant Samuel Strong.

But not enough to lose to him; the outcrop of rocks was coming up fast.

Stretching herself out over Defiant's neck, she whispered words of encouragement to him and moved her hands in a scrubbing motion that matched his rhythm. When she squeezed her legs and scrubbed faster, the big bay responded, altering his rhythm slightly to match hers.

From the corner of her eye, Louisa could see they were inching ahead.

She chanced a look in Strong's direction. The brim of his hat flattened practically over his eyes didn't seem to bother him. He was focused, determined, his very energy passing to his mount and seeming to make the chestnut move faster. The two horses were almost even again when Strong met her glance. A mistake on his end. He broke concentration.

Louisa took the opportunity to push Defiant past the rocky area nearly a neck length ahead of his former owner's mount.

She sat back in the saddle and shouted what she imagined to be a Comanche war cry. Her long black hair streamed around her. She'd rarely ever felt so free or light of heart. She was happy. Enthralled. Definitely not bored for the first time since returning home. And all because of *him.*

No sooner had she thought it than Strong startled her by grabbing her reins and stopping Defiant. They were all four, horses and riders, breathing hard. The lieutenant appeared angry as he danced his horse around hers and stopped when he was face-to-face with Louisa.

"Don't worry," she teased. "I won't tell anyone I bested you."

He scowled harder. "Is that what you think I care about?"

"You're a man, aren't you?"

Indeed, he was. One of the best-looking men she'd ever seen. More important, one of the best riders. Louisa had to admit she was impressed.

"And you're a foolish girl."

"Woman." She couldn't help herself. She tossed her head and threw back her hair, imitating one of Luz's haughty gestures. "Too much of a woman for you, obviously."

Strong's tanned face grew ruddy as a hand shot out to grab her arm. Louisa felt her heartbeat speed up. Confused by conflicting emotions, she tried to free herself from his grasp, but that only made Strong seem more determined to rein *her* in. He tugged, practically pulling her out of the saddle. Her body pressed into his, the contact leaving her excited.

And frightened.

Wide-eyed, she watched his perfect, handsome face draw closer. And then he was kissing her, stealing away her breath. She'd been kissed before a couple of times. By boys. Or by spoiled young men like Eusebio. Never by a man. Never with anger. Never like this.

Not with such deep-seated passion.

Louisa was about to throw her arms around the young lieutenant's neck and return that passion when he broke the kiss and pushed her away.

He still looked angry.

"Now see what you made me do!" he accused.

"What *I* made you do?" Louisa's temper flared. Why was she always being held responsible for other people's actions? "*I* didn't invite you to kiss me!"

"You dared me to!"

"I challenged you to a race, nothing more!" Though she had fully appreciated the reward until he had to go and ruin it. Louisa tore Defiant's reins from Strong's hand. "But don't worry, Señor Lieutenant," she said, mocking him as Eusebio had, "because it won't happen again!"

With that, she dug her heels into Defiant's sides and held on for dear life as the gelding bolted for home. Only then did she realize they weren't alone.

And that the heated exchange had not gone unnoticed.

Breath coming in painful spurts, Belle sat frozen to her carriage seat as her daughter rode toward her. Is this what Louisa did when she supposedly went riding on her beloved horses? After all that she'd gone through for the girl, after all that she'd done to protect her, to make a better life for her, how dare Louisa betray her trust?

Though she wasn't close enough to see the dust-coated man clearly before he rode away in the opposite direction—the setting sun near blinded her—Belle hadn't missed the fact that her daughter had been in his arms. And this after hearing gossip in town about

Louisa taking a furtive carriage ride with a young caballero. That Eusebio Velarde had much to answer for.

Louisa seemed intent on allowing herself to be compromised by one man or another and Belle wouldn't have it.

Louisa eyed her warily as she rode right up to the carriage. "I didn't expect you home for dinner—"

"I just bet you didn't!"

The girl's smile faded and her dust-covered face took on a serious expression. "Ma, it isn't what it looked like."

"You weren't in a man's arms? You weren't being mauled?"

"Well, he did kiss me, but that wasn't supposed to—"

"I'll say it wasn't!" Belle's anger was winding up. "I've given you too much freedom, young lady, and you've taken advantage of me. Hell, you've been running wild!"

"I haven't, I swear!"

"Don't you sass me! You've been the topic of gossip around here since you came home. There's only one thing for it. No more leaving the house unescorted."

"Ma, you can't mean that!"

"If I gotta, I'll sell your damned horses!"

"You wouldn't."

"Try me!" Belle yelled, ignoring Louisa's stricken expression.

She would lock the girl up if she had to. Her daughter would never end up like she had. She'd put Louisa in a nunnery first.

And, as for the men . . .

Belle stared at her beautiful, innocent daughter through a haze of anger as red as the dust covering her and vowed she would cut out the heart of any man who tried to ruin Louisa.

She was familiar with the taste of death; she wouldn't hesitate to kill again.

Frances couldn't rid herself of thoughts of death as she and Chaco finally rode into Santa Fe at dusk. First the Navajo. Then the Apache. Was Chaco next?

He'd seen the skin-walker twice and expected to see her again. Surely he would do so if he went after the *diablera* as the Jicarilla war leader had demanded of him. And if this fantastic tale of a shape-changer were true, then what? Which of them would be the one to die? Frances saw no other outcome. She wasn't certain how she felt about Chaco's killing this woman, guilty or not. Her feelings about killing hadn't changed, even if her feelings for the man had.

"Home at last," he said, stopping in front of the stable.

Looking as exhausted as she felt, he dismounted, then helped her before she had a chance to touch ground. His hands on her weren't unwelcome. But they scared her.

Or rather her easy acceptance of his touch did.

"Hey, Willy, come get these nags and put them up for the night!" Chaco called to the owner, who lurked in the shadows of the stable. "They need some gentle hands and pretty words to settle them down."

"Cost you extra," the grizzled man grumbled, stuffing a bottle into his vest pocket as he came through the opening. "Bad enough I gotta shovel the stinking horse hockeys. . ." His words dropped off as he noticed Frances. He tipped his filthy gray felt hat. "Beg pardon, ma'am."

Holding her breath against the strong fumes of the alcohol, Frances gave him a tired smile. After being around Belle awhile, it was near impossible to be shocked by rough language from a man.

"Hey, Jones, you know an hombre by the name of Martinez?" Willy asked, taking the reins from Chaco.

"Yeah. He and I worked together . . . awhile back." Chaco gave Frances a worried look. "Why?"

"Stabled his horse here. Looking for you. Told him you worked at the Blue Sky."

Chaco didn't say anything. He tipped Willy for the extra care of the horses, then, waiting for a wagon to pass, took Frances's arm. She was too tired to protest that she didn't need help crossing the alleyway. But once on the other side, Chaco didn't seem inclined to let go and Frances was not inclined to ask it of him. For a moment, he made her feel safe and protected.

And more confused than ever.

"Who's this Martinez?" she finally asked.

"Worked for the Ralston Double-Bar."

"A cowhand?"

"Not exactly."

She didn't prompt further explanation. Martinez had to be another gunman, a subject she was happier avoiding, especially if he were in town to lure Chaco back to his old life.

The very thought of Chaco's possibly leaving, of her never seeing him again, made her go all hollow inside.

Entering the Blue Sky Palace a few minutes later, Frances took her leave of Chaco, put the threat of Martinez out of mind and looked for Belle. The madam was nowhere to be found. None of the girls had seen her for hours. About to give up and head for her own room, Frances finally caught sight of Belle entering a back way. She looked drawn and tight-lipped, making Frances wonder if she was sick.

Hating to make her feel worse—or to get her upset as she had been with Avandera—Frances nevertheless quickly caught Belle up on the events of the day, ending casually with, "Luz and Adolfo will be in some time tomorrow."

Her expression unchanging, Belle merely nodded.

"Is something wrong?"

"It won't be, not if I have anything to say about it." Her comment confused Frances, but she could see the madam was in no mood to explain. Undoubtedly Belle was having problems with Louisa again.

"I'd better get cleaned up."

Belle didn't seem to hear. Frances limped to the stairs and tried not to wince as she ever-so-slowly climbed them. On entering her room, she heard a familiar splashing. Someone using her tub again? Without thinking, she opened the door fast . . . only to see Rosa lifting a bucket of steaming water.

The maid smiled. "Señor Chaco asked Juanita and me to do this."

A hot bath, complete with a thick layer of heavenly scented bubbles. "Oh, how considerate."

While Rosa finished adding water, Frances went back into the bedroom with barely the energy to remove her boots and clothing. She left them where she dropped them on the floor. No sooner had she slipped into a silk robe than she heard Rosa leave the next room by the hall door. Brushing the dust from her hair, she pinned it up in a knot and headed for the tub, dropping the robe on the floor beside it.

"Heavenly," she moaned as she slid down into the water.

She lay there for a few moments, allowing the hot water to do its work on her muscles. Then she found a fresh cake of fragrant soap and ran it over her wet arms, sighing with contentment as she left trails of bubbles down them both.

"Need some help with your back?"

Startled, Frances whipped around to see Chaco leaning against the wall just inside the door to her bedroom. The soap went flying. How long had he been standing there, watching her? Her heart beat faster as she sank lower into the tub under cover of the fast disappearing bubbles. "What are you doing in here?" she demanded, too tired to act as indignant as she should.

He hesitated a moment, as if he were waiting for something. An objection from her, perhaps? When she made none, he eased from the spot, crossed to the other door and locked it. "I wanted you to know you don't have to make an appearance downstairs tonight." He retrieved the cake of soap. "I cleared it with Jack and the boys."

"I'm so glad my bartender and other employees are willing to let me have the night off." She thought she ought to do something about the inappropriateness of their situation. "You can leave now that you've given me the message."

But he didn't seem so inclined. He stared down at her with those gray eyes that for once looked warm instead of cold or spooky. And Frances noticed he had already cleaned up and changed into fresh clothing. He'd even shaved the beard stubble and had tied his thick black hair back from his face.

Having trouble breathing, she forced out, "That was nice of you to arrange for my bath," then realized how stupid that must sound. Why wasn't she ordering him out of her rooms? No man had ever seen her bathe before. Not even Nate.

"I remembered you liked a hot bath."

Nate. She could hardly conjure his image in her mind, Frances thought guiltily. Could hardly remember what he looked like. And she was trying extra hard.

But Chaco wasn't the same man who'd shot her husband, she told herself. He'd turned his back on his profession. He'd been willing to try to stop bloodshed between the Indians and the whites rather than create more. He'd committed himself to a dangerous quest to save countless lives.

If there was a God—which she realized she believed despite her falling out with her father, despite her questioning her own faith—then didn't Chaco's self-sacrifice count for something in the grand scheme of things?

He reached over her and took a big sponge from a shelf. Without a by-your-leave, he dipped the sponge into the tub, then briskly rubbed the soap against the wet surface.

"Lean forward." When she looked at him uncomprehendingly, he explained, "I can't do your back with you like this."

Mesmerized . . . insane . . . too tired to fight his will—one of these would have to be a good enough reason to do as he commanded instead of screaming for help. She edged forward, arms crossed in front of her, protecting her breasts. Even the thought of his seeing them sent a thrill curling through her.

At the first touch of the sponge along her back, Frances closed her eyes and sighed. "Are you trying to get even for last time?" she asked. "When I made such a big deal about your using my tub?"

"Does it feel like I'm trying to get even about something?"

It felt as if she were being seduced. So why wasn't she fighting it? Fighting him? She remembered that hollow sensation that had gripped her when she'd thought of his leaving Santa Fe. She had her answer.

"Why are you here?" she asked, touching her forehead to her drawn-up knees.

"To take care of you. You shouldn't be alone tonight."

"A premonition?"

"Instinct. After all that talk about the skin-walker..."

Did he only feel obligation to protect her then? Because of Nate? "What if there was no skin-walker?"

"I'd be downstairs," he began, disappointing her. "Though I'd still want to be here with you."

She raised her face to look at him and recognized the longing in his expression. The same longing she had for him. Maybe she had become a wanton, but she couldn't stop the admission from escaping her.

"I'd want you to be here with me, too," she whispered, "even if there was no skin-walker."

12

Chaco looked deep into her eyes as if he were trying to read her very soul. Then he dropped the sponge and got to his feet. Stifling a protest, turning her head away so he wouldn't see her disappointment, Frances never expected him to reach down into the tub.

"What—?" she choked out as his hands slid along her back and her derrière.

In answer, Chaco lifted her, freeing her from the soapy water, hefted her against him, then carried her into the bedroom, dripping water and suds. He gently laid her on the bed and loomed over her, his knee pressing into the mattress beside her naked hip. Frances breathed heavily as he unbuttoned his shirt. The sleeves and the front where he'd held her against him were as wet as she. The very slowness of his actions gave her the opportunity to protest.

She didn't say a word. She watched . . . suddenly

breathless... fascinated... as unbearable heat coiled through her.

Surely her living at the Blue Sky had changed her, after all, for she had never felt this same hunger, this overwhelming desire, for her husband. Memories of her short time with Nate threatened to intrude, but Frances banished them lest they stop her. She didn't want to stop. She wanted Chaco Jones with every fiber of her being.

While he stripped off the shirt, she boldly reached out to unbutton his denim pants. He sucked in his breath and his nostrils flared. Head thrown back, eyes closed, he reached down, pressed her hand into him through the material. Too impenetrable. She wanted to feel *him*. Freeing her hand, she slid it inside the denim, startled when she found no other barrier. She grasped him and he fell over her, raining kisses on her face and neck and breasts.

Then he turned to her mouth, seduced from it a sensuality she hadn't known herself capable of. He began a rhythm she couldn't resist, neither with her tongue nor her hand. Soon she was breathless, writhing with anticipation, stroking him with something akin to desperation. And she didn't understand why he caught her wrist in a fierce hold and stopped her from continuing.

"Slow and easy," he said, finally stirring from her side to remove his boots and pants. "I want to remember this night. I want you to remember, too."

As he undressed, her eyes sought the most exciting part of him. Eyes wide, she licked her lips and swallowed hard, trying to imagine him inside her.

But Chaco was in no hurry. He spread her legs and enticed her into trusting him, first with his hands, then with his mouth. His teeth nipped the sensitive flesh of her inner thighs, making them quake. Then his tongue laved a path to the heart of her passion, making her quake harder.

Though this new and surely unusual act startled her, Frances didn't consider stopping him. Through slitted eyes, she observed his every movement as he loved her in this strange and wonderful way. She reached down, found the rawhide binding his hair and tore the strip free. Watching the long black strands feathering her thighs, she imagined she was being seduced by a savage.

Smiling, she curled her fingers in the thick pelt, lifted her hips and rocked, soon losing herself in the heat and the pleasure.

Just when she thought she could stand it no more, that surely she would shatter if he didn't stop, Chaco slid up and into her, filling her with even more pleasure. Her legs wrapped around his back of their own accord and her hips tilted so that she sheathed his entire length. They fit perfectly, she thought, as if they were made for each other.

Chaco was breathing hard. Watching her face. Waiting? Frances wanted to wait no longer. She wanted to return the pleasure he'd given her. And so, as she began moving, as he bent his head so he could suckle her breasts, she was amazed when her own arousal escalated. Within seconds she was digging her nails into his back, urging him to move faster.

"Frankie," he whispered, his mouth finding hers as his body went taut, triggering a response that sent her reeling.

They cried out together and Frances was lost, caught up in the sensations that pulsated through her until she was too weak to move or speak or breathe. She gasped for air and Chaco fell on her, rolling to his side, gathering her to him with arms and legs so that she couldn't tell where one of them ended and the other began.

Her head tucked into the crook of his neck, Frances thought she would be content to remain so always.

But it wasn't to be.

Her heart had barely slowed before a knock at the door disturbed them.

"Tell whoever it is to go away," Chaco muttered.

"What if there's a problem in the casino?" She felt his sigh. And called out, "Yes, who is it?"

"Juanita, Señora Gannon. Señor Chaco . . . have you seen him?"

Placing her hand over Chaco's mouth, Frances asked, "Is there a problem?"

"A man, he is looking for Señor Chaco. His name is Martinez. He says it is urgent."

"Thank you, Juanita. If I see Chaco, I shall tell him."

He tore his mouth from her fingers and raised both brows. "If you see me?"

"Well, what would you have preferred? That I announce to the maid that Señor Chaco is right here in my bed?"

He gazed at her steadily. "Why not?"

"I have a reputation—"

"Yeah, right." Face pulled into a thundercloud, he started to rise.

"Chaco, please." She grabbed his arm. "I'm not sorry this happened between us." Not yet, at any rate. "But I'm not used to people thinking . . . that is, I've never . . . I mean . . ." Because he was staring at her uncomprehendingly, she took a deep breath and said, "Nate was the only man . . ."

"Before me?" he finished, his expression turning to amazement.

A flush heated Frances's neck. Now thoroughly embarrassed by the admission, she pulled a pillow from the head of the bed to cover what she could of herself. "He saved me from being an old maid."

Chaco's laugh made the flush spread. But, as if to reassure her, he leaned over, tossed the pillow and cupped her hip with wickedly enticing fingers. "Old maid? You're a hell of a passionate woman, Frankie."

Falling from his lips, the shortened version of her name seemed right. "Passionate enough to keep you here awhile longer?" she asked.

He kissed her. "You bet." Another kiss. "Though Martinez seems pretty anxious to find me." His hand slid from hip to breast. "He might be pounding at the door next if I don't find him first."

"So? We don't have to answer it!" she said, desperate to keep him with her.

He studied her for a moment. "What're you afraid of?"

"Your leaving . . . for good."

"Who says I am?"

"But Martinez—"

"Is no friend of mine. That's why I'm extra-curious about what he wants. I'm through being a gunman, Frankie. I thought you believed that."

"I—I want to."

He gave her one last reassuring kiss before rising. "Then believe it."

Even so, as he quickly pulled on his clothes, Frances remained unsettled. Her sense of impending danger intensified, only now she wasn't certain whose it was. Maybe the premonition had never been meant for her, but for Chaco. Maybe she was being warned that something terrible would happen *to him*.

For danger awaited Chaco in every direction, she

realized, no matter which way he turned. Indians. A skin-walker. Now a gunman.

More than anything, Frances wanted to belong somewhere. And to someone. But with belonging came responsibility. Realizing that she had fallen in love with Chaco Jones no matter his gunfighter past, Frances feared she could easily lose him in any number of ways... especially if she tried to hold on too tight.

So when he leaned over her to give her one last kiss and said, "Be back when I can," she didn't renew her protest.

Praying she was wrong, that all the talk of witches and visions had merely incited her imagination to do its worst, Frances pulled the bedding around her now-chilled body and watched him go, whispering, "And I'll be waiting."

On entering the casino, Chaco immediately spotted Raul Martinez, belly up to the bar, an arm around Ruby's waist. He stood back and studied the hired gun for a moment. Martinez hadn't changed—same rumpled clothes, shaggy hair and drooping mustache. But while he had both drink and woman in hand as usual, he seemed truly uninterested in either. Instead, he appeared to be oddly alert. Waiting.

For him?

Chaco chose not to keep the gunman waiting any longer. He surged through the growing crowd surrounding the bar. "Martinez. Heard you were looking for me."

As he approached the Mexican, Martinez gave Ruby a pat on the behind and sent her away. Chaco thought the little blonde seemed relieved.

"Jones, my old friend!"

They'd never been friends. Chaco didn't even like the other man, and he figured the unspoken disaffection went both ways.

"Taking yourself a rest from the Double-Bar?"

"The permanent kind." Martinez downed a shot and poured himself another. "Quit. Went to work for Murphy."

Instigator of the Lincoln County War, businessman L. G. Murphy had the backing of the so-called Santa Fe Ring, a group of corrupt officials.

"He's here in town?" Chaco asked, thinking Martinez might be acting as bodyguard.

"Nah, he's back in Lincoln. Sent me to find you. He's tired of the war and especially William Bonney and wants to end things fast. Figures you could take The Kid if there was to be a meeting set up. Pays good. More'n twice what old Ralston put out."

For a shoot-out with Billy the Kid, a ruthless murderer? "Not interested."

Martinez made a face and surveyed the poker and monte tables. "You like this place so much then?"

"Not a bad way to make a living."

The Mexican snorted. "For a man used to the open range? Used to the power of a gun?"

"Problem was the smell of death. I never wanted to get used to that."

Chaco smelled something else right now. Something rotten. Instinct warned him Martinez wasn't exactly being straight with him.

And when the gunman said, "Any rules against the manager sitting down for a coupla friendly hands of cards with an old *compadre*?" Chaco replied, "None."

Maybe a little time with Martinez was all he needed to read through the other man's bluff.

She had been furious when her spells had failed to work on her enemy, more furious that the Indians had dared to rise up against her. But now she had a new plan, one that almost soothed the savage beast in her. One that had best not go wrong. She was thinking about the details as she headed back out of the cursed town when a carriage came whipping around a corner and almost ran her over.

Jumping to the side of the road and into an adobe wall, she shouted, "Idiots!"

The driver brought the horse under control, and the passenger leaned out toward her. "Ah, Señorita, our apologies," he said, waving a bottle.

The other's dark eyes glittered as she approached the stopped carriage. "Can we invite you to join us?" he asked after getting a good look at the Mexican peasant's outfit—short, red skirt and low-cut white blouse, both without benefit of undergarments. "Eusebio Velarde at your service. And this is my younger brother Enrique."

"Eusebio," she repeated, licking her lips. "And Enrique."

Perfect.

They both wanted her. She could see it in their lust-filled eyes that could not stay away from the hollow between her breasts. Her breath quickened at the thought of having them both at the same time, and she tugged at the already too-low blouse so the swell of her flesh was better displayed, her dark nipples peeping out from the ruffle. They were so hungry for her, their tongues were practically hanging out.

Why not take them? A reward for her ingenuity in

hiring the gunman. Brothers would be a special treat to satisfy her jaded appetite.

And they were ricos. Her lips curled as she realized that, while doubling her pleasure, she could use them not only to teach the Jicarilla a lesson well-deserved after their attempted betrayal, but to avenge herself on all Spanish men who were as arrogant as these two.

Lowering her eyes, she said, "I would join you . . . but not here."

Enrique jumped out of the carriage and vowed, "We would go to the ends of the earth to please you."

"That you shall," she promised as he helped her up.

She clenched her jaw against the twinge of her shoulder, and she remembered the difficulty of removing the bullet. Her flesh was still healing. The last weeks had been hard on her, and taking her pleasures with these two would be even more draining. Not as taxing as obtaining her powers had been, of course—she had almost died then—but enough to leave her weak and unable to work her witchery on anyone else for a while.

No matter. Martinez would take care of Chaco Jones. She was only sorry she would not be there to watch.

In a celebratory mood, she guided the Velarde brothers into a nearby clearing, away from the road at the edge of town.

"A blanket," one said, producing the item from under the seat with a flourish.

The other held out his half-empty bottle. "And wine."

"How thoughtful," she said, lowering her lashes and reclining on the covered ground.

She cared nothing for comfort, but she indulged the

drunken, laughing young men. Neither would be laughing much longer.

When the bottle was drained, Eusebio made the first move. She watched as he boldly placed a hand on her breast, pulling her blouse down so he could pinch a nipple. So he enjoyed pain? Her nostrils flared and she gave him a slant-eyed look as she thought of how much she would enjoy his pain.

She let the men do what they would, stroking, touching, exploring under her skirts. Inside her. They roughly removed her garments, then their own. They were both ready and quite pleasing to look at. She was vividly reminded of what autocratic bastards Hidalgo men were when Eusebio tangled a hand in her hair and tugged her onto her knees—as if he could force her to his will! He arranged himself under her so he could pull her face close to his engorged member. To encourage her, he slid his tongue along her already wet cleft.

"Are you certain this is what you want?" she asked as the fires began burning deep inside.

"I want it," Eusebio said.

From behind her, his drunken brother slurred, "So d—do I."

Slipping onto his knees, Enrique covered her like a dog. Or a wolf, she thought with a feral grin.

"Then you shall have more than you bargained for."

She went at Eusebio with relish, taking his entire length into her mouth, nipping hard with sharp teeth as she released him a tiny bit at a time. He squirmed, he moaned, he shoved his tongue along her fired flesh. It was gratifying to imagine that he was pleasuring not only her, but his brother who was working up a sweat from behind.

Imagining Eusebio tasting Enrique, she grew more excited than she could bear. While pressing her swelling flesh into the one's mouth, she tilted her hips and buttocks so the other brother could better fill her.

Being taken like this—both like a woman and a wolf simultaneously—was more exhilarating than she would ever have imagined.

"Aiyee," Enrique breathed from behind as he loosened his hold on her. "Your skin is so hot!"

Indeed, heat poured through and out of her . . . not that it made him think of stopping.

She felt herself stretching, tightening, changing, even as Enrique cried out and gave one last powerful shove that sent her tumbling over the edge of her control. When Eusebio grabbed onto her head and thrust his hips higher so she would be forced to take all of him as he released his salty seed deep into her throat, she reacted out of instinct—growling, biting, tearing the flesh at its base.

His scream of agony and his brother's of horror were only the beginning of her reward.

Awakening a few minutes after three the next day, Frances dressed quickly. Chaco had joined her sometime during the night. She vaguely remembered his climbing into bed if not his leaving. He'd pulled her body into the curve of his own, and, comforted by his heat, she'd quickly drifted off. Exhaustion had allowed her to sleep deep and long, and but for the sore muscles mostly in her lower back and thighs, she felt better than she might have expected.

Hunger making her stomach growl, she left her room in search of food and was drawn to excited female voices coming from the hotel lobby.

"Don't you think it's romantic?" Ruby was asking.

Magdalena's, "Romance, hah!" stopped Frances cold halfway down the stairs. "Belle will throw another fit when she finds out about this."

"And I intend to be far away from her when she does," Sophie stated.

Frances forced her legs to move and joined the girls who huddled at the foot of the staircase. "What's going on?" She feared the gossip was about her and Chaco, though she didn't know why Belle should care.

"Avandera ran off with her shepherd," Luz told her, the news making Frances grin.

"I gave her a potion for love," Magdalena bragged.

"Seems you've been spreading it around," Luz muttered darkly to Magdalena's placid smile.

Frances stared at the Pueblo woman who knew so much about *brujeria*. And she was the one who'd originally brought them all the news of the *diablera*, too. The reminder made all thoughts of romance pale.

"Magdalena, could I speak with you?" Frances asked. "Alone?"

"We are not wanted." Giving Frances a questioning look, Luz pushed Ruby and Sophie toward the doorway leading to the saloon and casino. "Let's have a drink for Avandera and you can tell me more about her shepherd."

Frances drew Magdalena toward a small alcove to one side of the lobby. The area was framed with tasseled red curtains and held a velvet-upholstered couch, two matching spindly-legged chairs and a wooden table with a glass-fringed lamp. Being that the lobby was clear but for the young clerk behind the desk, she figured this was as private a place as any to discuss a sensitive topic.

No sooner were they seated than she dived right in. "You seem to know quite a bit about witchcraft."

Magdalena's expression was at once cautious. "Are you angry with me for Avandera's love potion, Señora Gannon?"

"No, Magdalena, of course not. I'm glad she found some happiness." At least one of Belle's girls had been given a second chance to lead a more respectable and fulfilling life. "It's that I, uh, need your advice."

The Pueblo woman drew her brows together. "*You* need a love potion?"

"I need to know how to recognize a skin-walker."

Magdalena's eyes grew big and she made a strangled sound. "Searching for a skin-walker? This would be lunacy, Señora Gannon. You must not go looking for such trouble."

"What if trouble is looking for someone I love?"

The Pueblo woman swallowed hard. "I cannot—"

"Please. She's come after him twice. I'm afraid that next time she might succeed in hurting"—she couldn't say killing—"him. Helping me recognize the *diablera* would be in your own best interests, as well, because if she could be stopped, then you would be able to visit your own pueblo whenever you wanted. I remember your saying you were afraid to after the Navajo was found."

Silent for a moment, Magdalena gave her a measured stare, then finally said, "There are different kinds of looking. Gazing into obsidian or rock crystal might reveal her identity, especially if you had something that belonged to her . . . or something she had touched."

Frances could think of two examples, but they had both been taken away by their tribes and presumably buried. She swallowed hard. "And say we couldn't determine the witch's identity. What then?"

"There are certain protections. You can guard your house or quarters with sacred prayer sticks or feathered wands. Or you can burn cachana."

"Cachana?"

"Witch root. The Pueblo people gather it in the Jemez Mountains and from nearby mesas. Cachana can also be added to personal medicine bags."

Well, she'd asked, Frances reminded herself, not knowing what to think. To take Magdalena's advice, she would first need to stretch the boundaries of her imagination.

"I'm not certain I even believe in such things as skin-walkers," she admitted. How could she when she'd lost the capacity for faith in anything other than the tangible? "I find it far more difficult to think of using rocks and feathers and some mysterious plant as weapons against evil."

"These things are not simple solutions," Magdalena warned her. "A powerful shaman must prepare them, for it will be his spirit that fights the skin-walker."

"If that's so, then it must take an even more powerful medicine man to *destroy* a skin-walker."

"I am afraid you are correct, Señora Gannon."

Her flesh was crawling, and Frances was tempted to dismiss the feeling as being prompted by the conversation. But some instinct made her glance over her shoulder to be certain. Just outside the alcove, Ynez de Arguello stood frozen and wide-eyed, her face too pale against the deep-green silk of her dress. She had obviously been listening to their conversation, and her demeanor reflected her horror.

Not knowing what to say to the woman—though she owed her no explanation—Frances was relieved when she heard the hotel door swing open and Don Armando's voice boom, "Doña Ynez, are you feeling well?"

Expression a mixture of embarrassment and confusion, the Spanish woman said, "Yes, Husband, of course."

"Then why are you standing like a pillar of salt? Have you sent for my son?"

Ynez's mouth gaped open as if she were about to answer, but Ruby came running back into the lobby, looking around wildly, her relieved, "Mrs. Gannon, there you are!" drawing all eyes toward her.

"Ruby, what is it?"

"Trouble in the casino!"

"What the hell's your problem, Jones?"

"I don't have one." Though Martinez was trying to change that quickly, Chaco thought, staring down at the Mexican who'd been playing poker since noon. "Why don't you let me buy you a friendly drink at the bar?"

"A drink won't get my hundred dollars back."

Two of the three other players had a good number of chips stacked in front of them, but they didn't look happy about their winnings.

"Neither will my giving you credit."

"You don't know that."

He didn't, not for certain, but Chaco suspected he would be throwing good money after bad. Normally Martinez was a sharp poker player and came out ahead. If he were a suspicious man, he would think Martinez was cheating.

To lose.

Something was keeping the gunman around, and Chaco doubted it had anything to do with Murphy or with trying to change Chaco's mind in helping to bring a swift end to the Lincoln County War.

"If I lose," Martinez was saying, shuffling and reshuffling his hand of cards, "You get your money in a coupla days."

"I can't take that chance."

"You calling me a goddamn welsher?" His hands stilled.

The skin on the back of Chaco's neck began to crawl. "I'm telling you policy."

"For a *compadre?* We go way back!"

"I know a lot of men, Martinez." Chaco was watching him carefully now. Though he was aware of concerned voices, of movement around him as people began clearing the area in alarm, he focused on the Mexican. "Fact is, I wouldn't give any of them credit, either."

"What if I don't believe you?"

"You're entitled," Chaco said more calmly than he was feeling.

"An' I don't take insults lyin' down."

"You're free to leave any time."

Martinez threw the cards to the table so hard they went flying along the surface and off the other side. "No one throws me out! I leave when I'm ready."

"As long as you settle down, I don't have a problem with that."

"Now you're sayin' I'm outta line."

Chaco eyed Martinez coldly. No matter what he said, the man was bound and determined to start a fight, no doubt his purpose in being at the Blue Sky Palace in the first place.

"You're out of line," he agreed.

Martinez gave him an evil grin. "Then I guess you're gonna have to throw me out."

"If I have to."

"If you can."

So that was it. Martinez wanted a face-off. Chaco

realized someone fancied him dead and had hired the gunman to do the dirty work. No doubt if he'd agreed to the Mexican's offer to work for Murphy, he never would have made it down to Lincoln. Undoubtedly Martinez counted on jumping him and leaving him somewhere along the trail, his body fodder for the coyotes and rattlers and scorpions.

A familiar and unwelcome tension gripping him, Chaco suggested, "Why don't you just get out now, while you can?"

He heard a commotion, and from the corner of his eye, saw a flank of bodies surge into the casino through the saloon. Frances was in the lead.

Damn it all, anyway!

"Or maybe we should take it out to the street, Jones, and settle this like men."

"No!"

Chaco heard Frances's shout, though he dared not take his eyes off the gunman for a second. While Martinez had given up his gun belt as required when entering the Blue Sky, he probably had both pistol and knife hidden on him.

Knowing there was no way out of this, Chaco growled, "Then let's get to it."

Speculation buzzed around the room. Part of him heard. Part of him was aware of Frances, who stared at him with a mixture of disapproval, disappointment and downright horror. And damn if that wasn't de Arguello and his haughty young wife with her. But most of Chaco remained focused on Martinez as he carelessly downed a whiskey, pushed his chair away from the card table and got to his feet. The Mexican might be half drunk, but you'd never know it, Chaco thought. His eyes burned clear and his hands were steady.

Martinez started for the door. "You wouldn't shoot a man in the back, now would you?"

Chaco didn't respond to the insult. He kept a safe distance as he followed the other man. Harder to do, he ignored Frances, who shadowed him.

"Chaco, please, don't go out there. He's not worth it. You told me you were through with gunfighting!"

So he'd thought. But he wasn't about to let a man kill him, and Chaco had no doubt that's what Martinez was being paid for.

The Mexican collected his double-holstered gun belt and led the way outside. A crowd followed them through the *placita* and onto the dusty narrow street. Passersby, as if sensing the tension in the air, hurried along, seeking shelter in doorways or other nearby plazas.

Chaco never took his eyes off Martinez, not for a second. He watched the man's every movement, especially his hands.

The sun hung low in the west, and Chaco tilted his hat forward to keep it from blinding him. He flexed his shoulders, neck, back, arms. Martinez stopped. Turned. His hands slowly moved to his chest. He separated the front of his jacket and drew the dusty material back behind the holsters of his twin Peacemakers.

Chaco's blood began to rush. His heartbeat drummed in his ears. The taste of fear soured his mouth.

Fear that this time he wouldn't be fast enough or accurate enough. That this time he would be the one laid in a pine box, hands crossed over his chest for eternity. That he would be the one buried with no one to mourn him.

A sob from somewhere to his right reminded him that Frances would mourn him.

The thought steadied him, gave him more reason for living than he'd had since he'd buried his mother.

"It's your call," he told Martinez.

The Mexican grinned, revealing a mouth of rotting teeth. "It's your funeral, Jones. Don't worry, I'll give you a good one. And dance on your grave."

Then his hands moved like lightning. Chaco went for his Colt as gunshots echoed along the *trazo* and the air thickened with the stench of burned powder. Martinez jerked, but his guns were still blazing. Chaco hit the ground and rolled, continuing to fire.

When the smoke cleared, Martinez was laid out on the street, too.

Unmoving.

As Chaco rose, people swarmed out of nearby buildings. A grizzled old man was the first to reach the other gunman. He squatted, checked for any signs of life.

"Dead as a doornail," he pronounced, closing Martinez's eyes.

Shouts of congratulations assaulted Chaco's ears. Someone slapped him on the back. More than one man offered to buy him a drink.

He stood there, staring. Wondering why. Another man dead. More blood on his hands. He hadn't wanted this. Had tried to avoid it. Was, in fact, somewhat sickened by it.

"I had no choice," he found himself telling Frances.

She stood a yard away, separated from him by well-wishers, her expression appalled. By the death? The partylike atmosphere that so often followed a shoot-out? Or him?

"You always have a choice," she was saying. "You can always choose to be a civilized human being."

Is that what she thought of him after everything he'd

told her? That he chose this? That he enjoyed killing? Why did she have to look so damn accusing . . . and brokenhearted? Why couldn't she try to understand?

Angry that she turned her back on him without asking him what had happened—if that would make a difference—Chaco holstered his Colt and strode away from the Blue Sky Palace, possibly forever.

13

A swell of pride practically bursting through his thin chest, Armando de Arguello rushed after Chaco.

"Don Armando, where are you going?" his wife called. "Husband!"

Armando was irritated by her wails. No doubt she was upset by the sight of death—she was only a woman, after all—but she should learn to be more stoic. "Wait for me in the hotel lobby," he ordered. "I shall return shortly."

He hurried on, desperate to catch up to his son, who was now nowhere to be seen. His old heart was beating too fast as he stepped off the side street and onto the plaza, where people were milling, many of whom were soldiers. Then he spotted Chaco, a lonely figure near the gazebo, eyes cast to the ground as if he were praying. Armando gave himself a last push lest Chaco decide to move on and perchance disappear back into the crowd. Winded, sweating and nearly exhausted, he tried his best not to show his weakness as he stopped next to the man who was both his flesh and a stranger.

"You made me proud, my son," he puffed.

At first he thought Chaco had not heard him. Or did not want to. And then, expression grim, the younger man turned his head.

Spooky gray eyes sliced straight through Armando. "If my taking a life made you proud, then you're a sick man."

He ignored the sarcasm. "Not the death itself. The way you stood up to him. So proud. So unafraid."

"Who says?"

He accepted the response as one of modesty. "That could have been me thirty, perhaps forty years ago."

Chaco's gaze seared him. His son was not at all receptive to compliments. Or perhaps it was being compared to a man who had abandoned him . . . was he insulted?

"What is it you want, old man?"

"You. The land—"

"I'm not for sale. Not anymore."

"I do not seek to buy you. I choose to give you your birthright." He spoke straight through Chaco's barked laughter. "I want the de Arguello name to go on."

The laughter stilled and the eyes grew cold and deadly, making Armando sweat harder.

"Sorry. Name's Jones."

Was that all? "This can be taken care of," he began with a regal sweep of his hand.

"Reuben Jones was the best pa a kid could want," Chaco said in a low, skin-prickling tone. "I wouldn't sully his memory by throwing away the name he honored me with."

Realizing his mistake, Armando lied. "No, no! I did

not mean this. I can have papers drawn up to recognize you as my son, so that when I die . . ."

"Are you ill?"

He saw a break in Chaco's composure. Perhaps his son cared, even a little. Chaco had come to his rescue when he thought the Apache would attack his *estancia*. He chose to play up on this side of his son's nature. Loyalty had kept Chaco close to his mother until her death. If he were clever, Armando schemed, perhaps he could instill some of this sentiment in Chaco for himself.

"I have been weakening, having terrible stomach pains." Though not for a while, thank God. Whatever had been troubling him had for the most part passed. "I am afraid our time to become better acquainted with each other is limited." Truthfully, he was not at all certain this was an exaggeration. "Life can be so fragile," he reminded Chaco, feeling only a little guilty saying this after praising him for bringing down the Mexican gunfighter.

With an exaggerated sigh, Armando grew silent and watched his son digest all he had said. Emotions flickered over the hard features that held Oneida's stamp.

Finally, Chaco said, "Get to know each other, huh? And what do you suggest?"

Knowing that he had won despite the hostility in the younger man's voice, Armando stifled the smile that threatened his lips.

"It's Satan's work!" shrilled Minna Tucker, as Martinez's body was lifted by two men and put into a wagon. "And this is his house. How long will the good people of Santa Fe stand for it, I ask you?"

Other voices echoed her sentiments if with less enthusiasm.

Still in shock, Frances turned from the cries and confusion to seek the shelter of the hotel, but the Tucker woman stepped in her path and grabbed her arm roughly.

"Pardon me," Frances gritted out at the rude gesture.

"Ask the *Lord's* pardon," Minna intoned, reminding Frances of her unbending father.

"For what?"

"For luring young men into this house of vice, this den of iniquity." The Bible-thumper's voice rose. "For sheltering Satan himself—"

"Drivel!" Frances interrupted.

As she wrenched her arm free, the material of her sleeve gave and she heard a tearing sound, but she was too agitated to check the damage. She stalked inside, feeling as if her heart had broken. More fool she . . . to have believed Chaco when he'd shared his regrets, but it seemed he wasn't through living by the gun, after all.

She passed through the casino and saloon and was about to head upstairs to have a good cry in her own room, when she noticed Ynez de Arguello pacing the length of the hotel lobby. The woman's expression was one of anguish.

Upon spotting her, Ynez stopped and asked, "Don Armando—have you seen him?"

"I'm afraid not. All the confusion . . ."

"Yes, the gunfight. The killing. Oh!" Ynez's dark eyes flickered and her body started to go slack.

Realizing Ynez was about to faint, Frances rushed to her side and grabbed onto her. "I think you'd better sit down."

"I am but a foolish woman worried for my husband."

Ynez sounding convincing . . . and yet Frances wasn't persuaded. Supporting the Spanish woman's weight, she led her to the seating area.

"I'm certain Don Armando will return soon."

Perhaps it was the way Ynez glanced at her from the corner of her eyes as she slid down onto the sofa. Sneaky-like. Even while wondering why Ynez should playact for her, Frances remembered their meeting the day before. She'd thought the woman was two-faced then.

"Tell me, has Chaco told you about Don Armando?" Ynez asked, hanging onto Frances's arms.

"That your husband is his father?"

Something flickered deep in the dark eyes. "And what he intends to do about the fact?"

So that was it. Ynez was trying to elicit her sympathies to get information on Chaco.

"As far as I know, nothing," Frances said truthfully, not wanting to get into a discussion about the man who had disappointed her every bit as much as Nate had. Freeing herself, she took a step back from the sofa. "Would you care for some tea?"

"That would be very kind of you. It is so seldom I have the opportunity to speak with a woman of refinement."

"Sorry I can't join you. I have a business to run."

With that, Frances took her leave, asking Rosa to get the tea. Finally, she climbed the staircase to her room to find another surprise awaiting her.

Belle was staring down at the rumpled bed, her expression odd. Did she know about her and Chaco, or was she thinking of Avandera running off with the shepherd?

"Belle, what are you doing in here?"

Wide brown eyes focused warily on Frances.

"Frankie, honey, I gotta talk to you. Damn that Louisa! She's becoming impossible."

"She's young and impulsive."

How could the woman be so focused on a fairly normal domestic problem when one of their customers had just been killed by one of their employees. Unless she didn't know . . . Why hadn't Belle been drawn outside to investigate the gunfire? And what was she doing in Frances's room?

"Louisa's running wild, taking secret carriage rides, and now she's doing even worse."

Belle appeared wild herself. Her face was white, her red hair puffed out carelessly. She looked a bit . . . unstable. Thinking Ynez had put her in an odd and even suspicious mood, Frances reminded herself that the woman was not only her business partner, but her friend.

"Maybe she needs some time." Hoping Belle wouldn't take this the wrong way, she added, "And understanding."

But Belle didn't seem to digest the suggestion. She went on, "Louisa wouldn't give me her promise not to sneak out and ride alone, so I had to take away her horses. Now my own daughter won't speak to me."

With that admission, she burst into tears.

Wanting to cry herself, Frances put her arms around the other woman and patted her back instead. Belle wept so hard, Frances thought she might make herself sick.

"What should I do?" she sobbed into Frances's shoulder. "I only want to be a good mother, make sure she don't go through the terrible things I did. What the hell kinda life would that be for her? But I couldn't make the kid understand. I just made her hate me is all."

"Louisa's a good girl, and she loves you. I remember how excited she was to be coming home."

"Because she loves New Mexico and those galumphing horses of hers."

"And you. She told me how much she missed you."

It took some doing, but Frances finally convinced Belle to give Louisa some time and a lot more patience. The woman also promised to sit down and have a lengthy heart-to-heart talk with her daughter the next day, to see if she couldn't smooth things over. Maybe compromise.

When Frances changed the subject and told her about Martinez, the news of his death hardly seemed to touch Belle. She shrugged her shoulders, said gunfights were the way of the west and left to see to her girls. Frances figured she'd let one of them share the news about Avandera with their madam.

She was all washed out.

Giving the bed a longing look, Frances was tempted to crawl under the covers, have a good cry and a better sleep. But as she'd told Ynez earlier, she had a business to run. Not knowing whether Chaco would now show after he'd gone stalking off, she had to get herself in a better mood so she could act as floorman for the night if necessary.

A glance in the mirror startled her. She hardly recognized herself. Over the space of a few weeks, she had changed. Not only hairstyle and clothes . . . but the inner person she had become seemed to be reflected on a face that was at once softer and more mature. Though both inside and outside were pretty much a mess at the moment, she thought, picking up a brush to smooth her hair, she liked herself better than she ever had. For the first time in her life, she wasn't living by someone else's rigid standards or rules. She was making her own decisions without worrying about someone else's opinion.

And she was starting to feel like she belonged.

In the midst of straightening her hair before the mirror, she noticed the ruffle on her right sleeve hung crookedly. "Oh, fine. Ripped."

Another job for Ruby. Thinking she would have the girl give the material a few stitches before she went down on the floor, Frances realized the solution wasn't so simple. She'd lost the bow. Either she'd have to find it or remove the bow from the left sleeve, as well.

Where could it be? She remembered the material giving when she'd pulled her arm free from the Tucker woman's grasp, so she hurried back outside. Because the crowd had dispersed, she had no trouble checking the ground thoroughly. Still, she didn't find it. Returning through the now-empty lobby, she investigated the area around the couch where she'd left Ynez. Not there, either.

With a sigh of resignation, she gave up. What did bows on her sleeves matter anyway, she thought, going in search of Ruby and ignoring the odd feeling—*not* a premonition, she told herself sternly—that threatened her composure at the loss of the silly bow.

Bile rose in her throat at the thought of her latest failure. How did disaster keep shadowing her? Was someone more powerful on her scent? This time she had not even tried to use her special gifts, which were admittedly drained after her delicious encounter with the Velarde brothers.

Instead, she had used money, which, to her horror, had not worked either.

The gunman was dead.

Flames danced like fiery tongues against the brooding darkness of the desert. Feeling the chill, she huddled closer, looked deep into the burning embers of the crackling, fragrant juniper, as if the fire might reveal where she had suddenly gone wrong.

As if it might tell her why she could not seem to take the revenge she craved against Chaco Jones.

She had been successful for so many years, since she first sought her powers. She had been little more than a child when her safe world had been ripped from her. When she had been introduced to the truths of life that still haunted her. When she had been savaged like an animal with no feelings.

She had killed to protect herself then.

Over the years, she had killed as often as necessary.

And somewhere along the crooked path she had chosen, she had grown to enjoy killing, especially in ways that frightened most poor fools. Lately, her bloodlust had grown stronger than the one that occasionally burned between her thighs.

She would kill the woman, if she could.

"Frances Gannon."

She uttered the name aloud with such contempt that a nearby night creature scurried off into the brush.

Too bad her recent activities had drained her so. For the time being, her powers were diminished and she would need a few days to recoup. Until then, she was limited as to what destruction she could render.

If she could not kill the woman, then she could frighten her, hopefully into running back East where she belonged. Frances Gannon was a threat in more ways than one.

Good thing the stupid woman had been so trusting . . . and that she herself had been quick of hand. She turned the token over and over before the fire, taking pleasure in the bow's thick satin feel.

Drinking the potion she had specially mixed, she squeezed the scrap of material in her fist and waited. When she felt the power slide along her limbs, when her lashes fluttered, slitting her eyes, she pressed the satin to her forehead and uttered the invocation.

"Free me, oh powerful one, from this earthly body. Let my spirit cut through the night like a knife. Let the wind cast no shadow . . ."

Shadows everywhere. And somewhere deep within them, Frances sensed danger.

Another premonition.

Only a full moon lit the deserted, windswept streets of Santa Fe. The earthen buildings glowed a deep blue around her. A middle-of-the-night quiet pressed down so heavy she could barely breathe.

So as not to twist an ankle, she hopped over a rut made long ago by a wagon wheel. Despite her caution, she was hurrying, spurred on by this sense of urgency that she couldn't explain. The wind rose, its howl mournful, and her gaze flitted in every direction as she raced toward home. Still, no matter how fast she moved, how far she went, the Blue Sky Palace remained elusive, frustratingly out of sight.

She turned an unfamiliar corner. Then another. Panic set in when she realized she'd gone in the absolute wrong direction. Empty-eyed warehouses near the railroad's spur line loomed over her like dark ghosts.

Frances remembered Nate's body being loaded onto a funeral wagon here.

She had stopped and was trying to conjure his image when she heard a low grunt and a steady padding too light to be a person's footsteps. And yet something was heading her way. Following her? She strained to hear. A low animal noise. A growl. The padding drawing close enough to raise the hair on the back of her neck.

Keeping her gaze trained on a narrow street between two of the buildings—she was certain the sounds came from that direction—Frances backed up and almost fell when her leg rammed into the boardwalk beneath a portal. She was distracted long enough for whatever it was to draw closer. For her to hear the rapid panting indicating an animal's excitement.

Then she saw the eyes.

They glowed unnaturally. She was caught. Mesmerized. Trapped by their very intensity.

The panting grew louder, echoed from building to building. Reverberated inside her mind. Her mouth went dry and she forgot to breathe. Light-headed as the creature drew inexorably closer, its path straight for her, she began edging away.

When it crossed the street drenched in moonlight, she gasped in horror. A wolf. Jaws slathering. Eyes burning, coveting. Frances sensed it wanted *her*.

The skin-walker.

Flying along the boardwalk, Frances knew she didn't stand a chance in the open. The wolf's lazy lope narrowed the distance fast.

An open doorway. She sped over the walk and through the maw, slamming the heavy panel in the wolf's very face. Heart hammering, she sucked in the dusty air before moving away from the clawing, tearing noise on the other side. Away from the throaty growls of frustration.

Careful to make no noise herself, Frances crept through the near-dark—a single window gave some sense of where things lay. She found a staircase and had just reached the landing, had barely stepped through a doorway into some kind of hallway when the sound of splintering glass sent a rise of flesh straight down her back.

She felt her way through the dark, her silence magnified by the furious growls from below telling her the creature would soon be inside. Her stomach roiled and she thought she would be sick. No, not sick. Nor would she be the creature's prey if she could help it.

She kept moving.

At the end of a long room swept by moonlight shafting through the lone window, Frances found a hidey-hole, a small storage area beneath a back stairway. She crouched to enter. Pulled the door shut even as she heard the click of nails against the wooden risers. Waited in the dark, heart pounding. Found herself praying for help, or lacking that, forgiveness for any wrongs she might have committed against others.

She grasped onto a spark of faith that hadn't died, after all, and realized that forgiveness was a gift to be given as well as received. If she survived the skin-walker, she would remember that when dealing with mere mortals.

Scratching at her door, the wolf waited directly outside her hiding place. The wooden panel shuddered with the unnatural creature's strength.

Frances prepared to die.

She closed her eyes, allowed a few tears to slip through her lashes. Her only thought: she would never see Chaco again. She'd never told him that she loved him and now it was too late. She'd judged him and he'd turned away from her.

"Chaco, think of me," she whispered into the dark as the door shuddered and, with a horrible tearing sound, gave way.

Smelling the acrid scent of evil descend upon her, Frances screamed and lunged forward, grasping the wolf by the neck. Bodies entangled, they went flying into the empty room. Blindly, Frances shoved her fingers into the wolf's mouth so fast and hard that it didn't have time to bite her. Now, with her fist keeping its jaw open, it couldn't.

Rolling over and over across the floor, Frances felt the body against her change. Wolf to woman. Woman to wolf. It made human gagging sounds. Tried to claw her. Claws became nails. But whose?

They rolled into the shaft of light.

A shot rang out.

With a terrified-sounding screech, the creature ripped itself from her grip and went flying into the dark where it disappeared.

Panting, Frances gasped, "Who . . .?"

A silhouette separated from the shadows. "You called me, Frankie."

"Chaco?"

He was holding a gun whose smoke curled through the moonlight. A gun that had killed a man earlier, and that now had saved her life.

She plunged to her feet and threw herself into his arms, but even as he kissed her, her head began to spin and her knees refused to hold her. Unable to hold on any longer, knowing she was safe, she let go . . .

. . . coming to with a start sometime later.

She was in her own bed. Alone. Sweat-soaked and shaking.

A dream. All a terrible dream. No one had been chasing her, after all. Her breath came in choked spurts. The last days had affected her more deeply than she'd realized.

The talk of a skin-walker.

Her fear for Chaco.

Her disappointment in his taking up his gun against Martinez.

He'd shown up in the casino to work as scheduled, though he hadn't exchanged so much as a greeting with her. He'd reverted to his old self—closed and dangerous—and had seemed to be looking for another fight. None of the customers had been stupid enough to give him that opportunity. When the casino had shut down, Chaco had disappeared into the night like the skin-walker in her dream.

Frances wondered where he was now. Sleeping? Or was he, in truth, walking the empty streets of Santa Fe? Surely he would be safe . . .

Remembering she'd dreamt of forgiveness, of asking and giving, Frances knew she and Chaco had a lot to talk about. She needed to hear what he had to say about the gunfight just as she was sure he needed to tell her. She'd been unfair to turn her back on him.

Tomorrow she would listen.

Frances lay back against her pillows and started to adjust the covers, stopping when pain shooting through her left hand made her wince. What could she have done to herself while sleeping?

Not wanting to light her room lamp, she rose and moved toward the window where she saw that the knuckles were scraped, the back of her hand bruised. Her flesh crawled and she gasped for breath. In her dream, she'd used this hand to stop the skin-walker from savaging her.

She stared out over the rooftops onto the deserted streets of Santa Fe.

Had the dream truly come from deep within herself, from the problems that had been plaguing her . . . or had it been sent by a very dangerous woman who walked in a wolf's skin?

14

She would not *be a prisoner* in her own home, a furious Louisa decided shortly after a late breakfast. How dare her mother stable her horses in town, leaving instructions that Willy was not to release any of them to Louisa unless she was properly escorted?

Just let the drunken old geezer try to stop her from taking Defiant and she would give him what-for.

She was on foot, storming toward a confrontation, when a woman's scream made her whip around to see a familiar if driverless carriage. The lathered horse was wild-eyed, slowing its frenetic pace, yet spooked by more female squeals and the excited shouts of men trying to stop him. Uncaring for Eusebio's possible inconvenience, but feeling badly for the horse, who was sure to break down if not stopped, Louisa placed herself in its path and spoke to him in a loud if calm voice.

"Whoa, boy. Where are you off to in such a rush, my friend?"

Knowing the horse recognized her, she held out her hands as he slowed and took advantage of his hesitancy by grabbing hold of his halter and reins. Only then, up close, as she easily brought the animal to a full stop, did she realize the carriage was not empty. She caught a glimpse of bare flesh on the floor of the fancy rig before the small crowd that followed closed in, cutting off her view.

Stroking the horse's nose to calm him, Louisa also noticed a despised visage bearing down on her.

Minna Tucker.

"Oh, God save us all!" shouted a man in shopkeeper's apron, the first to inspect the carriage's contents. "They've gone and killed 'em, too."

Louisa's heart was beating hard. While she'd lost any respect for Eusebio, she hadn't wanted him dead. Him? The man had said *them*.

"Who?" she asked, meaning whoever was on the floor of the carriage.

"Injuns." The grim-mouthed shopkeeper was focused on the murderers rather than the victims. "Mutilated 'em worse'n the others."

An elderly Spaniard crossed himself. "*Dios*, both Eusebio and Enrique Velarde."

Louisa elbowed her way closer to get a better look, then nearly fainted at the sight that widened her eyes and brought a surge of bile to her throat. Mutilated was a kindly way of describing how the men had died. Both throats were ripped out and Eusebio was missing his . . .

For the first time in her life, Louisa's knees went weak and she was glad for the support of the man next to her. "Thanks," she whispered.

"Here now, Miss," he said, attempting to turn her away. "Ain't nothing for a lady to be seein'."

"She's no lady!" Quiet until now, Minna Tucker thundered the accusation. Her face was red and her eyes held a crazed cast. "And it wouldn't surprise me if *she* did this," the woman said, indicating Louisa.

Regaining strength in her limbs, adrenaline overcoming her horror of the murders, Louisa gasped, "Me? You are crazy!"

"Everyone knows how wild you are, how terrible your temper is—and I saw you in this very carriage only a few days ago."

"So what? Eusebio took me for a ride and—"

"You were leading this young man on." Hanging onto her cross with one hand, Minna was working herself up, spraying spittle on those closest to her. "And he was taken in by your evil ways, poor young man, until he learned the awful truth about your tainted blood."

"What's that?" the shopkeeper asked, now eyeing Louisa with suspicion.

"Why, she's a no-account, bloodthirsty half-breed!"

Voices rising in shock, several people moved away from Louisa as if she might kill them, too.

"I didn't do anything wrong!" she insisted, but she noted fear and doubt on many faces, glee on Minna Tucker's. "So what if my father was a Comanche, you old biddy?"

"You see, she admits it!" the hateful woman screeched, pointing an accusing finger straight at Louisa's chest. "And she wears the sign of the heathen."

Gaze stuck on her bear claw, one of the men stepped closer to her, his expression threatening. She glanced around the crowd but saw no help. No friendly faces. It seemed that with a few malicious words, Minna had convinced the others of what they wanted to believe: that they had the killer right there, in their power, to do with what they pleased.

Clear in Louisa's mind was a vigilante hanging of a young man accused of, but not convicted, of rustling. Only seven at the time, she'd gotten a good look at his bloated face and the way his head sat cocked on his broken neck before her mother found her, covered her eyes and pulled her away.

Panicked, not knowing what else to do, she ran, closing her ears to the yells that trailed after her. Young and well-muscled from riding, she quickly put enough distance between her and the crowd to duck around a corner and into a doorway unseen.

But, as they rushed by, voices rising, she heard Minna yell, "She probably headed for the Blue Sky Palace and her harlot of a mother!"

Pressed up against a wooden door, Louisa squeezed her eyes shut and tried to breathe naturally without making a sound. Oh, Lord, now what? She'd had little enough reason to stay in Santa Fe after her last row with her mother. Now she had none. She had to leave before she ended up at the end of a rope.

Once certain the mindless mob had passed, Louisa sneaked toward the stable, zigzagging in and out of doorways, trying not to think about Eusebio or his brother. No matter that she tried, she couldn't vanquish the image of their mutilated bodies. Defiant would take her from this horror. She would choke Willy if he so much as put up a fuss. But once at the stable, she found the grizzled owner curled up in an empty stall where he'd made friends with a bottle of whiskey.

Defiant was glad to see her and full of spit. Dancing around her when Louisa entered his stall, he pushed his great head into her shoulder and almost knocked her into the wall.

"Yeah, I missed you, too," she whispered, placing a finger on his nose as if that would keep him quiet.

Thankfully, she hushed him long enough to tack him up, fill a canteen with fresh water and "borrow" a knife she found in the back of the stable.

Lastly, she kissed Susie and Mancha on their velvety noses, and whispered her grief-stricken good-byes in their ears. "I wish I could take you with me, but you'd just slow me down."

She'd have to find feed and water for three horses instead of just one, not an easy task in the wilderness. She would rather leave them to strangers than take them with her if she couldn't properly care for them.

Heart pounding, she cautiously peered out the wide doorway, fearing that, since they were in sight of the Blue Sky Palace, one of the rabble-rousers might be on the lookout for her. Coast clear.

She made her escape unnoticed.

It was only when she got to the edge of town, coming within spitting distance of home, that the enormity of running away hit her. She'd never see Ma again. She no longer had a home. Tears filled her eyes and she kicked Defiant's sides, turning him south and urging him to leave the area as fast as his long legs would carry him. The thunder of his hooves covered the sounds of the dry, racking sobs that would surely embarrass her to death should anyone hear them. Thank heaven, she was alone.

Although not for long.

Ambushed by a flurry of chestnut hide that appeared out of nowhere, Louisa didn't have the time or sense to make a clean getaway before Lieutenant Samuel Strong grabbed hold of Defiant's reins and yelled, "Easy, boy."

Though furious at the intrusion, and ready to explode at the pretty tin soldier, Louisa stalled out and let him take control. But when they faced each other, she realized he wasn't playing some game with her. Wasn't trying to bully her. Concern lent strength to his features, and it was all she could do to stop herself from bursting into humiliating tears under his intense and worried gaze.

"I admit you're a good rider," he said, "but are you out to break your neck?"

Louisa mustered a ghost of defiance. "If I do, it's no concern of yours."

"If you do, who'll be good enough around here to race me?"

If only she had that to look forward to. Eyes filling once more, she turned her head away from him. "You'll have to find someone else anyway."

"Why? From the way you were just riding, I doubt you're about to give it up."

"I won't be here," she insisted, taking charge of Defiant's reins and moving him out. "I'm leaving."

Strong rode alongside her, took a moment before asking, "Your family's moving?"

"*I* am."

"You're not getting married?" he asked, voice oddly tense.

She gave him an astonished look. "What's it to you? No!"

His expression changed subtly, as if he were relieved. "Then why are you leaving . . . and where will you go?"

"Because I'm not wanted here any more . . . and

I don't know. About the where, that is. Maybe Albuquerque. I'll decide when I get there."

"You're going now?" Finally comprehending the immediacy of her situation, he looked over her tack. "Like this, without extra clothing or food?" Silent for a moment, he then said, "You're running away from home." When she didn't deny it, he asked, "Does your father beat you or something?"

"I don't even remember my Pa. He's been dead for years."

"Mother?"

Her insides twisted at the thought of losing the one person who loved her. "Nah, Ma just yells a lot."

"Then why?"

"Mind your own business!" she blurted, swallowing the tears that threatened her once more.

He stopped asking his infernal questions but made no move to leave her side. They rode together in silence.

Louisa couldn't help but think about the situation that had prompted her to leave Santa Fe. She should be used to it by now, people calling her a half-breed like she was something they'd found clinging to the bottom of their boots. She should be used to nasty names and nastier accusations. She should be used to being different.

But she wasn't.

She wanted to fit in. Wanted people to accept her. It had been bad enough when the girls at the city schools had made fun of her and made her life miserable, but now the people in her own town weren't any better. She'd thought Santa Fe with its mixture of cultures was different, that there were so many people of mixed blood—Anglo, Hispanic, Indian—that she fit right in. She'd been wrong. People in that mob had been ready to believe her a murderer, maybe string her up, all because her father had been Comanche.

She didn't understand what gave people the right to think they were better than anyone else because of who their kinsfolk were. She gave Strong a sideways glance and wondered if he'd figured out her blood was tainted. Probably not, or he wouldn't be here with her.

The thought ate at her as they traversed mile after mile, heading deeper into unfamiliar country.

"You can go back to your fort now," she said tightly.

"I'm in no hurry."

"I thought you were always in a hurry. That you always have work to do whether or not you're on duty."

"I'm working now." When she gave him a disbelieving look, he said, "My job is to protect the citizens of this Territory. That's what I'm doing."

"Me? You're protecting me? From whom?" She might as well tell him. Maybe then he would leave her alone. "If you're worried about the Indians, don't. I'm one of them. My pa was a Comanche."

If she expected him to appear disgusted and turn tail, she was disappointed. His blue-green gaze stayed steady on her, and his expression remained nonjudgmental.

"Didn't you hear me? I'm a savage!" Louisa yelled. "If you're not nice enough to me, I might decide that pretty gold hair of yours would be a perfect souvenir."

His eyebrows shot up. "Then I'll have to be careful that I don't make you too mad until I can convince you to turn around and go home."

"I'm not going home!"

"We'll see."

Part of her wanted to scream at him, to chase him

away. But another part, the part that realized he hadn't registered any contempt at her admission—had actually seemed amused at the way she'd blurted her threat—was relieved that he wanted to be with her, even for a while. She didn't really want to be alone. And she had to admit she liked Sam Strong, now more than ever.

It wouldn't hurt to have his company for a while, especially since she was staying away from the main road to Albuquerque and other possible traveling companions. She was afraid that vigilantes might even now be searching the main routes for her. Using the sun as her guide, Louisa headed southwest over far more difficult terrain than was normal for the trip.

Hours passed and Strong seemed no more inclined to leave her on her own than when they'd started out. Midafternoon, they stopped by a narrow ribbon of a stream where they watered their horses and refilled their canteens. Beneath a box elder, they shared some jerky he produced from his saddlebags. Since she wasn't inclined to talk—her mind drawn to the horrid deaths and the possibility of meeting up with a real skin-walker—he told her about his home, a farm in Ohio, and his father and uncles who'd been Union Army cavalrymen during the Civil War.

When they were rested, Louisa expected Strong to give her an ultimatum, to say he was heading back with or without her. But he silently remounted his chestnut and waited patiently until she was ready to leave.

"Why are you doing this?" she asked as she settled on Defiant's back. "Staying with me when you shouldn't?"

"Because I don't want anything bad to happen to

you, Louisa," Strong said, his sincere words thrilling her. "And when you change your mind, I want to make sure you make it back to Santa Fe safely."

If she were to change her mind. And *if* she knew how to get back. Taking a long look around, Louisa realized she didn't have the faintest idea of where they were.

Early evening shadows grew long in The Gentleman's Club sitting room where Frances was listening to Ruby's excited plans for Avandera's wedding dress—the other girls would pay for the material and Ruby would design and sew it—when Belle rushed in, gasping for breath.

"She's gone!" Belle wailed, grabbing a sofa-back to steady herself. "Damnation if Louisa ain't run away!"

"What?" Frances asked with a start, wondering if Belle weren't merely exaggerating. She'd been getting more and more off balance on the topic of her daughter. "Did you and Louisa have another fight?"

"No. I never even got the chance to talk to her like I said I would."

"Then how do you know she's gone?"

"I been looking for her all day, finally checked the stable. Defiant ain't there. And then a neighbor told me he saw Louisa riding south, hell-bent for leather late this morning."

"Maybe she's just angry you took her horses away and wants you to worry," Ruby ventured.

Shaking her head, Belle sank onto the sofa and choked back a sob. "Ain't that at all. That Velarde boy and his brother are both dead, killed like the others. Mutilated. Minna Tucker got some of the townsfolk riled up and believing Louisa's a savage and that she did it . . . all 'cause her Pa wasn't white."

"That's ridiculous!" Frances stated, feeling her very flesh crawl.

In addition to being angry that once again Louisa was the brunt of stupid prejudice, she was aware that more similar deaths pointed to the work of the skin-walker. Since waking from a dream to find her hand battered, she couldn't help but believe, at least on some level.

"They scared her, so she took off." Belle began sobbing. "I can't lose her. I can't lose another child!"

Another? Frances turned to Ruby. "Could you get Belle something to calm her nerves?"

"Sure, Mrs. Gannon."

No sooner had the blonde swept out of the room than Frances asked, "Now what's this about another child?"

Wild-eyed, Belle said, "I was hardly more'n a child myself when I ran away with Ralph Janks. Ma had a dozen kids and couldn't give us nothin'. Ralph said he loved me and would take care of me." Her tone grew intensely bitter. "He took care of me, all right."

"He beat you." At Belle's surprised expression, Frances explained, "Louisa told me."

"What she couldn't tell you was about Tommy. He was the sweetest little boy. Didn't once deserve the back of his Pa's hand. I tried to stop Ralph . . . and then I had to watch him beat a three-year-old to death."

"My God!" Tears sprang to Frances's eyes.

"I held his little broken body in my arms and cried until I had no tears left," Belle whispered with a terrible sob. "Something snapped in me, Frankie. I don't really remember much. One minute, I had Ralph's hunting knife in my hand. The next I was standing over him, still holding onto that thing, only the blade was bloody. *His* blood."

"You killed him." Though she had a hard time accepting the concept of one human being taking another's life, Frances realized she had no sympathy for Ralph Janks.

"That time's still like a buncha bad dreams," Belle was saying. "I was locked in a jail cell for a while. Later I learned the judge wouldn't hang a woman, and then someone realized I wasn't right in the head. So they shipped me to an asylum in New Orleans."

And Frances had thought she'd been through some rough times. "That must have been awful for you."

"Only once I got my wits back, which was more'n a year later. I escaped that hellhole and headed west. Paid my way as a working girl. A bunch of us were headed for a new bordello in Amarillo when the Comanches attacked."

"That's how you, uh, met Louisa's father," Frances assumed.

Belle wiped the tears from her cheeks. "Whites call them savages, but he never beat me like Ralph did. He mighta been a horse thief—the thing that got him killed by a posse just before Louisa was born—but he never did to a child what Ralph did to Tommy." Eyes red and still swimming with tears, she asked, "Frankie, honey, you don't think Louisa's dead, do you?"

"No, of course not," Frances said, unable to think of that vital young life snuffed out. "She hasn't even been gone a day. She can take care of herself, Belle."

"Out in the wilderness? Oh, she talks big and rides good. But she ain't never been on her own. She's so young and beautiful. She had a *future!*"

Frances noticed Ruby standing in the doorway,

whiskey in hand, big eyes filled with tears. Wondering if the young woman ever dreamed of a different future than the one she now faced, Frances waved her in and took the glass, which she handed to Belle.

"Drink. It'll steady your nerves."

Belle obeyed, swallowing the liquor in one big gulp. "What am I gonna do? I can't lose my girl."

"I'll find her for you," Frances promised. There'd been enough deaths. She wouldn't let Louisa be next.

"*You?*" Belle gave her a look of astonishment. "You barely learned to ride. And you ain't familiar with the country."

"But I know someone who is."

Frances longed for a shot of that whiskey herself. Maybe it would give her the courage to ask Chaco for his help.

Chaco was downing a drink, steadying his nerves so he'd be able to spend another evening watching Frances ignore him when she suddenly appeared at the saloon's bar.

"I have to talk to you."

He studied her grim expression, wondered if she was about to fire him. "You're the boss lady."

"Not as your employer."

"You want to talk about us?" he asked, afraid to get his hopes up.

"Louisa Janks."

The spark of hope died. He should have known it wouldn't be anything personal. Should have known it was a mistake to come back to the Blue Sky at all. Maybe he should have taken de Arguello up on his proposition rather than promising he'd think about it.

"Drink?" he signaled Jack Smith.

"No, nothing, thank you." Frances waved the bartender away.

When she turned back to him with an intent expression, Chaco admitted, "Heard about the girl. A crying shame what lies narrow-minded folks can dream up. And the things they don't believe in." He didn't say skin-walker, didn't know if Frances believed.

His thoughts turned to Louisa. He felt for her, maybe because they had a lot in common. From his childhood, he'd been called all kinds of rotten names and had been accused of all kinds of things for no good reason other than his mixed blood. He'd learned to handle himself—and a gun—in self-defense.

Frances asked, "Did you know she's missing?"

"When?"

"Sometime this morning. She ran away and now Belle's frantic thinking the worst will happen to Louisa." Taking a deep breath, Frances added, "I need your help to find her."

He frowned. "I don't know the girl well enough to figure where she might be."

"A neighbor saw her heading south on Defiant, the blooded horse she bought over at Fort Marcy. Since you at least know the road she took . . ."

Chaco thought about it. "Should be able to pick up her tracks, then, unless a cavalry regiment's been in the area recently." When she gave him a questioning look, he explained, "The army uses different shoes than the town blacksmith. I can recognize the marks." He realized he was, in effect, agreeing.

"You'll take me, then?"

"Take you?" Not wanting to torture himself by spending time alone with a woman he ached for, but who didn't want him, he shook his head. "I'll go alone."

"And what about when you find her. Louisa doesn't know you very well. It's doubtful you'd be able to talk her into coming back to Santa Fe with you."

"Don't have to talk. I can just bring her whether she wants to come or not."

"She's a very scared young woman. I won't have you terrifying her on top of what's already happened," Frances insisted. "I'm coming with you."

Chaco didn't like it, not one bit. He could go alone if he chose, could leave Frances Gannon in his dust if she tried to follow. But Louisa Janks was the important one here. Frances sure as hell was right about the poor kid being scared. Thinking about being hounded by a woman of Minna Tucker's ilk, he didn't blame her. And he didn't want to put her through more torture either. Undoubtedly, Louisa would be relieved to see Frances, so his objections faded before he could put them in words.

He gave her a curt nod. "First light."

"Can't we go now, while the tracks are fresh?"

"No use in it. Kid's got a good head start on us. Sun's already down. By the time we get provisions and our horses, it'll be dark."

Nodding, Frances started to turn away. "I'll tell Belle." Then stopped. She was swallowing rapidly and he could tell whatever she had to say wasn't coming easy. "Chaco, you didn't have to do this, not after . . . I mean . . . I want you to know how I—"

Coldly, he cut her off. "I'm doing it for the girl."

Chaco watched her walk away, back stiff, head high.

He tried convincing himself he was doing it for Louisa just as he'd told himself he'd come back to the job merely to thwart de Arguello's plans for him.

Truth be, he was becoming a practiced liar.

There was nothing he wouldn't do for Frances, he thought, until he remembered Martinez.

Almost nothing...

Dawn had barely broken before they were on their way. Belle pointed out the area where the neighbor had spotted Louisa, and, to Frances's relief, Chaco easily picked up her trail. Giving Belle a hug and an assurance that they would find her daughter, Frances mounted the sorrel without assistance and followed Chaco, who headed south. Her saddlebags bulged with food Elena had prepared, but she hoped they would return with Louisa before seriously depleting the supplies.

Chill nipped the early morning air and the eastern sky was streaked with vivid colors as the sun peaked over the horizon. It would be a romantic escape if their mission weren't so serious—and if Chaco himself weren't so grim. After he'd rebuffed her halting attempt at squaring things between them the night before, she wouldn't try again. At least not until she had some sign that Chaco was ready to talk about what happened . . . and to see her point of view.

Until then, she would try to put what had passed between them out of mind. She would try to look at him and not be affected by the hard planes of his face or by the sensual curve of his mouth or by the seductive way his loose hair fluttered against his neck as he rode. She would try not to ache for his touch or for the feel of his arms around her.

She would try . . . but Frances feared she would not succeed. An empty place within her awaited him.

A short piece down the road, Chaco dismounted,

squatted and inspected the trail. "Looks like someone joined up with Louisa here."

Frances was immediately alarmed. "Oh, no, what if one of the townspeople—"

"Army," he cut her off. Straightening, he led the buckskin several dozen yards further, then checked again. "Here they're riding together side by side."

"You're saying Louisa has an official escort?"

"Official?" He shrugged and got back into the saddle. "She's not alone. Or wasn't."

Frances tried to cheer herself up with that news. But, remembering how young Belle's daughter was, knowing that all men didn't have the proper respect for a female of any age, she only hoped Louisa was safe.

Not too long afterward, Chaco led her off the main road into rougher terrain. One hill rolled after another, the pale earth dotted with vegetation. Pinons turned and twisted their reddish trunks as they attempted to get the most of land and sky, and were interspersed with patches of bushy and freely branched juniper. Lower to the ground grew sagebrush, gray and shredded with age.

"Looks like Louisa was afraid someone would catch up with her if she headed straight for Albuquerque," Chaco explained of his detour. Before she could panic, he added, "Don't worry. I'll still be able to track her."

Frances took a relieved breath. "Did she go off alone?"

"Nope. Still two sets of tracks. Her escort is sticking with her."

They rode for hours, keeping to an easy pace, stopping only the few times Chaco needed to check the tracks up close. Frances got wise enough to dismount when he did, if but for a few minutes, so that she could relieve her legs and back of the awful monotony of the saddle. He only spoke to her when necessary. The silence that stretched between them didn't seem to bother him a bit. It was as if he didn't care, as if she meant nothing to him.

Frances felt her anger grow and feed on his neglect.

Eventually, she eased her mare alongside him and forced a conversation. "After we find Louisa, what then?"

"We go back to Santa Fe." He turned cool gray eyes on her. "Or did you have someplace else in mind?"

"I was talking about the true murderer. How do we find her?"

"*You* don't want to find her."

"No, I don't," Frances admitted. "But you have to. Until then, Louisa—none of us—will be safe."

His eyes turned spooky and stared right through her. He didn't say anything.

"Magdalena insisted going after a skin-walker would be lunacy."

That got a reaction out of him. His gaze connected with hers. "You talked to Magdalena about it? What else did she have to say?"

"Only that a more powerful shaman could stop the *diablera*. And you talked the war leader out of going after the evil one on your . . . on the de Arguello property," she said, thinking of the Jicarillas Chaco had intercepted.

"He's probably sitting back waiting to see how far I get before she kills me, too. Then he can learn from my mistakes."

Frances felt sick at the thought of Chaco being some kind of scapegoat. Not wanting to pursue the conversation, she dropped back into position behind him.

Suddenly she had difficulty breathing. Her chest felt heavy and she was certain her heart was to blame. She'd thought it had broken when he'd killed Martinez. Then why did she feel so awful at the notion of Chaco himself dying? Honest with herself, Frances knew she loved him no matter what he had done, her feelings going far deeper than she had even guessed.

She was brooding on the matter, weighing her options, trying to decide what to do about this self-discovery, when her mare nosed into the buckskin's rump and stopped. Before her, his horse unmoving, Chaco sat straight in the saddle, his back stiff, his hand held out to her in a silent command. About to demand an explanation, she let the words die in her throat.

She sensed . . . danger.

A sweep of the rolling land before and around them didn't reassure or enlighten her. She saw nothing. Heard nothing. The very air was still as if the earth itself were holding its breath.

But her skin crawled and her heart drummed as the sensation of being watched shot through her.

Frances waited for Chaco to give her some signal, to explain what was happening, to tell her what to do. Anything. But he remained stiff and silent in his saddle. Seconds stretched into minutes. Interminable. Tedious.

Frightening.

Then she heard it. The near-silent whisper, the muffled sound seeming to surround them. Drawing closer.

"Chaco!" she whispered to no avail.

She could only watch in horror as the hills came alive with armed riders and realized they were surrounded by an Apache war party. Trembling inside, not knowing what to expect next, she looked to Chaco, wondering why he did nothing to protect them. Her gaze shot back to the heavily-armed Indians. They, too, sat still and silent above them, as if in some kind of standoff.

Her heart practically beat out of her chest as Frances watched a final warrior, older than most of the others, move his pony into a break in the line. His nose was broad, his forehead low and wrinkled, his chin strong. His eyes were dark, two bits of obsidian with a light behind them, and his mouth was a thin-lipped gash without a softening curve. His loose shoulder-length hair was capped by beaded buckskin and he was wearing both breechcloth and moccasins, but his pants, shirt and jacket were of the white man's cloth and cut. She was certain he was the leader.

Now Chaco lifted his arm in greeting and spoke directly to the older warrior, his foreign-sounding words delivered in a staccato rhythm. He sounded at ease using their language, as if it were a part of him.

Frances understood not a wit of what he was saying until he uttered the name, "Geronimo."

15

Chaco sensed Frances's need to panic but would not allow it lest she shame him before his uncle. He sought her gaze, connected, and without words reassured her she was safe. Gradually, her too-white face regained its natural color.

He signaled to her to follow him. They joined the Apache who led them to a nearby stream where they allowed their ponies to drink and then gathered in small groups to eat or talk. Chaco and Frances, along with Geronimo and another warrior, his lifelong friend Juh, sat along the bank, beneath the shade of several peachleaf willow trees.

"What brings you so far from home?" Chaco asked as soon as they were settled.

Geronimo and his men were hundreds of miles from the area they normally traversed in playing hide-and-seek from the army, not to mention the San Carlos Reservation where many of the Chiricahua were interred.

"A vision summoned me."

"What kind of vision?"

"A she-wolf. An evil witch."

Giving Frances a reassuring glance since she had no idea about what they spoke, Chaco then asked his uncle, "You have heard of the skin-walker?"

"I have felt her presence. And her kills." The old warrior had a far-off look as if even now the visions haunted him.

"The witch condemns those she stalks to range through the afterlife mutilated as she leaves them," Juh said. "This, even though Apache blood runs through her cursed veins."

"Someone must exact vengeance against this evil one," Geronimo said gravely. "Soon."

Knowing different bands of Apache had no particular affection for one another, Chaco found it hard to believe Geronimo had ridden so far north to avenge the Jicarilla. The Navajo and Spaniards were even less to him.

"There must be more."

Geronimo nodded his agreement. "You, the son of my sister."

At which Chaco's skin crawled. "You have seen me in this vision of yours?"

Once more his uncle nodded gravely.

"Does she . . . kill me?"

"This I cannot say. The shape-changer threatens you. But you are stronger than even you know, Chaco. Like me, you are *di-yin*. Accept this gift from our ancestors and use it as a weapon against the evil that plagues our land."

Though he'd mostly ignored his own potential as a medicine man over the years, Chaco figured it might be the right time to explore the gift further.

THE WIND CASTS NO SHADOW

"So you traveled far from home merely to warn me?"

"You are of my blood. You are all that is left of Oneida." With that, Geronimo sank into silence.

Next to him, Frances whispered, "What does he say?"

"That he has seen the *diablera* in his visions and has sought me out to tell me that I am in danger."

"Do you believe that's all there is to it?"

Figuring Frances feared Geronimo was on the warpath, Chaco attempted to ease her mind. "My uncle lost a mother, wife and three children to the Mexican soldiers in a single raid. Considering he's been avenging their spirits for nearly three decades now, I guess it isn't too much to think he'd take the time to warn me."

Then, in an oddly tight voice, she asked, "His visions . . . are they the same as yours? Or might they involve someone else also?"

"What do you mean? Who?"

"I, uh, had this really awful dream the other night," Frances admitted, appearing uncomfortable under his steady gaze. "A wolf trapped me in a deserted warehouse. I grabbed onto her and she kept changing from wolf to woman and woman to wolf, only I couldn't see her face. In the end, *you* drove her away."

Chaco didn't want to believe that Frances, too, was in danger. If so, then he was to blame. "You had a lot on your mind."

"That's what I thought . . . before I realized my hand was hurt."

She held it out to him and Chaco frowned at the fading signs of bruises and scrapes. "You didn't do anything to—"

"Nothing."

Chaco suddenly realized Frances had his uncl

undivided attention. Geronimo was staring at her as if weighing her worth. She realized it, too. Her eyes widened and she swallowed hard, but he could tell she was trying not to show fear.

"Doesn't he like me?" Frances whispered, holding the obsidian stare without flinching.

"You are the woman of my sister's son," Geronimo said slowly and in English. "Though I have no love for the White Eyes, I accept you as my family."

"Thank you. I—I am honored," Frances told him.

Geronimo inclined his head, then removed something from a buckskin bag hanging from his gun belt. A small beaded pouch. He held it out to her.

Hesitantly, Frances took it and inspected it more closely. "Is this a medicine bag?"

"War charm," Geronimo told her. "For protection and good luck." At her surprised expression, he said, "In the papers all over the world they say I am a bad man, but this is a bad thing to say. I never do wrong without a cause. There is one God looking down on us all. We are children of the one God. God is listening to me. The sun, the darkness, the winds are all listening."

Frances stared down at the pouch in her hand, then at Geronimo. "Yes, children of one God." Her eyes shone as she said, "This I, too, believe. I accept your gift with respect and with my heart."

As she slipped the pouch into the pocket of her split skirt, Chaco slid back into the Chiricahua dialect and asked his uncle about his plans now that he'd shared his vision. Geronimo was purposely vague and Chaco didn't press him.

A while later, after they'd shared a meal with his uncle and Juh, Chaco figured they'd better get on with their search for Louisa. He and Frances gathered their horses, but before leaving, Chaco couldn't help giving Geronimo advice that came from his head rather than his heart.

"The world is changing, uncle. The old way of life is gone. You must think on how you can let go of what no longer is . . ." he said with more eloquence than normal for him, ". . . and how you can accept what is to be."

The old man's voice was thunderous when he returned, "I am Geronimo. Until the White Eyes find a way to stop me, I will continue to move about like the wind. I will be free to roam and will stay less time than it takes to cast a shadow. I am not an animal to be caged on a piece of arid, inhospitable land. I am Apache."

They clasped shoulders in affection and Chaco turned away from his uncle and mounted his buckskin.

The reticent Juh spoke. "From a thin cloud of blue smoke seen across a chasm, thousands of soldiers in blue uniforms marched against us. Ussen sent me this vision to warn us that, despite our struggle, we will be defeated, perhaps all killed by the government of the White Eyes. With their strength in numbers and powerful weapons, the Bluecoats will eventually exterminate us."

Chaco looked down on his uncle and saw the effect of those words in his grim visage. "I hope this vision is one that can be altered, then."

"Even I am not powerful enough to accomplish this," Geronimo admitted ruefully. "I can only trick such a fate for a while."

"Then make it a very long while, Uncle," Chaco said.

He took off, Frances following close behind. There

would always be war and its casualties. Nothing he could do to stop it. He couldn't save an entire tribe. But with luck and persistence, he could find one scared girl who'd done nothing wrong but to have been born of a union not blessed by the white world; and he could see that the real murderer was punished for her evil deeds.

Fighting exhaustion, Frances wondered how long it took a person to get used to riding all day. If ever. Chaco appeared nearly as tired as she, and he'd practically been born on a horse. He was relentless. He never lost sight of Louisa's tracks, never stopped to rest more than a few minutes. They were on the ground now, several hours after taking leave of Geronimo and his band of warriors.

Chaco trailed tracks on foot aways before saying, "I think Louisa and her friend are lost."

"Why?"

"Because they've looped back in nearly the same area twice now." He remounted and kept going. "Too bad the sun couldn't hold on a while longer. We'll have to make camp soon."

Camp. She'd known it was possible, but she'd prayed it wouldn't happen. They rode until dusk began to settle over the high desert. The thought of sleeping out on the hard, cold ground, prey to things that crawled and slithered in the night, spooked her. If there were rattlers in the area, Frances was nearly certain one must know her name.

Her only comfort came in the thought that Chaco would be nearby. She didn't want to imagine how near that could be . . . if only they could somehow make amends with each other. Though she didn't see what good a temporary truce would do in the long run. Some differences were impossible to gap to make a lasting relationship work. She certainly couldn't condone killing, and whether he would or no, that seemed to be his way of life.

As they began stripping their horses of tack, she asked, "Are Geronimo and his band heading back south?"

"He didn't say."

"You didn't ask?"

"I asked."

"Do you think he's hiding something from you?"

"Being evasive has kept him alive," Chaco said. "I think he's sticking around to look for the witch himself."

Frances knew a moment's panic and almost dropped her mare's saddle on her foot. The heavy leather hit the sand with a resounding smack. "Louisa . . . what if he thinks *she's* the one?"

Chaco shook his head and easily scooped up her saddle, moving it to an open area big enough to stretch out and build a fire. "Geronimo will know his enemy when he faces her. He won't hurt Louisa any more than he would hurt you."

"Because he thinks I'm your woman."

"Aren't you?"

If Frances thought he would follow the provocative question with an assault—physical or emotional—she was wrong. Chaco turned his back on her and started setting up a fire ring.

Yet the implication wouldn't go away.

Was she Chaco's woman? Did she want to be? Yes. She admitted it. But given the differences in their temperaments, in their very code of ethics, was it possible?

Slipping a hand into her pocket, she fingered the war charm Geronimo had given her. A man who had vision, who could see into the future, who could work magic had accepted her into his family. She'd sensed the old warrior's strength and pride. Not unlike Chaco's. Warriors engaged in combat, she told herself. Sometimes they took lives. An accepted fact, especially in the West.

Only she didn't think she could accept it.

She busied herself unrolling blankets into makeshift beds. "Chaco . . . about Martinez."

His back stiffened. "What about him?"

"What exactly happened?"

Still on his haunches where he'd set rocks in a ring, he glanced over his shoulder. "Someone hired him to kill me. I killed him first."

"He told you that?"

"Not in so many words." He rose and began gathering small pieces of dried dead wood from the area. "But he made his intentions clear by his actions."

"What if you were wrong?"

"I wasn't."

"Are you ever wrong?"

He looked up from what he was doing. "Are you?"

They were at an impasse.

It wasn't until much later, after dark cradled the desert and a small fire licked the inky sky, and a pot of something savory warmed at the heart of the blaze that Chaco brought up the gunfight again.

"Killing Martinez sickened me, Frankie." He sat barely a foot away from her on his bedroll. "I didn't know how much I could hate the smell of death until he was sprawled out in the dust."

Her heart beat unevenly at Chaco's nearness, and the softness of his voice combined with the note of regret sent a thrill through her. "Are you telling me you wouldn't do it again?"

"That'd be a fool's promise. A man can't know everything he might be up against in the future. Not even a man who sometimes has visions."

She swallowed her disappointment that he refused to be more definite. "I just don't understand why one human being has to kill another."

"That's the way of the world, the way it's always been."

"Can't things change? Become civilized? People don't go around killing each other back East anymore."

"You sure of that?" He removed the pot from the fire. "Maybe they just don't kill each other in public." He ladled the stew-like contents onto two metal plates.

"Well, murderers are arrested and tried."

"And hung? Think I should be at the end of a hangman's rope for protecting myself?" he asked, his voice soft, yet edgy as he held out her supper.

"I don't want to see you hang," she vowed with passion. "That's the point. Or part of it. I don't want to see any more people die, either. A shoot-out isn't exactly exciting and fun like dime novels make it out to be."

"And I wouldn't kill anyone unless I had to."

They ate in silence, though Frances couldn't keep her mind from the subject. Or from Chaco himself. If she loved the man, shouldn't she be able to accept him just as he was? A product of the rugged, as yet untamed West, he'd survived the best way he knew how. To his credit—or his mother's—he had a heart. And a conscience.

Maybe promises were too much to expect. Maybe *she* was being too rigid in this instance and was the one who needed to change. To learn how to place her trust in what was inside of Chaco rather than fear the image he projected. She had to believe that he would do the right thing and hope that would be to avoid further bloodshed if at all possible.

But was that enough for her?

When they finished eating, they cleaned up, working side by side so close they invariably touched. Longing for more as they sat close to one another, Frances shivered.

"Cold?"

The air *was* cool against her suddenly heated skin. "A little."

He reached across her, the back of his arm brushing her breasts as he brought the blanket up around her shoulders. "Warmer?"

Frances nodded. Staring at his hard features silhouetted by the fire, she felt heat coil deep within her. Her breathing slowed but blood rushed to her extremities.

The silhouette shifted even closer, slowly, allowing her time to move away if she so desired. She stayed where she was, lips parting in anticipation of Chaco's kiss. Covering hers, his mouth was hot and demanding, his tongue seductive, drawing a moan from deep in her throat. Their differences instantly forgotten, Frances was left a woman to his man, and that's all she wanted to consider.

She touched him, at first hesitantly, and then when he deepened the kiss in response, more freely. Her palm smoothed the flat of his muscled stomach, longing for the heat of his skin that his shirt kept from her. He caught her hand and forced it downward until she was cupping the fullness straining his denim pants.

Chaco groaned into her mouth, then pulled away, murmuring, "Ah, Frankie, what you do to me . . ."

Then he sank his mouth into the soft flesh of her neck and sent a streak of goose flesh down her spine. She unbuttoned his denims as he did the same to her split skirt. He was far more adept at this than she, and a moment later had her stripped from the waist down except for her boots while she'd barely uncovered him. To rid him of the denim pants, they'd first have to take off *his* boots.

Stroking him into even greater hardness while considering the boot issue, she was startled when he pulled her over him and quickly sheathed himself inside her before she so much as had time to react. One roughened hand flashed up, over her belly and below her clothing—vest, shirt, camisole. Chaco thumbed a nipple until the flesh pebbled and hardened.

His other hand sought their juncture. He was moving in and out slowly and without depth. A clever finger captured some of her essence and pulled it forward to moisten her sensitive nub. He did this over and over until she couldn't stop herself from moving against his hand. She raised her hips until he nearly slipped free . . . then plunged down hard to recapture his entire length. Each time she repeated the motion, she did so faster, harder, until she was breathing arduously with the exertion and excitement.

Her tender flesh swelled around him and sweat trickled down her spine. Her entire existence came down to three pleasure points where his ingenious hands and pulsing maleness assaulted and filled her.

Riding him hard—not unlike a horse, she realized—Frances threw back her head and sucked in long drafts of cool night air. Never had riding the sorrel pleasured her so intensely.

Then pleasure turned to torment as every fiber of her being labored to reach the pinnacle. Chaco's fingers turned seductively cruel, edging her ever closer. Her mouth opened in a fevered gasp. Her neck muscles strained as a sound started deep within her, straining for release. Through fluttering lashes, she watched the stars shatter into thousands of sparkling pinpoints and her piercing cry echoed through the night.

Chaco shot his hands to her waist, anchoring her in place while he swept up deep inside her, a strong surge of wet warmth pleasuring her even more.

Then he urged her toward him. She fell against his chest and he wrangled her to the ground, his body and arms and legs tangling with hers until she didn't know where one of them ended and the other began. Panting, she was content to lie there staring up at him, nuzzling her cheek into the free strands of his loose hair. He kissed the planes of her face and rolled to his side, finally breaking their intimate connection.

As passion subsided, Frances found humor in their situation. Her smothered laugh was met with a growl.

"What's so funny?"

"Us. We still have our boots on, not to mention other assorted garments."

"Easy enough to fix."

Within minutes, they were both naked and resting together on one bedroll, flesh against flesh.

Holding her tight, he asked, perhaps too casually, "Still planning on going back East?"

Frances remembered threatening to do so as soon as she had enough money . . . before this sense of belonging had grown inside her.

"I don't quite figure what I'd do when I got there," she murmured, placing a soft kiss in the hollow of his throat.

"Teach?"

"I'd say that particular career is over for me."

And not merely because she had no references. She couldn't see subjecting herself to such a restricted life again. She never wanted to relinquish the sense of freedom living in the West had offered her.

"But you do miss civilization."

"Sometimes."

After the gunfight especially.

But she kept that to herself, not wanting to allow the troubling topic to spoil their union. She would have to deal with the problem herself. Resolve it to her own satisfaction. Sometime. Only not now.

"What about you, Chaco? Any plans for the future?"

"Don Armando made me a new offer yesterday," he said, stroking her spine with a gentle hand.

"What sort of offer?"

"Land. He suggested he could spare a few hundred acres of his southeast range, about an hour's fast ride out of Santa Fe. There's water. And a small cabin."

Though she tried, Frances couldn't tell whether or not he viewed the proposal favorably. "And what does he want in return?"

"Me. He wants to me live on the land and either raise my own cattle or come to work for him. My choice. And in return, I would agree to spend time with him, to get to know him better."

"Would that be so bad?"

"My mother—"

"Would probably want this for you."

"He can't bribe me to be his son if I don't want to!"

"Then don't let him. Just give him a chance."

"So, you think I should do it. Give up my job at the Blue Sky and become a rancher."

His hand continued to move along her spine, but the strokes were tense rather than sensual.

"I think coming to terms with your past is more important than managing a casino." Frances would have given anything for her father to bend, to admit he wanted to heal the rift between them. And while she didn't want to give up seeing Chaco every day, neither would she be selfish. "Yes, I think you should do it, but for your sake, not his."

Suspecting she hadn't responded as he'd hoped, for he seemed stiff and withdrawn, Frances curled a leg around his hip and nuzzled his throat. Chaco responded to her like a man who'd been starved for a woman's touch rather than one who'd so recently spent himself in her. If they were to be separated soon, then she wanted to take advantage of each moment they had together. She suspected every relationship between a man and a woman had its problems.

They had more rough spots than most, and that wasn't counting the trouble a *diablera* could cause.

Daybreak saw them back on Louisa's trail. After a night of loving, Frances figured she should be relaxed, but a short sleep had brought with it another nightmare, as if her thinking about the skin-walker no matter how briefly had summoned the evil spirit.

The day had dawned gray and cold, unusual for New Mexico whose skies were normally a vivid blue and temperature was typically a sight more pleasant. Frances only hoped the odd weather didn't portend added obstacles.

It wasn't long before Chaco dashed that fear. Checking tracks on foot he said, "I think we're about to catch up to our runaway."

"How can you tell?"

"They rode straight into that canyon."

"So?"

"I know this country pretty well. And I don't know of another easy way out."

Relief flowed through Frances. "Then we'll be back in Santa Fe before dark."

"I expect so."

The canyon was much larger than Frances might have guessed. The floor had every bit as much growth as the desert outside. She could imagine wandering into the area, then spending twice the time trying to find a way back out again.

"Louisa!" she called a moment after passing through the entrance. "It's Frances!"

Her words bounced around the canyon walls that rose practically straight up to flat-topped mesas. She waited until they reached the area's heart before trying again. The striated reddish rock stared down on them blankly. No sign of life anywhere.

"Are you sure they couldn't have left the way they came?" she asked Chaco.

"No fresh tracks showing they did," he assured her. "They're here somewhere, all right."

They kept riding and Frances noted openings in the rock face high above them. "Could those be caves?"

"Living quarters of a people long gone," he said. "Anasazi."

A more intense inspection revealed what looked like chiseled hand- and footholds leading up to the openings. "If Louisa and her traveling companion took shelter in one of them," Frances asked, "where did they leave their horses?"

A whinny answered the question. "Over there." Chaco pointed to a stand of juniper, through which she saw movement at the base of a cliff whose face was etched with toeholds leading to a sheltered opening.

"Louisa!" Frances yelled, spurring her mare forward.

Before she and Chaco reached the tethered horses, a faint, "Frances?" echoed in return. Then Louisa appeared in the opening above. "It is you!"

Without hesitating, the girl scrambled down the wall, clinging precariously to the rock face. Heart pounding, fearing that with one misstep, Louisa could turn Belle's greatest fear into truth, Frances dismounted. She'd barely caught a glimpse of a blue uniform in the opening before Louisa threw herself into Frances's arms.

"Are you all right?" she asked the girl, whose hair was tangled and clothes disheveled.

"I am now that you're here. I was so stupid."

Holding onto Louisa, Frances stared accusingly at the young officer who had reached the ground but kept his distance and looked decidedly uncomfortable. "Belle is worried sick about you, Louisa."

"I thought Ma'd be glad to be rid of me."

"Your mother loves you. She thought she lost you and that her life was over." Remembering Louisa had vowed she would never take off with some man like her mother had before her, she asked, "You didn't run away because of him, did you?"

Shaking her head, Louisa freed herself but avoided looking at the golden-haired young officer who stood up straighter. "Lieutenant Samuel Strong, U.S. Cavalry, at your service, Ma'am."

"He just thought he could get me to go home," Louisa said. "Instead I got him lost."

"I would have found our way given the chance," Strong protested.

The young officer stayed where he was, staring at

Louisa with a familiar hunger lighting his eyes. Frances didn't know whether to thank him for trying to protect the girl . . . or to have Chaco horsewhip him. From the way they were both acting, *something* had gone on between them.

"We're taking you back to Santa Fe, Louisa," Chaco told her.

"I can't go back."

"A sixteen-year-old girl has no business wandering out on her own." Frances kept her eyes focused on the lieutenant. Sure enough, his tan faded and his expression revealed his surprise at Louisa's tender age.

"They think I killed those men!" the girl protested. "If I go back, they'll hang me!"

"No one's going to hang you," Chaco promised. "I'll see to that by finding the real murderer."

"In the meantime, I'll ask Adolfo to protect you," Frances added. "None of those cowards will argue with his knives."

She was infinitely relieved when Louisa swallowed and nodded her agreement.

As soon as Defiant and the chestnut were saddled, they set off for home, Chaco in the lead, Louisa riding close to Frances, Sam trailing behind.

They stopped a few times to rest the horses and fill their stomachs, but Louisa avoided the lieutenant all the way back to Santa Fe. Frances kept looking at her like she was wondering exactly how close they had come out on the trail. To Louisa's shame, she'd gone against everything she'd told the other woman about how she'd act with a man. After all her fine words, she'd foolishly lost herself in Sam's embrace. Now he had to think she was just like Ma and the girls. Louisa couldn't stand it.

And she worried about Ma's reaction when she learned what happened.

Thankfully, when they rode into Santa Fe and arrived at the Blue Sky just after sunset, all her mother seemed to be concerned about was getting her back in one piece.

"My baby, don't ever scare me like that again!" Belle sobbed, pulling Louisa to her ample bosom in the *placita.*

Feeling like a kid—one that wasn't too bright—Louisa hugged her back. "I won't, Ma, I promise."

"Frances and Chaco, I don't know how to thank you."

Belle's girls poured out of the building and gathered round, all talking at once. Mother and daughter hugged one another and sobbed on each other's shoulders. Frances let Chaco stable their horses while she stuck around, probably to see if there was anything else she could do.

Louisa sneaked a peak at Sam, wishing he would say something—anything—to reassure her.

Silently watching their reunion from the back of his horse—as if he were waiting for *her* to make the first move—Lieutenant Samuel Strong finally turned the chestnut toward Fort Marcy and never looked back.

16

Frances didn't want him. That's the only conclusion Chaco could reach after their talk out in the desert. He didn't understand it. She'd made love to him so passionately . . . though if she had any real feelings for him, she hadn't voiced them. What had he expected from a woman who yearned for civilization, who'd practically pushed him out of his job at the casino and onto a stranger's land?

Well, he wasn't about to waste any time dragging his boots. He'd taken a day to catch his breath and to make certain no lynch mob was roaming the town. Now, he was about to take Frances up on her offer for him to leave.

He'd just thrown his saddlebags on the bed and was about to pack them when she stopped in the doorway to watch.

"So you'll be gone, what? Two, maybe three days?"

Chaco hardened himself against the sight of her.

"Sounds about right." He would be on his way to the de Arguello spread in no time. Rather than quitting outright, he'd taken a few days off. "Just enough time to get a lay of the land." And of the man who would be his father. Then if he didn't cotton to what he learned, he could come back whether Frances liked it or not. "How's Louisa?"

"Still scared," she said, drawing closer. "Though Adolfo is doing his best to entertain her with tales of his youth in Mexico."

In reality, Chaco had yet another purpose for wanting to spend some time on the de Arguello spread. He'd promised to find the real murderer and doubted he could do so by normal means. But he hadn't yet tried the Apache way. That took time and a quiet place. No interruptions. If he truly had the makings of a *di-yin,* even as untrained as he was, perhaps he could seek a vision that would reveal the skin-walker's identity.

For a while, he'd almost been convinced Magdalena had been to blame, but her being a *bruja* didn't mean she had turned her knowledge to the dark side.

He thought about the other women he knew.

"I wonder if Minna Tucker's accusing Louisa isn't the pot calling the kettle black," he said, shoving a change of clothing into the worn leather pouch.

"You think the Tucker woman is capable of killing these young men?"

"Anyone is capable of killing . . . possibly with a few exceptions," he said, giving her a steady stare. He had to hold himself back from grabbing her, throwing her down on the bed and trying to change her mind about wanting him to go. "That Bible-thumper's crazy as a loon. And from what I hear tell, she's a mean drunk when she gets into her patent medicine."

"But the skin-walker's been after you. Does Minna Tucker have something against you?"

"Maybe she thinks *I* shot down her husband." He added his razor and a cake of soap to the clothes. He could smell the lingering fragrance that clung to Frances from her bath last evening—one he'd kept himself from interrupting. "Tucker was a railroad man who was killed by some gunfighter down South."

"But not you?"

Giving her a disgusted frown, Chaco wondered if Frances blamed him for every unnatural death in the Territory. "No, Frances, not me."

Then there was Belle herself, he thought, his mind back on the *diablera*—though he didn't say so since the two women were friends. Frances had told him about Belle's knifing her first husband and ending up in an asylum. That proved she was capable of dangerous behavior. Frances had also told him Louisa's father had been killed by a posse. He'd been a deputy in Texas about that time and had killed a few Comanches himself in the line of duty. Belle's husband? He didn't know.

"Did you ever think about Ynez?" Frances asked as he strapped the saddlebags shut. "I know she's your father's wife, but—"

"I've given her some thought."

Frances nodded in approval. "There's something about her that's odd, certainly not in keeping with the modest Spanish wife she pretends to be. And the way she looked at you at the *estancia* . . ." She flushed. "You said the *diablera* would wear two faces. I've seen both of hers."

"I'll keep that in mind," Chaco promised, wondering if she could possibly be jealous of Ynez's interest in him. Wishful thinking.

Though he, too, was wary of Ynez. He suspected that while his father's wife was willing to sacrifice herself to him, it wasn't because she liked him. No doubt she'd figured on being a rich widow someday until he'd shown up. Given that de Arguello so desperately wanted an heir—even an illegitimate one—that made problems for Ynez and she no doubt was trying to make the best of the situation. He still couldn't believe the arrogance that made her think she could control him with her body.

Shouldering his saddlebags, he said, "I'd best get started."

Frances backed off, her expression strange. Chaco would swear she was covering some emotion she didn't want him to see. "You'd best," she said in a small voice.

He couldn't help himself. He couldn't brush by her as if she was nothing to him. Pride be damned. He didn't know how much longer he'd be around the casino . . . or she'd be in Santa Fe.

Who was to say she might not pack her bags and head back to her precious Boston before he even returned?

Wrapping his free arm around her waist, Chaco swept Frances into his chest. He stared down into the face of the woman he loved more than life itself. Her eyes widened, her lips parted, her breath quickened. He quickened, too. Within seconds, before his mouth sank over hers, he was in pain. Physical. Heartfelt. He was a fool. But for a moment, he allowed it.

He kissed her like there was no tomorrow for them . . . no doubt the truth.

Then he set her aside. She blinked as if waking from a dream. He thought she might say something. Ask him not to go, maybe? But she pursed her lips together and moved back to let him pass.

Chaco strode by her without another word, wondering if she would really disappear from his life, as if taken from him by the unfeeling wind . . . .

Dark shadows filled the room as she huddled in the chair before the fire, staring into the flames, sipping at the liquid that gave her added strength.

Rested, she was fully recovered, more powerful than ever. A good thing since Chaco Jones was trying to fight her on her own territory. She ignored his puny attempts to summon her. To command her to enter his vision.

More fool he . . if she answered . . .

Taking another draft of the magic potion, she thought long and hard about meeting him head on. She hungered for revenge, for the taste of his manhood and his throat. But something was stopping her. A recognition of a sentient power greater than hers hovering nearby. Instinct had kept her safe through all these years, and she was not about to spit in its face.

Could Chaco be the source of this disturbance, after all? Surely not alone. Perhaps he had gained strength from the woman. Frances Gannon had power she did not even recognize in herself, a power that had assisted her when they met in the dream.

That had to be the danger she sensed—the two of them together—what else could it be? Perhaps she could find a way to play one against the other.

Just as her juices began flowing, a voice called her, stirring her from her liquid reverie. Setting down the cup, she hid her annoyance and went to answer.

She would think on the solution to her problem later.

* * *

Frances had never been inside a jail of any kind before. The very idea of being locked up, caged like an animal, frightened and sickened her. And that's exactly what had happened to Lieutenant Samuel Strong for desertion of his duty, temporary and as noble as it had been. She felt obligated to visit the young man the morning after Chaco rode north.

The sergeant left them alone in the narrow, dank room. The first thing she noticed was how disheveled and tired Strong looked as he stood at respectful attention.

"Mrs. Gannon, I didn't expect to see you here."

"You thought Louisa would come?" When he tightened his jaw rather than answer, she explained, "We're keeping a close watch on her in case anyone decides to pursue this murder accusation again."

"That's ridiculous!" Breaking his rigid military stance, he grabbed the bars. "Louisa couldn't . . . I mean, Miss Janks wouldn't hurt a fly."

She looked deep into his guilt-ridden, blue-green eyes. "You care about her?"

Once more he withdrew, though not quite so far. "That would be inappropriate."

"Because she's a half-breed?" Frances asked quietly.

"I don't give a damn who her father was . . . pardon my language, Ma'am."

"But your commanding officer does. I understand that's why you're behind bars." Or so Adolfo had passed on this gossip to her. A graduate of West Point, Strong had supposedly sunk beneath himself by taking up with a heathen. "For how long?"

"Until my transfer to Fort Sill, Oklahoma, comes through."

"You're leaving?"

"I'm afraid I was given no choice." He drew himself up tight and looked straight over Frances's shoulder. "Would you be so kind as to do me a favor, Ma'am?"

"What's that?"

"If there's any . . . results . . . if Louisa finds herself in . . ." He swallowed hard rather than put his obvious concern into words. "Would you find a way to let me know?"

"I'll let you know."

Having learned what she'd come for, Frances left Fort Marcy on foot. Though he appeared even younger than he let on, Strong seemed to be in love with Louisa and willing to do right by her if only she'd let him.

Louisa, on the other hand, pretended she barely knew Lieutenant Samuel Strong existed. She refused to talk about what happened during those two days in the wilderness. Not to Belle. Not to her. More odd yet, she spoke of being eager to return to school, had even agreed to finish her education under the tutelage of the Sisters of Loretto.

Belle had been too happy to see what Frances had—that something was terribly wrong.

Beneath Louisa's newly cooperative facade, Frances recognized a very unhappy girl. Young woman, she corrected herself. For Belle's daughter had lost something of her youth these past days, both physically and emotionally. Frances suspected she'd also lost her heart.

That made two of them, Frances thought, Chaco's image clear in her mind. She realized she was equally reluctant to discuss her own situation with anyone. Was love always so frightening? She felt as if the emotion addled her senses so that she didn't know what she wanted. One moment she was pushing

Chaco toward a reconciliation with his past. The next, fearing that she was driving him away forever, she wanted to hang onto him for all she was worth.

She was still ruminating over the unfairness of it all when she walked into the Blue Sky Palace and Luz jumped up from the sitting area to intercept her.

"A message . . . I did not know where to find you . . ."

"Luz, you're scaring me. What happened? Is it Louisa?"

The Mexican shook her head vigorously. "Señor Chaco—he's been hurt!"

Frances felt as if someone had punched her square in the chest. She gasped for air and the room's walls seemed to be moving unnaturally. The next thing she knew, the other woman had a steadying arm around her and was leading her to a sofa. Convinced her legs wouldn't hold her another second, Frances gratefully sank to the upholstered cushions. Out of nowhere came the image of the man she loved, a bloody gash where his throat should be.

"He's not—?"

"Dead? No!"

But Luz's expression didn't put Frances at ease. "How bad is it? What happened?"

"Something spooked the cattle and Señor Chaco found himself on the ground beneath their hooves."

"He was trampled?"

Luz nodded. "His life is not in danger, but he is in great pain. A broken leg. And his shoulder. He asked for you."

Frances popped back off the sofa. "Then I must go to him immediately."

"There is no one here to take you. Adolfo—"

"Must stay with Louisa. I'll go alone. I remember the way."

"I can run to the stable and have your horse ready by the time you change clothes."

Frances hugged Luz. "Thank you." About to run upstairs, she asked, "Does Belle know?"

Luz shrugged. "She is nowhere. No one has seen her since last night."

"When she shows up, you'll tell her what happened and where I've gone?"

"Yes, Señora Gannon."

Halfway up the staircase, Frances paused. "Luz, one more thing. Please call me Frances."

A fleeting smile crossed Luz's face as she made for the front door.

Frances had no smiles in her. Not when Chaco was hurt, not before she could assure herself that he would be all right. That he had asked for her, was waiting for her, brought some measure of gladness to her heart as she quickly changed into her riding clothes. Geronimo's war pouch dangled from a leather thong at her throat. Though she hadn't thought deeply about her reasons for continuing to wear it, she hadn't been without the token since the old warrior had given it to her. She tucked the pouch inside her shirt, feeling an odd sort of security with it in place snuggled between her breasts.

After tugging on her boots, Frances raced to the stable where Luz was already waiting with the sorrel. As she started off, she heard the Mexican call after her, "May God go with you!"

Mere weeks ago, she would have closed her mind to the blessing. But things had changed. *She* had changed. Living with a new openness in which she'd heard varied versions—both good and evil—of peoples' beliefs, she'd been forced to face what she'd considered her own lack of faith.

Geronimo had spoken of the one God and that all people were God's children. Isn't that what she'd always believed deep in her own heart? Within every person, no matter his or her background, there existed the capacity for good or evil and all the conditions in between. Frances now knew that she didn't have to reject her own faith because it didn't correspond with her minister father's. She could choose her own path, find her own way.

Content with that . . . she, too, hoped God would ride with her.

The miles flew by, though she kept her mare alternating between a fast walk and a comfortable lope. Though she'd only been to the de Arguello spread once, the visit had been recent enough so she remembered her way. Assuming Chaco was at the *estancia*, she wouldn't have any trouble finding him.

After riding for more than an hour, knowing she was close to rejoining him, Frances pushed her mount a bit. The path they followed wound through a series of small brush- and rock-covered hills. An odd feeling began plaguing her, as if something was really wrong. Something more than Chaco having sustained a few broken bones.

The scent of danger filled the air.

The mare smelled it, too. She ignored Frances's attempts to make her go faster. Foamy white lather gathered along the sorrel's neck and she kept throwing her head as if fighting going forward at all.

"Easy, girl," Frances murmured more calmly than she was feeling.

A sudden movement to the side gave her a start and she whipped around in the saddle to see a shaggy body lope from a nearby copse of juniper at the crest of a hill.

A wolf?

The mare whinnied and bolted to the side, leaving Frances behind. Suspended in midair for a second, she saw the ground come up to meet her.

The wolf was coming, too.

Luckily some chamisa broke her fall and she scrambled to her feet uninjured, not for an instant taking her eyes off the creature that was larger than she imagined it should be. Its jaws dripped with white foam and a terrible snarl issued from its throat.

Was this a real wolf? Or a skin-walker?

Terrified, Frances ran with jaws snapping at her heels. Then the creature fell back. Ran along one side . . . then the other. It was playing with her.

Without any weapon with which to defend herself, she realized the beast could kill her if it chose.

A weapon?

Frances looked around frantically, but saw nothing she could use to threaten the wolf. Then she remembered the pouch. But did she believe it would work?

Hadn't she just decided she could take her own path? That in matters of faith she could make her own choices? Then she chose to believe that Geronimo was the powerful shaman and protector he was said to be, and that his magic was the good that would turn away evil.

Charging up a hill, she slowed to a stop a fourth of the way to the top. The wolf began circling her, each pass closer than the last. Fear pounded at her heart and dried her mouth. Praying to the God she had always believed in that she was doing the right thing, she freed the pouch from beneath her shirt and gripped it tight.

When the wolf made a move for her, Frances held

it out. "Evil, be wary of a greater power!" she shouted, trying not to feel foolish.

Halting immediately, the wolf let loose a horrible almost-human-sounding shriek.

Of frustration?

Frances backed away. Though it followed, the creature kept a wary distance, head hung low. Frances clung to the pouch for all she was worth. Her blood flowed fast and furious and she experienced an exhilarating sense of achievement.

It was working . . .

Encouraged, she looked around. Her horse was nowhere in sight. Uncertain of how far she might have to walk—and how unpleasant that experience could be with a wolf trailing her—she thought the sensible thing would be to wait someplace safe. Surely someone would come along eventually and give her a ride to the *estancia*.

After a better examination of the surrounding hills, she noticed an opening in the rock above a short distance away. A cave? It appeared cruder than the one Louisa and the lieutenant had taken refuge in, but it could provide her with shelter nevertheless. On closer examination, Frances decided that it would do.

Resting in the opening, she was protected on three sides. The wolf would have to come for her straight on. She watched the shaggy creature pace back and forth as if trying to make up its mind. Finally, it turned and came straight for her. Holding onto the pouch with her left hand, Frances picked up a rock with the right.

When the wolf was within mere feet of her, its muscles bunching as if it was ready to spring, she threw the rock and shouted, "Evil, begone!"

Yelping at contact, the wolf slunk away, belly close to the ground.

Frances took a shaky breath and sank to the floor of the cave, where she gathered more rocks into an ammunition pile. Hopefully, someone would come along before she had to use them. She had a clear view of a winding section of road below. All she had to do was to remain alert.

A harder task than she had imagined.

Minutes stretched into what seemed like hours. The early afternoon sun beat down on the cave's entrance. The growing warmth dried her mouth and made her eyes heavy. She fought the urge to doze lest she miss some movement from below.

She concentrated on Chaco. Thought about how much she loved him. Sent him a silent message that she would soon be at his side.

Surely someone was bound to come along before sunset.

What if no one came? What then? Should she have set off for the *estancia* on foot? It wasn't too late to do so now. While trying to make up her mind, she heard a scrabbling sound nearby, like loose rocks being disturbed.

Had the wolf returned?

Her heartbeat quickened. Increasing her vigilance, she picked up other sounds more clearly. Quick, light footsteps and a ragged sobbing.

Another woman?

Armed with a large rock lest she be fooled into letting down her guard, Frances inched out of the cave's mouth for a more encompassing view of the area. She was startled by the sight of a bedraggled dark-haired woman, clothes ripped, hair straggling around her face and neck, dragging a leather bag and stumbling in her general direction. Good Lord—Ynez de Arguello. Frances caught her breath. The Spanish woman didn't realize she was being observed. She seemed disoriented, running aimlessly, and rivulets of tears rolled down her dirt-streaked face.

Tripping and falling to her knees, she gasped, "Help me! *Dios*, someone help me!" while fearfully gazing over her shoulder.

Before Frances gave herself time to think about it, she yelled, "Over here!"

It was only when a sobbing Ynez turned wide eyes toward the cave that Frances remembered the skinwalker was a woman. And Ynez was certainly suspect.

But the woman's expression of relief and gratitude seemed real when she staggered toward the cave. "Thank God, thank God! A wolf frightened my horse and the carriage overturned. I was lucky to escape with my life!" Then her brow furrowed as she focused on Frances's makeshift weapon. "And you? Why are you here?"

The rock prickled her hand. "The wolf." But unable to bring herself to throw it at a fellow human being without proof of that person's guilt, Frances lowered her hand, though she kept a sturdy grip on the rock. Her suspicions were not completely eased. "You had no weapon?"

Ynez slashed a palm across her tear-ravaged cheeks. "I despise guns."

"Then how did you get away?"

"That creature was distracted feeding on my horse's throat." Ynez shivered delicately but kept herself in control. "Then it followed. It is there—the ears in the chamisa." She pointed. "You see?"

Frances didn't. She stiffened when the other woman drew closer. What should she do?

"You used mere rocks to keep the beast away?" Ynez asked, sounding amazed.

Frances edged the truth. "I didn't have a choice."

"You do not think . . ." Ynez licked her lips. "The creature the Apache were after. Could this be the one?"

"The skin-walker?" Frances gazed hard at Ynez. The woman seemed utterly distraught. "Possibly."

The Spanish woman touched her fingers to her forehead and chest as if to cross herself, saying, "Then mere stone would not be enough to protect you." When Frances didn't respond, Ynez focused on the base of her throat. "Is that a medicine bag?" Without waiting for an answer, she said, "That must be it, then! Magic kept you safe!"

Responding to Ynez's desperate tone, Frances finally admitted, "This was given to me by a great *di-yin*."

"You will share the contents," Ynez pleaded softly, "to keep me safe?"

"Share?" Frances's hand went to the pouch. Already feeling guilty at not instantly agreeing, she murmured, "I don't know."

"Have you no gratitude?" Tears spilled down Ynez's cheeks again. "I sent a servant to you with the message from your Chaco."

"You did? Luz didn't say."

Before she could ask how Chaco was, Ynez added, "And this after my husband forbade it. Don Armando was so furious with me that he made me afraid for my safety." She lowered her eyes. "How ironic that I was heading for shelter with a friend when the wolf . . ." Swallowing hard, she continued, "Surely you would not let another human being die when you could prevent it."

Frances knew Ynez was right. "But I don't know

what would happen if I disturb the contents of the pouch."

"They would work the same. Please," Ynez said, fumbling in her skirts and pulling out a lace-edged handkerchief, which she held out in the flat of her hand. "Just a pinch. I promise you won't miss it."

Guilt would plague her if anything happened to Ynez because of her refusal. Reluctantly, Frances dropped the rock, removed the pouch from around her throat and loosened it. As she made to pour a bit into the other woman's handkerchief, Ynez lunged forward, knocking the little bag out of her hands. The contents sprayed everywhere.

Ynez screamed and frantically rubbed at her face where some of the powder had settled.

Frances at once flew to the ground and tried to gather up the contents. But Ynez intercepted her—pushed her so hard that Frances sprawled on her back—and began stomping the white powder with her booted foot, scattering it and grinding it into the earth.

Too late, Frances realized her mistake in allowing her heart to rule her head.

Ynez's features seemed to change. Her teeth looked longer, her nails sharper, and her hate-filled eyes seemed to glow as they turned on Frances.

"Stupid fool. Your silly kindness has destroyed you. First coming to rescue your lover when he has no need of you. Then allowing yourself to be taken in by a simpering woman!"

Ynez wasn't simpering now. She was gloating despite the terrible burns marring her beauty. The powder had burned her badly, Frances realized, so that Ynez would probably be scarred for the rest of her life.

"Now you no longer have protection against me," the witch said with an evil laugh. "You, Frances Gannon, will die!"

17

"You mean to kill me?" Frances asked in a too-calm voice.

Furious that she might have been maimed by the insipid woman's potion—the skin on one side of her face still sizzled as if it had been torched—Ynez stared at her latest victim through hate-filled eyes. Beauty being her greatest asset in the mortal world, she would revenge herself for its slightest loss.

"I shall feast on your blood."

She could already taste it, all the more sweet because it would give her power over Chaco, as well. Unfortunately, having once turned herself into a creature by light of day—an incredible feat that exhibited the extent of her true strength—she could not do so again until sunset, when power once more would infuse her spirit.

"Why?" Frances asked, expression both puzzled and horrified. "What makes a human being turn into an animal?"

"Being treated as an animal. The man whom I

believed was my father raped me after my mother died when I was twelve." Ynez revealed this without emotion, for she had learned to believe this incident gave her the strength to become who she was. "That is when I learned that my true father was an Apache slave, making me nothing but chattel. The bastard could do what he wanted with me. And he did . . . until I killed him."

"And with that you turned into a skin-walker?"

"Of course not!" Annoyed, Ynez paced the narrow entrance of the cave. "I learned magic from my real father's mother who was an Apache *diablera*. She thought I would turn my gifts against the Anglos and Spaniards who decimated 'our' people." Ynez spat on the ground. "I never wanted to be Indian."

"There's nothing wrong with being part Apache."

Ynez held herself back from striking out at Frances now. This putrid Anglo did not understand the pride she had had in her Spanish conquistador ancestry. Pride that had died a quick and painful death. Even so, she had never let on to anyone that she was not descended from the pure blood of Hidalgos.

"Taking the wolf's spirit was a difficult, painful process." The little fool knew nothing of the rigorous ceremonies, the difficulty of capturing a wolf, tearing out its throat while it still lived and drinking its blood. "I almost died. But I was strong. I survived."

"You didn't make yourself better." Still on the ground, Frances shook her head. "You've killed so many people . . . and for what?"

"More than you can ever know . . . and for good reasons. My first husband and many, many servants. Armando's legal children and that cow Mercedes whom he worshiped."

Ynez remembered her horror at being forced to

marry an old Spanish Don her supposed aunt chose for her so many years ago, this before she had come to terms with her true strength. To think that her first husband had expected her to birth his little bastards. Disgusting. She had had no choice but to warm his bed, but she had used an ancient method of preventing conception.

After she had grown weary of his demands, she had slowly poisoned him to death, just as she had begun to do with Armando until the question of the inheritance had surfaced. She had married a second time merely to add to her own wealth, not to find herself placed back under the thumb of some distant relative. As powerful as she was, she was still a woman living mostly in a mortal world, and therefore subject to the vagaries of custom and law.

"Did you ever think of turning your strengths to something positive?" Frances asked.

Ynez was amazed. "Why?"

"You are a human being . . . or were."

"Human beings are ambitious and unafraid to crush those who stand in their way."

"If they're warped, yes."

"And if they are not, they are weak. Like you, Frances Gannon. Prepare to suffer a terrible death, as did the men who thought they might use me to their will."

Ynez smiled, baring her sharp teeth at the Anglo woman, who seemed unable to take this all in. The stupid fool was closing her eyes, moving her mealy mouth in what was undoubtedly a silent prayer.

More fool she . . . her god would be of no help to her now.

* * *

Sitting with his back against a twisted pinon trunk on a hill overlooking the land that was his for the taking, Chaco felt a sense of urgency he couldn't identify. Kind of a buzzing started at the back of his brain—a sound like a bee made—and he couldn't make it stop. As he stared out at the gentle slopes, and at the small cabin in their midst, the odd feeling that plucked at him intensified.

Maybe it was a sign. Maybe if he increased his effort, he might see the *diablera* at last.

He'd been trying to summon the shape-changer in her human form off and on for nearly a day now. After a short obligatory visit to the *estancia* the morning before, he'd made himself at home in the isolated cabin. Going without food or drink, he'd spent most of his time communing with nature. Earth. Water. Sky. Wind. All he'd gotten for his efforts so far was a light head and a naggingly empty stomach.

Calling up a vision wasn't as easy as he'd hoped, but Chaco was determined to keep trying until he succeeded.

Focusing on the buzzing, he closed his eyes and took deep, slow breaths. Inside his mind, he created the image of a wolf. Large, shaggy, open-jawed and red-eyed. The woman riding him in the dream had been red-eyed, so he concentrated on that part of the creature, as if he could mesmerize it to reveal the hidden human features behind the long nose and tawny fur.

He met resistance.

And sensed a wild terror that was not his own. His heart beat hard as he concentrated. The buzzing clarified into words. A woman's voice. But saying what? Dry as the air of the Southwest was, beads of sweat broke out along his skin as he tried to remove himself from everything but this presence that sought him.

Chaco, I need you.

A chill shot up his spine when he sensed rather than heard Frances's plea.

She'll kill me when the sun goes down. Find me, Please, But be careful . . . don't be fooled.

"Fooled by what? Who? Who is she?" he whispered, but the vision of Frances didn't answer.

He pictured her hazel eyes, wide with fright. Her generous mouth set in a grimace. Her golden-brown hair tumbling around her dirt-streaked, heart-shaped face. Dirt-streaked? Why? He pulled back, peered around her into the shadows.

He again sensed rather than saw . . . but this time the something was evil.

The skin-walker.

Inside his mind, he backed up even more, but no matter how far he went, the creature remained elusive. The harsh echo of her laughter was haunting. And maddening. She was playing with him and enjoying herself. He would enjoy wringing her neck when he could get his hands around it.

He backed up further until the sun bathed him with its fading light and saw himself sitting in this very spot overlooking the cabin.

Opening his eyes, Chaco rose, mounted his buckskin, and, as if still in a vision, turned the horse back on the road toward Santa Fe.

Chaco, I know I can make you hear me!

He urged his horse faster toward the voice carried to him on the wind . . .

He soon came across another mare. Frances's horse, loose, scared, but too exhausted to try to elude him. Using a gentle voice, he coaxed the horse into remaining calm. Calmer than he was feeling, for now he was certain Frances was nearby and in harrowing danger.

He gathered the mare's dangling reins, then tracked the horse's route to find its rider.

A while later, he slowed when he found the spot where the mare had dislodged Frances.

The hair on the back of his neck stood on end. He was being watched. He whipped around and his gaze connected with a dark maw. A cave. Waves of invisible evil assaulted him. Hatred. Bloodlust. Death.

Instinct kicked in, allowing him to sense more. Anguish. Fear. For *him*.

"Frances?"

"Chaco!" her voice echoed. "Be careful or . . . ah—h!"

His gut wrenched and a fist squeezed his heart at her cry. Frances was afraid for him when she was the one in imminent danger. Urging the buckskin up the face of the hill was a futile effort. His horse whinnied and side-stepped, and the mare lunged away from him, trying to tear her reins from his hand. The buckskin made to follow. There was nothing to do, but to dismount and free both horses. Then he could concentrate on the evil who posed as a human being.

Without taking his eyes off the cave entrance, he dropped lightly to the ground, and gave both horses a pat on the rear. "Stay close," he ordered softly, hoping they would respond to his firm tone if not understand his words.

At last, he would face the skin-walker.

He hadn't seen her in his vision, but he was certain he knew her identity. He'd guessed it, and now he felt a familiar chill that had enveloped him every time he'd visited the de Arguello *estancia*. And so, when he touched his boot to the ledge that spread before the rocky shelter, and Frances came flying out of the cave's mouth with Ynez's hand attached to her golden-brown hair, Chaco wasn't surprised. He continued moving toward the women, only to freeze when he saw the gun Ynez dug cruelly into Frances's side.

"Do not be too daring, Chaco, or I shall be forced to shoot her."

He could think of worse ways for a person to die, especially if Ynez was able to skin-walk on command. Totally attuned to her now, though, he sensed a weakness. If he remained alert, he might be able to use that to overpower her.

"What is it you want?" he asked.

"Something you were not willing to give, your interest being elsewhere." She gave the hair in her fist a cruel tug, making Frances cry out yet again. "You sealed your own fate." She waved the gun at him. "On the ground, face down."

Chaco did as she ordered. "You're going to shoot me in the back?"

"If you force me to it . . . but I would rather enjoy myself."

From where he lay, Chaco saw Ynez release Frances. Keeping the gun on the woman he loved, she backed up to the cave's entrance where she retrieved some lengths of rope from a leather satchel. She held them out.

"Hands behind your back, Chaco. And you may have the honor of tying up your lover," she told Frances.

"So that you can kill him? Never!"

"Then I shall kill you." Ynez took careful aim at Frances's chest.

Making Chaco frantic for her life. "Do what she says, Frankie!"

Ynez grinned triumphantly. "And tie him securely."

Chaco stared at Ynez's scarred face, unnerved her a bit, as Frances took the rope and went about the task. He made tight fists and held his wrists apart so slightly that Ynez would never be able to tell he was leaving room to free himself unless she checked. He didn't think she wanted to get that close, not now, not in her human form.

He smelled her fear.

And concentrated on that. Used his mind to bore into hers, to send her a vision of his breaking her scrawny lupine neck with his bared hands. He didn't miss the fact that she stepped back slightly.

Now it was his turn to grin, and he taunted Ynez while Frances tied his ankles together. "So what you got planned for this party?" He couldn't do as good a job keeping these bonds loose, but he did his best.

Ynez's eyes narrowed. "Why, I have a special treat for you, Señor Jones. When the sun sets, you shall see your precious lover's throat torn out." Her smile was feral. "And perhaps other more tender parts you are fond of. If you wish, we can share."

Chaco forced himself not to react visibly, but his heart was practically pounding through his chest. He'd never hated so much, never had the true urge to kill before. His taking part in gunfights over the years had been mostly business, and he'd been mostly removed.

But he would kill Ynez de Arguello for the sheer satisfaction of it if he could. She was responsible for ending untold lives. Now she was threatening the woman he loved.

He would savor her death.

Surely Frances would understand . . .

First he had to get loose. In the meantime, he would concentrate on sending Ynez visions of her own destruction that would hopefully keep her off balance until he could do something about it.

Frances watched Ynez pace. The woman's nerves were getting to her. *Chaco* was getting to the witch, for every so often she gave him a look of pure hatred that seared the very air between them. When Ynez wasn't looking at him, Chaco was working on freeing his wrists.

"What are you waiting for?" Frances finally asked, thinking to draw Ynez's attention to herself and away from Chaco. "If you're going to kill us anyway, why don't—"

"Frankie!" he protested.

"—you just do it?" she finished, ignoring him.

Ynez's teeth seemed to lengthen when she said, "I prefer to feed on fresh meat."

Frances tightened her stomach against the revulsion the words conjured. "That means you have to wait."

"I did not say this."

"How long?" Sensing Ynez's nerves were fraying, she hoped to do more damage. The less certain the witch was of herself, the better. "Sundown, right? Is that when you can easily turn into the creature?"

Staring into the other woman's eyes, Frances knew she'd scored a point.

"Dusk will be falling soon," Ynez countered.

From the corner of her eye, Frances noticed Chaco's progress. One hand was practically free of the bonds. Ynez was standing slightly in front of him and therefore would have to turn to see.

"But are you certain you'll have the strength to transform yourself again," Frances probed, "since you already appeared as a wolf in the daylight?"

The disfigured face snarled at her. "Stop this nonsense, or you will not live so long to see the sun set."

"What if I choose not to believe in skin-walkers?"

"Then you are more stupid than I thought," the other woman told her with a harsh laugh.

"Why? Are the gods you worship more powerful than mine? Perhaps if Chaco and I pray hard enough, we can prevent you from turning into this wolf-creature."

Ynez's uncertainty grew. "Shut your stupid mouth!"

"Did you know Chaco is considered *di-yin* by his mother's people?"

"This is true," Chaco said, hands still for a moment. "Geronimo is my mother's brother."

Ynez's fine nostrils flared and she turned wide eyes on him. "Lies!"

Frances used their bit of leverage. "Who do you think gave me that war pouch? Geronimo is responsible for the loss of your beauty."

"This disfigurement is only temporary!" Ynez screeched.

"He's looking for you, Ynez," Frances continued. "Can't you feel his power?"

"I told you to be silent!"

"Do you really think he would let you harm his nephew without seeking retribution?"

Ynez stepped forward and slashed out with a clawlike hand. Frances felt the sting of sharp nails ripping at her flesh, even as she pulled her cheek away. The distraction was thorough enough so Ynez didn't see Chaco free his hands.

"Are you afraid, Ynez?" Frances asked softly. "How does it feel to know your life might end?"

"Enough! You are the one who will die!"

Aiming the gun at Frances, Ynez took a step back. Suddenly, Chaco lunged forward, knocking his shoulder into the back of her legs. The gun discharged and flew from her grasp as she rushed Frances, who might as well have tried to fight a giant, such was the greatness of Ynez's strength. The witch grabbed her by the throat and squeezed. At once, spots of light hovered before Frances's eyes.

Aware of Chaco untying the bonds from his ankles, she prayed for the strength to hang on a little longer. She clawed at the burned side of the other woman's face, but her efforts were to no avail. Ynez's dark eyes seemed to glow as Frances felt the life drain from her, as if the witch stole her waning strength and made it her own. The hands choking her burned with an unnatural heat.

Then a huge jolt sent them both flying and the promise of death was ripped from her throat.

Choking, Frances tried to drag in air. She lay on her side, chest heaving, dazedly watching Chaco and Ynez roll one over the other across the rocky ledge, which was now thrown into deep shadow.

The sun had set . . .

Her heart drumming loudly in her ears, Frances pushed herself to a sitting position. Though he tried, Chaco couldn't subdue Ynez. She was wild-eyed and snarling. As she rolled up, straddling Chaco, a low-throated growl issued from her throat.

Wildly, Frances looked for the gun that now lay in the maw of the cave. Unable to rise, she crawled, Chaco's grunts of pain urging her on. A glance over her shoulder terrified her, for, holding Chaco's head pinned between both hands, Ynez thrust it down against a sharp protrusion in the rock. With a groan, Chaco went still. Panting down at her victim, Ynez grinned, her face seeming to stretch into something far more feral.

"God, no!" Frances gasped, lunging for the gun.

Ynez was shape-changing right before her eyes. Shakily rising to her feet, she clasped the weapon with both hands. "Leave him be, witch!"

But the thing that had been Ynez was beyond reason. Or recognition. She was neither woman nor wolf, but some creature in between. Her jaws slathering, she gazed hungrily—covetously—at Chaco's throat. Frances knew that if she didn't shoot to kill, he was a dead man for sure.

Praying her aim was good, she squeezed the trigger. The gun fired with a kick. Frances hung on, encouraged by the skin-walker's inhuman scream. Chaco stirred. He was regaining consciousness. Over him, the witch was holding her side, blood oozing between fingers that now looked all too human.

"You dared shoot me!" Ynez growled, as Frances held the gun up toward her once more. She meant to finish the job.

"Frankie, don't," Chaco called. "You can't."

"I have to." But the gun wavered slightly.

"She's weakened. You don't have to shoot her again. You don't have to kill her."

Chaco's words cut through her haze of hatred for Ynez. She lowered the gun. Tears spilled from her eyes as she realized she not only was able but was perfectly willing to kill another person under the correct circumstances. No, not a person, she reassured herself. A creature that hadn't one iota of the nobility of a real wolf.

Chaco struggled up from the ground and threw a dazed-looking Ynez to her backside. She didn't even attempt a struggle. He was right—she was through.

"Get the rope," he told Frances.

She found one of the freed lengths and handed it to him. He bound Ynez's hands together in front of her, so that she could use her arm to keep pressure on her still-bleeding side.

"I almost killed her," Frances said, still amazed at herself. In a haze of terror, she'd abandoned everything she'd believed in.

Not everything . . . she'd actually managed to renew her faith in an odd way.

"It's only a flesh wound," Chaco assured her. Though obviously serious enough to slow the witch down. Frances almost forgot about Ynez for a moment as the man she loved took her in his arms and whispered in her hair, "If anything had happened to you, I would have wanted to die, too."

Having felt the same, Frances burrowed closer, nodded and asked, "Now what?"

Chaco shrugged. "Supposing we bring her into Santa Fe—"

Ynez laughed weakly. "And tell everyone you've caught a skin-walker? Perhaps they'll lock *you* up."

"She's right," Frances said, for a moment almost regretting her aim hadn't been better. Then there would be no decision to make. "Maybe we should turn her over to the Jicarilla." She hadn't forgotten the Apache threat to Chaco lest he produce the witch.

"If they kill her, there'll no doubt be massacres, red and white, all through this part of the Territory," he said. "And then how do I explain my actions to my father?"

"The truth?" That he was recognizing Don Armando as his parent didn't escape Frances. "He's lived with her. Surely he has some sense of her evil."

"Fools!" Ynez spat from where she rocked herself on the ground. "Armando never even guessed that I was responsible for the death of his legitimate children

... and that he would have been next but for the inconvenient matter of the will."

Chaco's eyes went all spooky. "Then someone should tell him. Maybe he's the one who should mete out your punishment."

"Aiyee!" Face contorted with pain, Ynez drew up her knees and folded in on herself, bowing her head as if trying to hide her weakness and fear.

Frances was amazed that Chaco was so calm and rational, that he would even consider bringing Ynez in rather than kill her himself. But hadn't he told her he only killed when he had to? She hadn't been able to understand that kind of reasoning then as she did now. If he hadn't stopped her, the witch *would* be dead, and at her hand, Frances realized.

"Will Don Armando believe you?"

"If not me alone, he'll listen to us both."

Chaco's eyes bore into her and the next thing Frances knew, his mouth was covering hers. In his kiss, she recognized hunger for reassurance. She gave him all she had. The embrace lasted for barely a moment . . . long enough for Ynez to scurry away. By the time Frances realized there was a problem, the other woman was running down the dusk-dusted hillside, laughing at them, her teeth shredding the bonds at her wrists.

"She's getting away!" Frances cried, watching her literally chew through the rope like a wild animal.

"Never fear!" Ynez called as she threw the binding back at them. "I shall find *you* and have my tasty revenge later!"

Chaco was already on his way after her, Frances following close behind until he stopped dead in his tracks and she jarred into his back. For from every direction came horses with riders holding lit torches aloft. Ynez, too, crashed to a halt and screamed at the sight of Geronimo himself calmly placing a flaming arrow against his bow.

"Evil, you have met your match!" the shaman thundered as Ynez backed away and looked around wildly for an escape that was not hers. "Now die!"

Geronimo aimed quickly and released the arrow. The *thwang* reverberated up Frances's spine as she followed its path straight to the witch's black heart.

Even enveloped in flames and crumbling to her knees, Ynez was not spent. She raised her arms toward Geronimo and screeched, "A hex on you, old man! I condemn you to walk in the white man's shadow until the end of your cursed days!"

For a moment Frances watched in stunned silence as the flames crackled and Ynez screamed and collapsed on the ground. Then she had to turn her face away, sickened. Though a creature of nightmares, Ynez had once been a human being.

18

"You made this dress?" Frances asked Ruby in wonder as she entered the noise-filled sitting room of The Gentleman's Club.

Ruby nodded happily. "I never had much of a chance to make something this fancy before. You really like it?"

"It's beautiful."

"Wearing this, I will be the most envied bride in all of Santa Fe," Avandera exclaimed happily.

The bride-to-be then turned slowly, to give the full effect of the silk-trimmed, green taffeta with lace collar and cuffs. All the girls oohed and aahed, even Luz, who Frances suspected might be next in the market for such a garment. She didn't want to think about her own relationship with Chaco, which had been put on hold while he spent some time working things out with his father. Louisa was there, too, hanging back from the others, her expression enigmatic.

"Ruby, this is such a professional job—you should be doing this for a living."

The words were out of her mouth before Frances could think. She shouldn't be giving the young woman encouragement unless there was some real possibility of her changing professions.

But Ruby took the compliment in stride. "I'm happy to be able to sew at all."

Realizing Belle was about to enter the room, Frances waylaid the madam before she could spoil the festive mood. "Belle, can I talk to you? Outside?"

"Sure, Frankie, honey." She turned around and walked back toward the railing overlooking the lobby. "What's on your mind?"

"Avandera's here."

"I ain't blind."

"Trying on her wedding dress."

"That's what I came to see. Look, I mighta blown up at her before, but I got no reason to stand in the way of true love. Someone sure deserves it."

Judging her friend to be in a positive frame of mind for once, Frances took a chance. "It's a wonderful dress, and it would be a shame to let Ruby's talent go to waste, don't you think?" she asked, then caught her breath, lest Belle blow up as she'd done so often lately.

Indeed, censure crossed the madam's expression, but only for a few seconds. "I already lost one of my girls," she said with a sigh. "I suppose I can make do for a while without another. Who's Ruby gonna work for?"

Frances gave Belle a quick hug. "Herself, I hope. If we could give her a small business loan to tide her over."

"Now hold on, this ain't no charity—"

"Which she would have to pay back with interest, of course," Frances quickly added. "Ruby could start by working out of a room in the hotel, until she got some regular customers. Then she could open up a real shop."

"Giving her money means stinting around here some."

"True." She was amazed that Belle didn't sound altogether disagreeable.

"And you'd be stuck in town longer'n you expected."

Frances forced a sigh and said, "I'm willing to make the sacrifice."

Truth was, she had no intentions of leaving anyway, whether or not things worked out between her and Chaco.

Belle smiled. "Then I'll do it. I sure as shootin' expected you to hightail it outta town on the first coach or train after what happened with that de Arguello woman last week."

The story they'd told about Ynez had been a modified, more acceptable version of the truth: that Ynez had taken Frances hostage because Frances had figured out the other woman was doing the killing; that she'd threatened to kill both Frances and Chaco to keep her secret; and that Geronimo had cut her down to save his nephew. They'd claimed Ynez was insane, having admitted to brutal treatment at the hands of her father after her mother died, and that she had made up for it by killing other men. The word *skin-walker* had never been spoken.

"Ynez did have me wishing I was elsewhere," Frances admitted, "but there are other things about the West I love."

"Like Chaco Jones," Belle said wisely. "Well, good, 'cause I'm getting used to you hanging around. The way you went after my girl, well, I can't rightly show you enough appreciation."

"I love Louisa, too."

Frances looked through the doorway toward the girl who was now all smiles as she chatted away with Ruby. No more sullen moods. No protests about returning to school. Overnight, Louisa had become the perfect daughter to Belle. If the madam saw through the facade, she wasn't saying, undoubtedly too grateful to have her daughter back unharmed to question Louisa's new and improved attitude. She allowed the girl to visit the Blue Sky when she wanted and she'd even managed to "forget" Louisa had gone off with a man.

But Frances hadn't forgotten. If there were any consequences . . .

"Let's get a better look at Avandera's dress."

While spending the next half hour chatting with the girls and sharing tea and biscuits, Frances kept an eye on Louisa. While she talked and smiled, she was a shell of the girl she had been. Gone was the fire that had imbued her spirit and made her special.

Strong's request preying on her mind, Frances eventually said, "Louisa, I was going to check on my mare over at the stable. Want to come?"

"Sure. My horses could use some attention."

They were barely out of the Blue Sky when Billie Tucker came flying down the street, shouting, "Hey, Louisa Janks, wait up!"

What now? Frances wondered. Louisa didn't need more grief. But Billie looked embarrassed as he stopped before them. He took off his hat and crushed it between his hands.

"What is it?" Louisa asked, her suspicion ripe in her tone.

"I, uh, don't know how to say this . . ." He was turning red. "It's about my ma."

"She's not getting the town riled up about Louisa again, is she?" Frances asked.

"No, ma'am. You gotta excuse her for what she did, 'cause she's outta her head. Has been since Pa got killed. I tried to take care of her . . ."

"I'm sure you did your best," Frances said.

Louisa remained silent and stiff.

"Anyhow, you got my apologies." Billie wrung the felt brim between nervous fingers. "I don't know what else to say."

"How about that you'll keep her from doing what she did to me to anyone ever again," Louisa suggested.

"I aim to do that. I mean, I'm taking her away from here. We got family back East. Anyhow, I just wanted you to know how sorry I am."

Louisa nodded. "Thank you, Billie."

Nodding, the teenager backed off, squashed his hat back on his head and strode off, looking a little more like a man than he had a few minutes ago.

Frances waited until he was out of ear shot before asking Louisa, "Did you know Lieutenant Strong was leaving Santa Fe?"

Smile turned brittle, Louisa said, "No. Why ever would I care?"

"I thought you might have some affection for the man."

"For that no-account . . ." The girl looked appalled and quickly said, "Lieutenant Samuel Strong means nothing to me."

"You mean something to him. He asked about you."

"You've seen him?"

"I visited him in the brig where he's been confined

since taking off without leave. He was worried about you."

"He has no need. I'm not going to run away again."

"That's not what he's worried about."

Louisa flushed and avoided looking her way.

Frances touched her arm. "Louisa, if you ever need to talk to another woman about . . . well, about anything, please, come to me."

Nodding, Louisa allowed her emotions to show but for a moment. "Listen, I don't feel like messing with the horses right now, after all. I, uh, need to stretch my legs."

"You want company?"

The girl shook her head. "I'd rather be alone." Then, as if feeling Frances' distress for her, she said, "I'm all right. Please, don't worry about me. I just need some time to think about things."

"Don't take too long. Lieutenant Strong's transfer could come through any day."

Louisa hugged her. "Thanks for caring, Frances. I know I was your student and that I'm a lot younger than you, but I think of you as my best friend."

"That makes two of us," Frances assured her.

She watched Louisa walk away, a lonely figure, the weight of the world pressing down on her young shoulders, appearing far older than her sixteen years.

Though a trip to the stable had merely been an excuse to get Louisa alone, Frances chose to follow through. She was quite fond of the sorrel despite the beast's having dumped her, leaving her to Ynez's devices. Poor thing had been scared out of her wits . . . much as she had been.

Frances had been in the stall for only a few minutes, and was making over the mare, when she felt another presence behind her. She whipped around, eyes searching the shadows and finding a solid, familiar form.

"Chaco!"

A burst of pleasure filled her and she yearned to run to him, to throw herself in his arms and kiss him, but something held her back. Though he was obviously staring at her, she could see neither his expression nor his eyes. And his body was stiff, as if something disturbed him.

She had no idea of what until he said, "You're still here," without the slightest hint of emotion.

Was he happy about the fact or not?

Stroking the horse's nose to keep her hands from shaking, she asked, "Where else would I be?" in the steadiest voice she could muster.

"Thought you might have gone in search of that civilization you think so high of."

"Maybe I'd rather help bring civilization here. Not too much," Frances quickly added, her heart fluttering. Surely he was happy that she hadn't left! "There are things about this part of the country that I hope never change." When he still didn't respond positively, she grew irritated with his very denseness. "And I can't believe you would think me so poor-spirited as to turn tail and run."

"After what you've been through, no one would blame you."

"I came West seeking adventure. I merely got a bit more than I bargained for."

"You almost got killed."

"And I almost killed another human . . . well, whatever she was." Realizing uncertainty was keeping him at a distance, Frances thought it important that she tell him, "I understand now, Chaco."

"Understand what?"

"How a person can be driven to do things against his nature."

"You mean me? Don't fool yourself, Frankie. Don't make me out to be something better than I am."

"And don't make yourself out to be worse. I've met a lot of people who think highly of themselves, who believe they're good upstanding Christians when they're really narrow-minded and shallow like Minna Tucker. Maybe they never do anything terrible, maybe they aren't responsible for taking lives, but they're misguided, even cruel. I know you for who you are inside, Chaco. You're a good person, kind, someone I trust. And love."

As if her heartfelt declaration freed him from his own constraints, he swept forward and gathered her into his arms. "I love you, too, Frankie, only I was afraid . . ."

"Not of me," she murmured against his chest. "Don't ever be afraid of me."

He showed her his new fearlessness in a kiss that was both loving and demanding. She opened herself to him, poured every emotion she'd ever felt for this man into one heart-stopping moment. His hands left trails of fire where they touched her, and she shuddered with need when he pulled away.

"You serious about helping to civilize this Territory?" he asked, stroking her hair away from her face.

"Dead serious."

"How about me? Willing to have a go at a former gunfighter?"

"Absolutely."

"Mind changing your last name again?"

"Not a bit."

He kissed her again and held her so tight that her

heart raced uncontrollably. All her doubts were vanquished. They belonged together.

"The wind from the East might have blown you here, but I intend to keep you," Chaco vowed. "How does being a rancher's wife sound?"

"Like a new adventure." She couldn't contain her happiness. "You've worked things out with your father?"

"Some. He's having papers drawn up so those southeast acres are mine no matter what. As for the rest . . . we'll see. He's kind of distracted after his wife's death and all."

"But he believes she was a skin-walker?"

"Yes. And that she was very evil. Quite a few of his servants had tales to tell, as well. They found poisons she'd mixed up in a chest in her bedroom."

At the mention of Ynez, they were both silent for a moment. Frances's good mood was tempered.

But then Chaco returned to a more positive subject. "You won't mind leaving the Blue Sky?"

Frances smiled, imagining spending every day with him. "I'll gladly leave the whole operation in Belle's capable hands." Thinking of how things had worked out for Avandera and Ruby—and maybe even Luz— she said, "With a little luck, all the employees of The Gentleman's Club will have other prospects." Especially if she helped find them.

"And you won't mind living in a cabin?"

"It'll only be temporary. We'll build our own home."

"You don't like the *estancia?*"

"I don't like Ynez's having lived there," Frances admitted. Even though the woman was dead, she would always be aware of the witch's presence in her former quarters. "Besides, I think we both deserve a fresh start."

"And as soon as possible," Chaco said, taking her mouth with a groan of impatience.

The winds of change might sweep through New Mexico, Frances knew, and she and Chaco might have to bend, but they would never break or be forced to move on. In her heart, she hoped their legacy would be the marriage of all the Territory's cultures, a foundation for a rich, wonderful future.

Louisa and Sam's story continues in *Heart of the Jaguar*.

AVAILABLE NOW

FLAME LILY by Candace Camp
Continuing the saga of the Tyrells begun in *Rain Lily,* another heart-tugging, passionate tale of love from bestselling author Candace Camp. Returning home after years at war, Confederate officer Hunter Tyrell dreamed only of marrying his sweetheart, Linette Sanders, and settling down. But when he discovered that Linette had wed another, he vowed never to love again—until he found out her heartbreaking secret.

ALL THAT GLITTERS by Ruth Ryan Langan
From a humble singing job in a Los Angeles bar, Alexandra Corday is discovered and propelled into stardom. Along the way her path crosses that of rising young photographer Adam Montrose. Just when it seems that Alex will finally have it all—a man she loves, a home for herself and her brother, and the family she has always yearned for—buried secrets threaten to destroy her.

THE WIND CASTS NO SHADOW by Roslynn Griffith
With an incredibly deft hand, Roslynn Griffith has combined Indian mythology and historical flavor in this compelling tale of love, betrayal, and murder deep in the heart of New Mexico territory.

UNQUIET HEARTS by Kathy Lynn Emerson
Tudor England comes back to life in this richly detailed historical romance. With the death of her mother, Thomasine Strangeways had no choice but to return to Catsholme Manor, the home where her mother was once employed as governess. There she was reunited with Nick Carrier, her childhood hero who had become the manor's steward. Meeting now as adults, they found the attraction between them instant and undeniable, but they were both guarding dangerous secrets.

STOLEN TREASURE by Catriona Flynt
A madcap romantic adventure set in 19th-century Arizona gold country. Neel Blade was rich, handsome, lucky, and thoroughly bored, until he met Cate Stewart, a feisty chemist who was trying to hold her world together while her father was in prison. He instantly fell in love with her, but if only he could remember who he was . . .

WILD CARD by Nancy Hutchinson
It is a dream come true for writer Sarah MacDonald when movie idol Ian Wild miraculously appears on her doorstep. This just doesn't happen to a typical widow who lives a quiet, unexciting life in a small college town. But when Ian convinces Sarah to go with him to his remote Montana ranch, she comes face to face with not only a life and a love more exciting than anything in the pages of her novels, but a shocking murder.

COMING NEXT MONTH

STARLIGHT by Patricia Hagan
Another spellbinding historical romance from bestselling author Patricia Hagan. Desperate to escape her miserable life in Paris, Samara Labonte agreed to switch places with a friend and marry an American soldier. During the train journey to her intended, however, Sam was abducted by Cheyenne Indians. Though at first she was terrified, her heart was soon captured by one particular blue-eyed warrior.

THE NIGHT ORCHID by Patricia Simpson
A stunning new time travel story from an author who *Romantic Times* says is "fast becoming one of the premier writers of supernatural romance." When Marissa Quinn goes to Seattle to find her missing sister who was working for a scientist, what she finds instead is a race across centuries with a powerfully handsome Celtic warrior from 285 B.C. He is the key to her missing sister and the man who steals her heart.

ALL THINGS BEAUTIFUL by Cathy Maxwell
Set in the ballrooms and country estates of Regency England, a stirring love story of a dark, mysterious tradesman and his exquisite aristocratic wife looking to find all things beautiful. "*All Things Beautiful* is a wonderful 'Beauty and the Beast' story with a twist. Cathy Maxwell is a bright new talent."—*Romantic Times*

THE COMING HOME PLACE by Mary Spencer
Knowing that her new husband, James, loved another, Elizabeth left him and made a new life for herself. Soon she emerged from her plain cocoon to become an astonishingly lovely woman. Only when James' best friend ardently pursued her did James realize the mistake he had made by letting Elizabeth go.

DEADLY DESIRES by Christina Dair
When photographer Jessica Martinson begins to uncover the hidden history of the exclusive Santa Lucia Inn, she is targeted as the next victim of a murderer who will stop at nothing to prevent the truth from coming out. Now she must find out who is behind the murders, as all the evidence is pointing to the one man she has finally given her heart to.

MIRAGE by Donna Valentino
To escape her domineering father, Eleanor McKittrick ran away to the Kansas frontier where she and her friend Lauretta had purchased land to homestead. Her father, a prison warden, sent Tremayne Hawthorne, an Englishman imprisoned for a murder he didn't commit, after her in exchange for his freedom. Yet Hawthorne soon realized that this was a woman he couldn't bear to give up.

Harper Monogram **The Mark of Distinctive Women's Fiction**

ATTENTION: ORGANIZATIONS AND CORPORATIONS

Most HarperPaperbacks are available at special quantity discounts for bulk purchases for sales promotions, premiums, or fund-raising. For information, please call or write:
**Special Markets Department, HarperCollins Publishers,
10 East 53rd Street, New York, N.Y. 10022.**
Telephone: (212) 207-7528. Fax: (212) 207-7222.

larger room, then opened the door that led outside.

The moon shone dully, growing old. The wind blew south, making the pinons sigh and moan. She raised her head expectantly.

But there was no use going to him, not again. Not until she had found a way to combat the strength and power she had been surprised to find in her enemy.

And she would find a way.

Shutting the door again, she went to the great fireplace stretching along one wall, stirred the embers until they leaped up hungrily.

She smiled and threw in a twisted pinon log. "This for your appetite, little brother."

While it waited for the real offering . . .

Gazing at the piece of cloth she held, she brought forth several cactus needles from her pocket—long, sharp, capable of drawing blood.

She only wished they could draw his blood.

But she must be patient.

"Pain!" she hissed, jabbing one of the needles into the cloth, a fragment of a blanket that had warmed him as a child. "Fear!" She jabbed a second needle, then a third and fourth. "Sickness! Death!"

With the last, she tossed the cloth into the fire, curling her lip as it was eaten alive.

In life or the world of dreams, her enemy would soon be sorry that he had ever dared resist her.

Frances continued to wonder if she were dreaming as she rode the rails westward to New Mexico.

She had married Nathan Gannon that very morning following his proposal, then climbed aboard a train that had carried them to Chicago. Once there, they'd taken a two-day layover, had gone on a big shopping

He stepped closer again. "You think I'm proposing because I feel sorry for you?"

Yes, but she said, "Perhaps."

"Well, you're wrong. I like your courage, your plucky spirit. Not to mention your education and looks. I've always wanted a smart, well-spoken lady for a wife. You can help me run my hotel and restaurant in Santa Fe. So what do you say?"

He was gazing at her with an expression she'd never before seen on the face of any man. And for a fleeting second, Frances allowed herself to dream of love and belonging and a new home in the exciting West she'd only heard and read about.

Surely the dreams produced the answer that even surprised herself. "I say yes."

Before she could take it back, Nathan Gannon enveloped her in his arms. "Wonderful! You won't regret it . . . Frances. That's your first name, right? And you can call me Nate. We're gonna have a rollicking good time!" Then he kissed her.

Shyly, Frances wrapped her arms about his neck and closed her eyes, giving in to completely new sensations. Nate's mustache tickled and his breath was fragrant with a hint of brandy and coffee. Warmth coiled within her. A new home—a place where she might belong at last, and a man with whom she could share it. If this was a dream, she didn't want to wake up.

New Mexico

In the deep of night, restless, she rose to prowl, tearing off a small piece of the cloth she had stored in a chest at the foot of her bed. Clutching the material tightly, she glided down the corridor, turned into another again. The shuttle from Galisteo Junction was now an hour late. She hoped nothing was wrong.

While she couldn't wait to see her daughter, she was spittin' mad at Louisa for ruining yet another chance at being educated like a lady.

Controlling her exasperation, Belle wondered about Nate's new wife. Probably a charmer to get a bachelor of fifty-three to tie the knot. Belle had been mighty surprised to receive the telegram announcing Nate's marriage.

"Why aren't there separate areas for heathens and decent people?" came a strident female voice some yards away.

Belle watched a middle-aged woman mincing past a seated group of Pueblo Indians wrapped in bright blankets. Wouldn't be bad-looking if she didn't dress so plain and stern. Nose in the air, the woman pressed her skirts tightly to her side as if touching the Indians with her brown hem might dirty her somehow. When one of the Indians held out a clay pot he obviously wanted to sell, the virago made a terrible pinched face.

"No! I don't want anything! Get away from me!"

Belle frowned, recognizing the woman and her old-fashioned bonnet from an encounter she'd had at an open-air marketplace. The widow of a railroad man, Minna Tucker was a holier-than-thou Bible-thumper. She was certain Minna also recognized her when the woman glanced her way in passing and widened her eyes.

She intoned, "God is the punisher of sinners!"

Knowing a woman like Minna Tucker would hate it, Belle smiled directly at her and waved.

The woman looked set to blow some steam and nearly started into a dead run. "Get thee behind me, Satan!"

A conscience?

Finally, she and Louisa climbed aboard a passenger car. Frances glanced down at her suit, now dirty and blood-stained, before Louisa guided her to a seat.

"Ma will be there to meet us," the girl said matter-of-factly. And as the train started, she told Frances, "Uncle Nate was a good man, you know, no matter what mistakes he made or what he did for a living."

Frances had so little energy, she gazed at her companion blankly. "What do you mean?"

"He did tell you about his business, right?"

"The restaurant and the hotel?"

Louisa gazed at her closely. "Uh, oh." Then she sighed. "From the way you acted on the trip, I was afraid of this."

"What do you mean?"

"Well, Blue Sky Palace isn't exactly . . . uh, just a hotel. It's also a casino."

Despite her sorrow, Frances was stunned. "You mean a gambling parlor?"

"Uh, huh." Louisa seemed to be searching for words. "And Uncle Nate was more than the owner of the establishment. He played his own tables from time to time. You know, poker and faro—"

"He was a gambler?" Frances cut in.

Louisa simply nodded.

Truly shocked, Frances turned to stare out the window. Nate had been shot dead and his hotel was actually a den of iniquity. Her dream was rapidly descending into a nightmare.

Adjusting her parasol against the bright sun, Belle Janks checked the little jeweled watch she wore on a chain about her neck and gazed down the tracks

"Anglo?" Perhaps that's where he got his height and gray eyes. "Really?"

"One of my grandmothers was a Texan."

"An interesting mix."

"Not much different than a lot of people in Santa Fe."

"But very different from people in Boston, the city I came from." And to which she now questioned returning, having realized there was nothing there for her. "I was a schoolteacher before coming to New Mexico."

"I heard."

So Magdalena or someone else had also gossiped to him.

She wondered about the sad, hard background Magdalena had mentioned. Chaco didn't look sad. He appeared self-sufficient, tough and remote. "Does any of your family live in Santa Fe?"

"My mother died a long time ago. I didn't have anyone else."

So he'd probably been an impoverished orphan. Well, she admitted that could be sad and hard. Perhaps he'd only drifted into gunslinging because he needed to make a living. She wondered if she'd ever get to know him . . . or if she should want to.

"You don't talk much about yourself, do you?"

"Most people talk too much."

Did he mean her? "Conversation is the way people socialize, communicate their thoughts and feelings."

"You can usually tell what a person's thinking or feeling by watching him, paying close attention."

Perhaps *he* could tell what others were thinking. Maybe that's why he stared so hard with those spooky eyes. Frances only hoped he hadn't guessed what she'd been thinking and feeling when he'd sat on the side of her bed! Yet again, she started to go.

"So is there anything else besides cards and dice you want me to check on?"

She turned back to him. "The other things that are on that list."

He showed her the piece of paper and pointed at the second item. "You mean this?"

"Chips? Surely we have plenty of those." Considering they took the place of both Mexican and U.S. money. "But you should check."

"And this." His finger slid to the next item.

Was he trying to trick her into reading the list aloud? She recalled a student pulling a similar stunt, a girl who was semi-illiterate. She decided to find out for certain. "Could I have that please?" She reached for the paper. "I forgot to add something else."

Placing the paper on a nearby table, she wrote, *Can you read?*, then showed it to him.

"We might need pencils and some paper," he said slowly, obviously guessing. He didn't react to the question at all.

"Yes, we might. Oh, and I also need to add this." Once more, placing the paper on the table, she scrawled, *You are a big donkey.*

He didn't even raise an eyebrow when she handed the paper back.

"Any other questions?" she asked.

"No."

Obviously, she'd discouraged him, which meant he'd probably only go to someone else. Frances suddenly felt guilty. Perhaps he'd been too poor to attend school.

"Um, I need that paper again." When he looked at her measuredly, she forced herself to explain, "I wrote something bad on there."